Praise for

ANTi-iCE

and Stephen Baxter

"One of the most interesting newer hard SF writers . . . a thoroughly enjoyable novel and a provocative contribution to one of SF's more colorful emerging subgenres—psuedo-Victoriana."

—*Locus*

"Mr. Baxter has provided us with a cabinet of scientific marvels even more astonishing than Mr. Verne's! His convincing and detailed vision . . . takes us into space and to the Moon itself!"

—Michael Moorcock

"He writes like I used to. . . . I should have him assassinated before it's too late!"

—David Niven

"Highly original and satisfying . . . Clever science, bizarre settings, lots of pace and action in a truly exotic universe."

—Charles Sheffield

"Good hard SF of a kind rarely seen nowadays, with exotic science and engineering worked out in loving detail. . . . The people who inhabit Baxter's strange world are well drawn in their pain and confusion, their friendships and enmities."

—Joe Haldeman

MOONQUAKE

I soon lost track of time as I worked through that changeless Lunar afternoon. Boulder after boulder I tore aside, finding substantial caches of water under perhaps half of them. I filled the bag over and over, and returned several times to the *Phaeton,* soon amassing a small hill of crumbled ice in the shadow of the ship. Every few minutes the ground would tremble ominously; but I learned to ignore these small earthquakes. When the bag was more than half-full, though it did not weigh me down, its inertia, as it swung against my back, became a distracting nuisance.

Then came a massive tremor.

It was as if some giant had struck the surface of the Moon. I was thrown to the ground. I had the presence of mind to cover my faceplate with my mittens; otherwise the glass should surely have smashed. I lay there for long seconds, hardly daring to look up, expecting at any moment to be hurled into some Lunar chasm or smashed beneath a fall of rock. And the Moonquake continued in an utter and eerie silence!

[By the same author]

Raft
Timelike Infinity

ANTI-ICE

Stephen Baxter

This is a work of fiction. The characters, incidents, and dialogues are products of the author's imagination and are not to be construed as real. Any resemblance to actual events or persons, living or dead, is entirely coincidental.

HarperPaperbacks *A Division of* HarperCollins*Publishers*
10 East 53rd Street, New York, N.Y. 10022

A hardcover edition of this book was published in 1993 in Britain by HarperCollins*Publishers.*

Cover illustration by Bob Eggleton

First HarperPaperbacks printing: November 1994

Printed in the United States of America

HarperPrism is an imprint of HarperPaperbacks. HarperPaperbacks, HarperPrism, and colophon are trademarks of HarperCollins*Publishers*

10 9 8 7 6 5 4 3 2 1

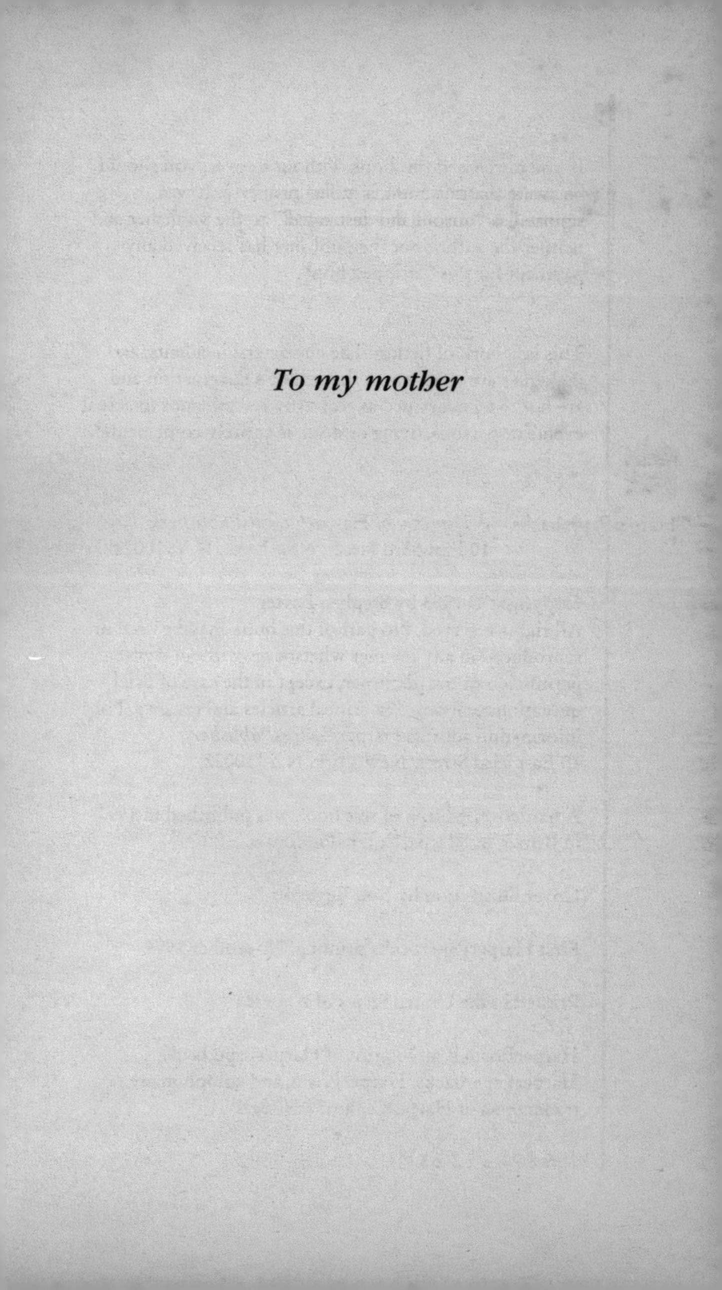

To my mother

[acknowledgments]

I would like to express my thanks to Eric Brown and Alan Cousins who read drafts of the manuscript; to David S. Garnett for his enthusiasm for the concept; and to my agent Maggie Noach, my editor Malcolm Edwards, and the staff at HarperCollins for their hard work on this project.

[prologue]

A LETTER TO A FATHER

July 7th, 1855
Before Sebastopol

My Dear Father,
I scarcely know how to address myself to you after the disgraceful conduct which caused me to leave home. I am well aware that a full year has elapsed without a word from me, and can only offer my great shame as excuse for my silence. I can assure you of my guilt at the thought that you, Mother and Ned might have imagined me lying in some dismal corner of England, alone, penniless and dying.

Well, Sir, Love and Duty have combined themselves with the extraordinary events of the past few days to prompt me to break my silence. Father, I am alive and hale and serving in the 90 Light Infantry in the cause of the Empire in the Crimean campaign! I begin this account seated in the remains of a Russian fortification we call the

Redan—named for its shape after the French "tooth," you see, an unimposing but effective affair of sandbags and earthworks—before the ruins of Sebastopol. I have no doubt that my news so far will astonish you enough—and I dare to hope that your heart will be touched by the tidings of my survival to date—and yet you must be prepared for still greater astonishment, dear Father, at the tale I have to tell. You have no doubt read in Russell's dispatches to *The Times* of the final disembowelling of the fortress of Sebastopol by this fellow Traveller and his infernal anti-ice shell. Sir, I have witnessed it all. And, in view of my eternal disgrace, I regard my survival as an unmerited gift from the Lord, as so many good fellows—French and Turks too, as well as English—have fallen all around me.

I owe you some explanation of my conduct since leaving *Sylvan*, that dark day last year, and how I arrived on this remote shore.

As you know I took with me only a few shillings. My mood was one of self-contempt, Sir, and shame; determined to atone, I made my way by Light Rail to Liverpool and there enlisted into the 90 Regiment. I joined as an ordinary soldier; I had of course no means of purchasing a commission, and in any event I had determined to descend, to mix with the lowest of men, in order to cleanse myself of my sin.

A week after my arrival in Liverpool I was sent to Chatham, and spent some months there being shaped as a soldier of the Empire. Then, determined to submit my life to the will of the Lord, in February of this year I volunteered to join the 90 Light Infantry, in order to be brought out here, to the Turkish war.

As I waited for my transport, convinced that only death waited for me in the distant fields of the Crimea, I wanted most desperately to write to you; but my courage—which has sustained me through the most terrible carnage here—failed before such a trivial task, and so I left England without a word.

We were fifteen days coming to Balaclava; and then we faced some days' march along the road north to the Allied encampments around Sebastopol.

I beg your indulgence to describe the situation I found here; while the campaign has evidently been reasonably well reported at home by such correspondents as Russell, perhaps the views of an ordinary infantryman of the Army—for such am I, and proud to be—will be of some interest.

Sir, you know why we are here.

Our Empire girdles the World. And our dominion is held together by the threads that are our lines of communication: roads, railways, Light Rail routes and sea lanes.

Czar Nicholas, seeking a Mediterranean port, had cast his envious eyes on the failing Ottoman Empire. So he threatened Constantinople herself—and our lines to India. Soon the Czar was worsting Johnny Turk on land and on sea; and so we, with the French at our side, went to war with him.

We entered the war under the command of Lord Raglan, who had once served with Wellington himself at Waterloo. Father, I once saw that great gentleman himself, riding through our encampment on his way to a conference with his French counterpart Canrobert. Sir, to see Raglan as I did that day, his back ramrod-stiff on his gray, his empty sleeve tucked into his coat (for the French had shot his arm off for him) and his grand, careworn, hawk's gaze raking over us all, the same gaze that had once faced down

Bonaparte himself—I can tell you I was not the only chap to cheer to the heavens and throw his cap high!

But, from the day I arrived, there were whispers against Raglan.

His head full of days of glory against the Corsican, Raglan apparently was wont to refer to the Russians here as the "French"! And, of course, there were mutterings about Raglan's conduct of the campaign. After all our first engagement with the Russians was at Alma, a good ten months ago, at which we administered a sound licking to the Czar's men. What a spectacle that was, by all accounts; the Allied lines were a forest of color highlighted by the glinting of bayonets, while the ear was assailed by a tumult of noise, drums and bugles of all descriptions, all immersed in the unending hum of an armed force on the march. A fellow here describes a charge by a unit of the Grays, their great bearskin caps high above the enemy as they fought back to back, hacking and slicing everywhere . . .

My only regret is that I missed all the fun!

But, after victory at Alma, Raglan failed to follow up.

Perhaps we could have chased the Russkies there and then out of the Peninsula and been home by Christmas! But it wasn't to be, and you know the rest of the story: the great battles of Balaclava and Inkerman, with, at Balaclava, the slaughter of the noble Light Brigade under the Earl of Cardigan. (Father, I might interject that early in May I had the opportunity to ride up that famous North valley, almost as far as the site of the Russian guns which had been the Brigade's objective. The ground was gaudy with flowers, and warm and golden in the rays of the setting sun; six-point shot and pieces of shell lay strewn thickly enough on the ground, with flowers growing through the rusty fragments. I found a horse's skull, quite clean of meat, pierced by a single bullet hole from left to right. We saw no traces of human bodies. But I heard tell of one fellow who found a jawbone—complete and blanched, with the most perfect, regular set of teeth.)

In any event the Russians survived, and—by Christmas—had holed up in their fortress of Sebastopol.

Now Sebastopol, Father, is the Russians' key naval base here. If we could take that city the threat to Constantinople would evaporate, and the Czar's Mediterranean ambitions would be as naught. And so we were drawn up here in great numbers with our trenches, earthworks and mines; and—since Christmas—besieged the town.

It was—or seemed to me—a farcical siege; the Russians were well enough supplied with ammo, and we had no way of imposing a sea blockade—and so the Czar's ships supplied victuals to the besieged almost daily!

But Raglan would entertain no way of dislodging the Russians other than patient attrition. And, of course, he adamantly refused to have anything to do with suggestions of anti-ice weaponry; a man of his honor would have naught to do with such modern monstrosities.

And meanwhile we waited and waited . . .

I can only thank a too-benevolent Savior that I, unworthy as I am, arrived after the worst ravages of the winter here. The lads who survived all that have some tales to tell. The summer months had been benevolent, you see, with good foraging to be had, and even sufficient time for games of cricket, improvised but played strictly to the rules! But winter turned the roads and trenches to mud. There was only canvas cover—if that—and the men had to snatch what sleep was possible in knee-deep, freezing mud. Even the Officers suffered disgracefully; by all accounts they were forced to wear their swords in the trenches as the only means by which they might be distinguished from the common footsoldier! Father, this truly was soldiering without the gilding.

And, of course, there was Dame Cholera, brought to all quarters of the Peninsula from the landing station at Varna. A Cholera epidemic is no fun, Sir, for a man can turn from a healthy soldier into a gaunt and careworn shadow in a few hours, and next day he is dead. To maintain discipline and composure in such circumstances says much for the mettle of these fellows; and, dare I say it, the common English have acquitted themselves far better than the French, despite the rumors of our allies' superior provisioning.

But I have my own ideas about the provision situation, Father. It is my judgment that the French starve better than the English! Deprive an Englishman of his roast beef and ale and he will growl, and lie down and die. But your Frenchman . . . One Captain Maude, a convivial fellow (who was later shipped home when a shell exploded inside his horse and lacerated his leg) told us of an occasion on which he was invited to supper with a lieutenant of the French army. Approaching the chap's tent our Maude was greeted by the scents of fine cooking and snatches of opera, and inside the tent boards had been laid out and a clean cloth spread upon them, and a three course meal was served! And on complimenting his host, Maude was astonished to learn that the sole ingredients of all three courses had been beans, and a few local herbs!

So there you have it!

But I would not complain of the conditions endured by the ordinary Englishman here by the time of my arrival. I found a billet in a hut which had been constructed by a platoon of the Turks. We receive salt Beef and Biscuit daily now, poor rations indeed compared to the comfort of home, but more than sufficient to sustain life. And the degradation of alcohol is not unknown to us, Father. Beer is difficult to come by and quite expensive—but not so spirits. There is a species of poison called "raki," for instance, which may be wheedled from the peasantry here. More than once I have seen men, Officers too, staggering drunk from the stuff; although such behavior, of course, is not condoned. I might relate the downfall of a splendidly made fellow in our company, a chap over six feet in height, a fine soldier but a devil with the drink inside him. Punishment parade is always held early in the morning, before the whole regiment; on this occasion the air was frost and a keen wind was blowing. Our soldier's wrists and ankles were tied to a triangle of stretcher poles and his bare back exposed; and a drummer plied the cat o' nine tails while the drum major counted the strokes. Father, the fellow took sixty lashes without a murmur, although the blood was flowing after a dozen strokes. When it was done he straightened up and saluted his Colonel. "That's a warm breakfast you gave me, your honor, this morning," he said; and he was walked away to hospital.

For what it is worth, Father, I can report that not a drop has passed my lips since the day I left your house in such unfortunate circumstances.

Now—at last, I almost hear you cry!—I shall describe to you the momentous events of the last few days; and, if you will indulge me so far, I will conclude with a report of my own disposition.

Sebastopol is a naval port on the Black Sea. Imagine if you will a wide bay running west, from the sea, to east; the town squats on the south side of this bay. And the town is riven in two by an inlet which extends south from the bay by some two miles.

The practical import of this, Father, is that two separate armies are required to invest the town; for a force attacking one side could not hope to offer support to a force attacking the other, because of the existence of the inlet. And therefore we and the French were drawn up on either side of the inlet—the French to the left, the British to the right.

The Russian defenses are—or were—slight in appearance, but occupied very commanding positions and were fortified strongly by nature herself. For example, I have already mentioned the earthen battery called the Redan, which was armed with seventeen heavy guns.

I remember one day walking up to within about a mile from the town, intending to inspect its environs. From a hillock I could see the fine Russian ships of war lying like gray ghosts in the bay, and the inhabitants of Sebastopol walking through the streets all unconcerned, as if the one hundred and forty thousand men investing their port were but a dream. But less dreamlike were the fortresses which looked down over our positions. Great black guns peered down at me through their embrasures, and when I showed myself too clearly there was a puff of smoke and I heard a hiss as the shot flew over my head; for they had their ranges very well and could drop them very close.

I have said that the siege lasted many months, and not a few men, growing distracted by the lack of progress, murmured that Lord Raglan, with his long memories and traditional ways, did not have the flexibility of mind to resolve this problem of Sebastopol.

Then, early in May, we had our first indication of such rumblings in more senior circles. A group of Officers joined us, evidently fresh from England, for their epaulettes shone brightly. They were led by General Sir James Simpson, a portly, fierce-looking gentleman. With them came a civilian: an odd cove about fifty years of age, over six feet in height and blessed with a nose like a hawk's beak, with muttonchop whiskers that were vast bushes as black as you please, and a stovepipe hat that made him look ten feet tall. (Legend has it that a stray Russkie shot—the like of which winged constantly through our midst like tiny, deadly birds—one day threaded a neat hole through this headpiece; and the gentleman, as cool as you like, doffed the piece, inspected the hole, and promised on his return to England to invoice the Czar's Embassy for the repair!) This fellow picked his way through the mud, peering into our earthworks and studying our amputees and other sick, and his concern and grim humor were evident for all to see.

You will, I hope, recognize from my description the famous Sir Josiah Traveller, author of all those engineering marvels which have made the Manchester industrialists so famous at home. But as far as I know anti-ice gadgetry had never before been employed in a theater of war.

Well, here was Sir Josiah come to the Peninsula to advise us on that very issue.

I was not, of course, privy to the debates which followed Traveller's arrival, and my report is necessarily based on hearsay. General Simpson was strongly in favor of the deployment of Traveller's new shells, the quicker to resolve the investment. But Raglan would have none of it. Would the old Duke have used such devilish devices, the same Duke who forbade even the use of the lash on drunkards? (So I imagine Raglan arguing.) No, gentlemen, he would not; and nor would Lord Fitzroy Raglan countenance such a deviance. The traditional methods of investment, as refined for centuries, could not fail; and they would not fail here.

Well, Raglan carried the day; and an assault on the fortress was planned.

Now, Father, only a slight study of the science of investment is required to understand that for us to assail such a fortress as Sebastopol, with little numerical superiority to the defenders, with nothing but field pieces at our command, and with our flanks and retreats insecure, was quite a desperate undertaking. Nevertheless, on 18th June, after nine months of a debilitating and fruitless siege, the Allied forces attempted just such a feat.

Our bombardment had begun as early as a fortnight before. Father, the shells and shot flew over our heads by day and by night, and back came answering fire from the Russians. In my kit constantly, and clutching my Minie to my chest, I had scarcely slept for those two weeks. And as if the racket of the guns were not disturbance enough to our peace of mind, the Czar's men were wont to send thirty-two-pound shot bouncing through our positions like cricket balls, without regard for the clock, which hardly made for a peaceful night's sleep!

At last, early on the 18th, we heard the bugles and drums which told us that the assault had started. We gave a ragged cheer—remember that this was my first taste of real action, Sir—and I poked my silly head out of my trench, the better to follow the action.

Through smoke and steam and across smashed-up ground I saw the French go in first. But the Russians were ready for them, and the fellows toppled as if scythed; those following tripped on the fallen, and soon all was confusion. I fear, Father, that some of those brave Gauls fell to misplaced Allied fire in all that turmoil.

At last the orders came for us to advance. Over the top we skirmishers went and on over the broken mud, yells burning our throats, our bayonets glinting before us. We made for the most formidable Russian redoubt, the Redan; our mission was to cover an assault force who carried ladders and woollen bags, the idea being to scale the Redan's stone walls. I blasted my Minie before me, and for a few seconds the fire of battle coursed through my veins!

Unfortunately the Russians would not play the game.

The Czar's men stayed in their fortifications and sent a most murderous hail of grape and musketry showering down over us. Quite how I survived those minutes I shall never know, Father; for all around me better fellows than I fell sprawling. At last my boot caught in the soft mud of a shell crater; I pitched forward and found myself lying at the bottom of the hole. Russian grape filled the air like a sheet inches above me, and so I lay flat in the mud, knowing that to rise at that point was to face certain death.

I hope you will believe that it was not cowardice that kept me down, Father; as I lay in that hole, the stink of blood and cordite in my nostrils, rage ate at my soul, and I promised myself that once I had the opportunity I would resume the assault and sell my life dear.

At length, with shot still sizzling around me, I clambered out of my shelter, raised my Minie and ran forward.

I was greeted by the most fantastic sight.

Siege ladders lay like pickup sticks about the plain; and men—and fragments of men—lay strewn among them, adorned with smoking shot and pieces of shell. Only one ladder, I saw, had by some miracle been raised against the redoubt's brooding wall: its bearers lay crumpled in a muddy pile, arms and legs everywhere, at its base. And the Russian guns stared undaunted from the redoubt's every embrasure.

The retreat sounded and, under a renewed hail of grape from our unwelcoming hosts, we limped back to our trenches.

And so ended my first experience of combat, Father; and that evening I lay sorely troubled. For how could the death of so many fine men be justified for such an absurd bungle?

The next week was a grim time. For hour after hour rough carts drew up among our tents and huts, and our poor injured lads were loaded aboard and hauled off for the jolting journey to the hospital three miles away at the coast.

Their cries and weeping were terrible to hear.

And day and night, as if to mock our failure and frustration, the Russian artillery bellowed.

No less disturbing to us were the hints we received of ructions among our Commanding Officers. Around the clock the conferences went on, and more than once I saw a grand gentleman emerge from Lord Raglan's tent and go stalking around the camp in high dudgeon, scarred cheeks blazing with anger, white gloves slapping against jostling scabbard. And several times we saw the engineer, Traveller, trotting across the camp site to Raglan's tent bearing mysterious plans and other specifications; and so we knew that the deployment, at last, of this strange stuff anti-ice must be under consideration.

But of Lord Raglan himself we saw no sign.

I imagined that gentleman, Father, his face drawn with care and sickness and his head full of memories of Waterloo and the Iron Duke, at the eye of a storm of disrespect and interrogation.

At last, on 27th June, our Captain called us together. His expression grim, he informed us that Lord Fitzroy Raglan had died the previous day, the 26th; that General Sir James Simpson had been appointed our new Commander-in-Chief; and that we should prepare ourselves for a fresh assault within twenty-four hours. This assault, said the Captain, would follow "a new artillery barrage of unprecedented ferocity."

Then he stalked away from us, his back stiff, refusing to say any more.

We were never told the cause of Raglan's death. Some say he died of disappointment, after that last, failed assault on the Russian redoubts; but I cannot believe it. For even a month earlier, when he visited our camp, Father, care and fatigue had seemed etched into that noble face. Now, God forbid that you should ever see a victim of the Cholera, Sir—I have seen too many—but if you do you will, I am sure, remark on the drained, troubled appearance of that unfortunate; and so I have no doubt of the cause of Raglan's doom.

Men like Raglan do not die of broken hearts, I say.

That night we retired to our muddy billets. I did not sleep well, Father, but not through apprehension, or excitement, or even the constant shouting of the artillery; rather I felt sunk in depression, I have to report, following the deaths of so many good fellows—and now of Raglan himself—to such little effect. It seemed to me that night as if the English Army itself were dying, there on the plains of the Crimea.

We were roused at dawn. The bugles and drums were

silent, but nevertheless we were told to draw up in drill formation and to prepare to advance.

And so I turned out, my fingers jammed into my cuffs to escape the gray cold of dawn, the webbing of my Minie chafing at my unshaven neck. The barrage from the artillery behind us went on unabated; as did, I noted, the replies from the redoubts of Sebastopol, and a sick apprehension gripped me. For if the Russian guns had not been subdued, our assault would be another suicidal charge. Once again, Father, I beg that you do not think me a coward; but I had—and have—no desire to sell my life without profit, and such seemed the prospect before me at that moment.

Then the guns behind us grew quiet, all of a sudden; and soon, as if in response, those of the Russians also lapsed into calmness. A silence fell over our camp, and it combined with the misty dawn light into a strangeness that made me wrap my arms around myself, shivering. The only motion was that of the Little Moon which rose above us, a dazzling beacon of light, setting off on another of its half-hour jaunts across the sky. I looked around, seeking reassurance in the lines of drawn, uncertain faces all around me; but comfort there was none. It was as if we had all, infantrymen, Officers and horses, been transported to some distant, gray star.

I held my breath.

Then, from the Allied emplacements behind me, I heard the speaking of a single artillery piece.

I was later given an account by a friendly Artilleryman of the few moments which had preceded that single shot. This gunner had watched as the engineer Josiah Traveller approached a particular emplacement, his stovepipe hat screwed tightly down around his ears. The fellow wore thick leather gloves which, according to my reporter, added up to a rather comical effect; and at arms' length he carried a large metal cask that shone with frost, as if it were as cold as death. Following Traveller came Sir James Simpson himself and several of his staff, their faces grim, their epaulettes and decorations gleaming. At the muzzle of the gun the engineer placed his cask on the ground and, by loosening clasps, cracked it open. Its central cavity was quite small, my friend reported, so that the walls of the cask were some inches thick and might, he speculated, have contained some substance which kept the temperature of the cask unnaturally low.

Inside the cavity was a single shell, of size about ten pounds. This the engineer lifted as delicately as if it were a child and placed it gently in the muzzle of the artillery piece. Then Traveller stood back.

The gun fired, with a muffled explosion like a cough. Within seconds that single, precious shell was arcing above my head, bearing a few ounces of anti-ice to Sebastopol.

From my position I could not see the town itself, but still I peered over the heads of my colleagues in anticipation as that shell made for the battered fortress; I even pushed back my cap and peaked my hand over my eyes, the better to see.

I have since learned something of the properties of that strange substance anti-ice, Father. It is mined from a strange seam in the frozen ocean of the South Pole, and as long as it is maintained at those frosty temperatures it is perfectly safe. Once it is heated, however—

Well, let me describe to you what I saw.

The shell shriek fell away.

Then it was as if the Sun had touched the Earth.

The horizon in the direction of Sebastopol exploded into a silent sea of light. It was a light that tore into the skin, so that one could feel the very blisters as they rose. I staggered back, my cries of shock and horror joining those of my companions. I dropped my hand from my forehead and stared at it; scorched and blistering, the hand was like a grotesque waxwork, not part of my body at all. Then the pain reached my dull wits and I yelled; and as I did so I felt my scorched cheeks crack and ooze, and I soon shut up. But, Father, I soon learned that I had once more been undeservedly fortunate; for my hand had shielded my sight from the worst of that shock of light, while all around me fellows had crumpled to the soil, pressing their burnt eyes. Then—only a few seconds after that great optical concussion—there came a wind like the breath of God. I was bowled over backwards, and I tucked my blasted hand into my uniform to protect it; I clung to the ground amid a hail of dust and screamed into the wind.

The heat was astonishing.

Long minutes later that gale subsided, and I staggered to my feet. Men, burned and weeping—weapons—the remains of tents—terrified horses—all lay scattered over the ground like the toys of some capricious child-giant. Father, within less than a quarter-hour our camp had been devastated to a far greater extent than either the Russians, Dame Cholera, or Generals January and February had managed hitherto.

Meanwhile, over Sebastopol, a cloud shaped like a black hammer rose into the air.

A fellow beside me lay weeping, his eyes pools of cloudy liquid—horribly like the eyes of a boiled trout. For the next minutes I crouched by him and grasped his hand, mutely offering what comfort I could. Then an Officer came by—his uniform was scorched and unrecognizable, but the remains of a sword still swung at his hip—and I called up to him. "What have they done to us, your honor? Is this some devilish new weapon of the Cossacks?"

He paused and looked down at me. He was a young man, but that infernal light had blasted lines of age into his face; and he said: "No, lad, not the Cossacks; that was one of our own."

At first I could not understand him, but he pointed to the dispersing cloud over Sebastopol, and I came to see the astonishing truth: that the engineer's single shell, impacting Sebastopol, had caused an explosion of such severity that even we—at a distance of three miles—had been incapacitated.

Clearly the power of the novel projectile had been grossly underestimated; otherwise surely we would have been confined to our trenches and foxholes.

Slowly I became aware that the Russian guns, a constant chorus since my arrival on the Peninsula, were stilled at last. Had we then achieved our main objective? With this one, single, devastating blow, was Sebastopol laid low?

A trace of exultation, of victory, coursed through my veins; but my own pain, the devastation around me, and that looming thunderhead over Sebastopol, all worked rapidly to subdue me; and from those left standing near me I heard not a word of rejoicing.

It was still only seven-thirty.

The Officers organized us quickly. Those of us reasonably able-bodied—which included me, Father, once my poor hand was salved, bandaged up and wrapped in a thick mitten—were put to work aiding the rest. We erected our tents once more and restored the camp into something resembling a British military operation.

Then the lines of hospital carts began to form.

So we were occupied until noon, by which time the sun was high overhead. I sat in the shade, salt sweat coursing into my burns, and ate Bully Beef and sipped water through cracked lips.

Though the thunderhead was cleared now, there was still not a sound from the Russian guns in Sebastopol.

At about two of the afternoon we were ordered to form up for the final assault. But, Father, a strange assault it was going to be: we carried our Minies and ammo, yes; but also we hauled trench shovels, picks and other tools, and we loaded up carts with all the blankets, bandages, medication, water we could spare.

And so we set off over the last three miles to Sebastopol.

It took two hours, I would guess. After ten months of artillery bombardment and siege warfare the land was an ocean of churned, crusty mud; continually I slipped into shell pits, and before long all of us were soaked by foul-smelling, brackish water. And everywhere I came across the rubble of warfare: cracked shell casings, abandoned kit, the wreckage of artillery pieces . . . and one or two ornaments of a more grisly nature which, with respect, Father, I will forbear to describe.

But at last we reached Sebastopol; and I stood for some minutes on a rise overlooking the town.

Father, you will recall my earlier description of that town as it lay intact within its walls, which had bristled with weaponry. Well, now it was as if a great boot had stamped—I can think of no other way to describe it. A crater perhaps a quarter-mile wide lay plumb in the center of the city, close to the docks; and I could see how the gouged earth continued to steam, the rocks and slag glowing red hot. And around this crater was a great circle, where the houses and other buildings had been razed, quite neatly; one could see the outlines of their foundations, as if one were staring at a giant architect's plan—although here and there a chimney stack or fragment of wall, scorched to blackness, clung defiantly to the vertical. Beyond that region of devastation the buildings appeared to have remained largely intact—but of windows and roof slates there was scarcely an example. And in several quarters of the town we saw great fires raging, apparently uncontrolled.

The stout defensive walls of the town were trails of rubble now, toppled outwards by the blast; the muzzles of wrecked artillery pieces pointed at random to the sky. And the redoubts lay shattered; Russians in their shapeless uniforms sprawled over the ruins of their guns.

Beyond this infernal landscape the bay lay glimmering blue, quite unperturbed; but the corpses of several vessels lay adrift in the water, their masts snapped.

For some minutes we stared slack-mouthed. Then the Captain said, "Come on, lads; we have our duty to perform."

We formed up once more. A bugle and drum struck up, their rousing sounds sharply misplaced, and we marched across the wreckage of the walls.

So, at last, at about four in the afternoon, the British Army entered Sebastopol.

At first we carried our weapons at battle ready and moved in good military order, with scouts and lookouts; but the only sound was the crunch of glass and smashed masonry under our boots, and it was as if we marched across the surface of the Moon. Even on the outskirts of town the buildings were uniformly scorched and blackened, and I was reminded of that terrible heat which had blazed from the heart of the city. We came across one house which looked as if it had been sliced open, so that we could see within to the furnishings and decorations of its unfortunate occupants. Smashed vehicles of all sizes littered the streets, dead or injured horses trapped in their harnesses still.

And the people:

Father, they lay everywhere as they had fallen, men, women and children alike, their bodies twisted and cast down like dolls, their dumpy Russian clothing torn, bloodied and smouldering. Somehow the attitudes of these unfortunate corpses made them seem less than human, and I felt only a sickened numbness.

Then we met our first living Russian.

He came limping through a doorway which no longer led anywhere. He was a soldier—an Officer, for all I could tell—and around me I could hear chaps murmuring and fingering their arms. But this poor fellow had lost his cap, carried no weapon of any kind, and, one foot dangling behind him, was managing to walk only by supporting himself on a crutch improvised from a piece of timber. The Captain ordered us to shoulder arms. The fellow began to jabber in that guttural tongue of theirs, and gradually the Captain worked out that there were several people, perhaps a dozen, trapped in the wreckage of a schoolhouse, some hundreds of yards away.

A detail of chaps was issued with shovels and other gear and sent with the Russian.

And so it went, for the next several days. Father, as far as I know not a shot was fired in anger in Sebastopol after the falling of the anti-ice shell; instead we worked side by side with the Russian survivors—and with the French and Turks—in the guts of that felled port.

I remember a child, lying on her back, a red scarf wrapped around her head. She held one hand up to the sky which had betrayed her, and her fingers burned like candles. One chap came out of the wreckage of a sailmaking factory, hauling himself by his arms only; he left a red, glistening trail as he moved, like some ghastly slug . . .

Father, I have chosen to relate these things to you; but I know that you will not allow Mother or young Ned to become distressed by a repetition of this account.

The greatest single labor was clearing the corpses; but this we could not achieve fast enough. After a few days under the hot Crimean sun the stink of the place was impossible to bear; and across our mouths we all wore kerchiefs soaked in "raki."

The strangest sight I saw came after a few days, when I was sent into that crater at the heart of the town. We had to wrap soaked rags around our boots as, even then, the masonry was still hot enough to burn the skin. Here I found a slab of wall which poked like a large, irregular tombstone out of the shattered earth. This wall was uniformly blackened—save for an oddly shaped patch close to ground level; and this patch, I realized after some time, was in the shape of an old woman, making her painful way along the street.

Father, the wall bore the shadow cast by that poor lady in the light of the anti-ice shell. Of the lady herself there was of course no sign; and neither did we find any survivors in that part of the city.

More than once I came across the engineer, Traveller, laboring with the rest of us; and once I saw tears coursing down his grimy cheeks. Perhaps, we speculated, even he had not appreciated the devastation to be achieved by his invention. I wondered how this Traveller would spend the rest of his days; and what other miracles—or curses—of anti-ice he might spawn.

But I did not approach him, and I know no one who did.

There is little else to say, dear Father. I was relieved of my work in Sebastopol once fresh troops and equipment arrived from Britain and France; now, after nine or ten days, the town—though wrecked—is a little less like a scene from the "Divine Comedy;" and the harbor is beginning to function again.

The months of siege are, of course, at an end, and the war is won. But since our occupation of the town we have learned that prior to the anti-ice bombardment the Russians were already losing a thousand lives a day, thanks to our artillery shots and the various privations they suffered. Their mood apparently had been growing increasingly desperate, and—I am told—their Officers had been considering a final gamble, a break-out and assault which, I am confident, we could have fielded and so won the war.

So, Father—did the anti-ice have to be used? Could we have won without such suffering among the population of the town?

I fear that only God, the Master of more Worlds than this, knows the answers to such questions.

As to myself: the Doctor has told me that I should regain partial use of my burnt hand, with time, though it will never be a pretty sight, and I will never hold a fiddle with it! And speaking of pretty sights—I must report this in advance of the meeting and reconciliation between us which, I hope, will one day come—I fear that my face has been scarred by the anti-ice flames, and will remain so marked throughout my life—all save the distinctive and quite unmistakable shadow of the hand which I had held cupped over my eyes, at the moment when that unusual shell fell on Sebastopol.

Father, I will close now. Please forward my love and devotion to Mother and Ned; as I say, I hope to see you all once more, if you will have me, on my return to England; at which date I will be able to thank you, Father, for the reparations you have made to the young lady whose honor I so carelessly mistreated with the actions of my youth.

May God keep you, Sir.
I Remain, with Love,
Your Devoted Son
HEDLEY VICARS

[1]

AT THE NEW GREAT EXHIBITION

It was at the opening of the New Great Exhibition, on the 18th of July 1870, that I first encountered the famous engineer Josiah Traveller in person, although I had grown up with my brother Hedley's tales of the devilism wrought by Traveller's anti-ice in the Crimean campaign. Our first meeting was brief enough and quite overshadowed in my mind by the wonders of the Crystal Cathedral and all it contained—not to mention the beautiful face of one Françoise Michelet—and yet the chain of events initiated by that first casual encounter were to lead link by link into the astonishing adventure which would lift me above the very stratosphere; and plunge me at last into the depths of a man-made hell at Orléans.

In that climactic year of 1870 I was a junior attaché to the Foreign Office. My father, despairing of my shallow character and shallower intellect, had been eager to find me a role in which I would be of significant service to the country. I believe he had toyed with the idea of purchasing a commission for me in one or other of the Services; but, blighted as he was by Hedley's Crimean experiences, he had decided against that course. Also I have always shown a certain facility with languages, and Father vaguely imagined that might be useful in overseas postings. (He was wrong, of course; English remains the common tongue of the civilized world.)

And so a diplomat I became.

You must picture me, then, at the age of twenty-three, somewhere beneath the bottom rung of the great Ladder of Diplomacy. I was five feet ten inches in height, of slender build, fair-haired and clean-shaven—of acceptable appearance, if I may say so, if not noticeably overbright. I was not long down from college but already rather bored by my work, which largely consisted of desk-bound paper-shuffling in a congested office deep in the bowels of Whitehall. (I had been looking forward to a posting to the capital, Manchester, but I soon learned that London had remained the administrative hub of the Empire, despite its reduced national status.) How I anticipated my first overseas posting! As I stared sightlessly at my blotter I strolled before the bejeweled palaces of the Raj princes; I confronted the wild Indians of Canada armed with nothing but Treasury tags and crocodile clips; and my teacup was a schooner in which I sailed in the wake of Cook into the dusky arms of South Pacific maidens.

With all that to do each day I didn't complete a great deal of work; and Mr. Spiers, my superior, soon began to show dangerously high steam levels.

Therefore I was more than happy when my facility with languages won me an assignment to attend the opening of the New Great Exhibition.

Spiers stood over my ink-stained desk, his gin-blown

cheeks aquiver and his sad little walrus moustache working over his mouth. "You're to be attached to the Prussian party," he said. "Old Bismarck himself will attend, I'm told."

I could sense an envious stirring among the fellows at their desks. To rub shoulders with Prince Otto von Schönhausen Bismarck, the Iron Chancellor of Prussia—who not four years earlier had given the armies of old Franz Joseph of Austria a damn good licking in under two months . . . Said Spiers, "The Prussians will be traveling by Light Rail to the Belgian ports, and then by fast packet to Dover. You'll be in the party to meet them when they land."

"Sir, why such a circuitous route? The Light Rail from Calais is much faster—"

He eyed me bleakly. "Vicars, every time I think I've underestimated you, you come through again. Because of the situation between Prussia and France, boy. Don't you read the newspapers? For God's sake don't talk to Bismarck or you'll start another blessed war . . ."

And so on.

In any event, I packed up my desk with a light heart and set off for Dover. The Prussian delegation traveled from that port by Light Rail to London; the Rail company had provided a carriage especially decorated with the arms of the Prussian King William, and the Prussian eagle flew on pennants at each corner. A fine sight we must have made as we soared along our single rail at fifty miles per hour a hundred feet above the rolling Kent countryside!

The party dined in the Imperial Embassy off St. James's Square, and a grand affair it was too. The dozen Prussians in their grand uniforms, their chests ablaze with medals, looked like a row of aging peacocks. I in my new cummerbund, the most junior of our party and utterly unbemedalled, felt tongue-tied; but once the wine and other liqueurs worked their spell my spirit seemed to expand to fill the airy, ornate spaces of His Excellency's dining room. I toyed with silver cutlery and savored the aroma of a brandy that had been casked before Napoleon was a boy, and my world of ink-stained desks seemed as far away as the Little Moon. At last, I fancied, I knew why I had joined the diplomatic service.

As the evening wore on Bismarck himself took rather a liking to me. Otto von Bismarck was a rotund, rather grandfatherly gentleman; and to him I was "Herr Vicars, my polite host." I smiled glassily and sought topics of conversation. Bismarck ate heartily but would drink only a foul-smelling Germanic beer from a great lidded tankard; I fancied that he strained the worst elements of the brew through his impressive moustache. The beer, Bismarck whispered to me in his halting English, helped him to forget the complexities of his life at the court of King William, and to fall into sleep each night.

On the morning of the eighteenth we rose early. The Little Moon was still visible in the dawn sky, a fist of light tracking steadily toward the horizon. We caught the Light out of Euston for Manchester Piccadilly, and thence made our way by hansom to Peel Park, at the north of the city. By noon we had joined the procession of dignitaries approaching the vast gates of the Crystal Cathedral which had been erected in the Park. Even Bismarck, Colossus of Europe, became just another face in the crowd; and I was amused—and impressed—to see the Prussian's round jaw grow slack as we neared this newest symbol of British ingenuity.

Like the first Crystal Palace—which had been erected in Hyde Park to house the Great Exhibition of 1851—the Cathedral was a monument of iron and glass designed by Sir Joseph Paxton. Laid out in Gothic cruciform style, its walls towered above us with the July sunlight blazing from a thousand panes. A Light Rail link soared from the east on graceful pylons and entered the building through an arched portal perhaps a hundred feet above the ground. Over the Cathedral's entrance stood a spire five hundred feet tall; its distant tip, sporting a bravely fluttering Union flag, seemed to scrape the light clouds.

I barely heard my colleagues' steady murmur of explanations to the awestruck Prussian delegation: "With over fifty acres of glass—twice as much as the Crystal Palace of '51—and with a hundred thousand companies exhibiting (double the number of Paris in 1867) this fair will truly be an Exhibition of the Works of Industry of All Nations; as well as a fitting celebration of Manchester's new status: Manchester and the North of England, workshop and capital of Britain and the Empire . . . the organizers anticipate ten million visitors in all—a hundred thousand this first day alone . . ."

We entered the building. I stood in that vast, hushed space; the clear glass roof seemed so high that clouds might form beneath it, and the iron frame of Sir Joseph's construction seemed fairy-light, surely incapable of bearing such a weight of glass. The overall impression was something of that of a great glasshouse—but with none of the heat of the glasshouse; in fact the air inside the building was pleasantly cool, thanks to twenty great fans set high in the walls and powered, I was given to understand, by anti-ice steam turbines.

The babble of excited voices that carpeted the building seemed confined to the few feet of atmosphere just above my head, as if the vast volume of air reduced human activities to insignificance. The Light Rail link swept across that great space without visible means of support, terminating in a small platform built into the inside of the wall; a Mechanical Staircase carried passengers from the platform to the ground.

A high dais had been set up at the far end of the building; already it bore an array of grand-looking gentlemen in frock coats and toppers—not to mention a full orchestra and a thousand choristers. Kings, Chancellors and Presidents formed into rows meekly before the dais. I led my party of Prussians to positions delineated by red ropes borne on brass poles. I stood in my place patiently, gloved hands folded before me; and, looking down, I was astonished to observe that the Cathedral's entire floor area had been carpeted with a thick red weave.

"It is indeed an expensive occasion."

I looked to my left, startled—and found myself gazing into a pair of female eyes, ice-blue and sharply humorous, set in a china face.

I essayed a stammered reply.

"Excuse me," she said tolerantly. "I caught you peeking at the acreage of carpet. I, too, was impressed." She smiled at me—and it was as if the sun had come out. My new conversant was perhaps twenty-five; she wore a small-bustled, elegant dress of a pale blue velvet which offset her eyes perfectly; her night-dark hair was restrained into a simple bun, although curls straggled endearingly about her fringe. About her neck she wore a choker of black velvet, and that neck, a sculpture in pale flesh, led my eyes smoothly down to creamy pools of skin—

And I, prize chump, was staring unforgivably. I was vaguely aware of a young man beyond her, a swarthy, slim specimen who watched me suspiciously. "Forgive me," I stammered at last. "My name is Vicars; Ned Vicars."

She proffered a small gloved hand; I held it gently. "I am Françoise Michelet."

"Ah—" Her accent was faint but unmistakable; "peeking" had sounded like "picking," with the soft intonation of the southern Gallic provinces, perhaps of Marseilles. "You are French, mam'selle."

"You should be in your Foreign Office," she said drily.

"I am," I replied like a fool—and then grinned at myself as I worked out her joke. "I am on duty here, I fear."

"There are duties more onerous, I am sure."

"And you?"

"Strictly pleasure," she said, her voice light and a little bored. "This is one of the highlights of the season; and soon I shall be winging my way to Belgium for the launch of the *Prince Albert.* You British certainly throw good parties these days."

"And if all the guests are as charming as you, I am sure the trouble is worth while."

She raised her eyebrows at this clumsy gallantry. "Will you attend the *Albert* launch, Mr. Vicars?"

I frowned. "I fear my assignment with Herr Bismarck's party will keep me occupied until after the launch. But," I went on hurriedly, "perhaps we—"

But there was no possibility of further discussion with this intriguing stranger; for, to a peal of choral voices which dazzled from the glass walls, the royal procession was proceeding grandly up a shallow flight of stairs to the dais. His Imperial Majesty himself was a neat figure in black, almost lost amid scarlet and silver uniforms. A little behind Edward marched Gladstone, the Prime Minister, his gray suit a splash of drabness in the military glitter.

The choir fell silent, last echoes rattling around the panes like trapped birds. Then the Archbishop of Canterbury stepped forward, miter and all, and called us, in sonorous tones, to prayer.

A reverent hush descended on the grand multitude.

Then Edward himself stood up. I was far away in that vast field of a building, but I could see how he adjusted his pince-nez and referred to a small notebook. His voice was low, yet it seemed to fill the great glass hall.

His words plain and unaffected, he recalled the first Exhibition of 1851 which, like the present one, had been intended to "wed high art with the greatest mechanical skills;" that earlier fair had been inspired by Edward's father, the Prince Consort Albert, since lost to the typhoid; and Edward remarked how proud Albert would have been to see the events of today.

As the King spoke I was assailed by a sense of dislocation. Heads of state like Bismarck and Grant stood respectfully, here at the heart of the most powerful Empire the world had ever known: an Empire whose ships owned the seas, and whose anti-ice mechanical marvels girdled the globe.

And yet here was nothing more than a thin, rather shallow-looking young chap, quietly speaking of his lost father.

His Majesty concluded and retired, and the choir ripped into the Hallelujah Chorus.

Françoise leaned close to me and murmured through the music, "Rather a subdued performance from your new King."

"I'm sorry?"

"The stories are that young Edward, with his circle of well-to-do friends like Lipton, is something of a—what is the word? a sybarite? Such a shallow hedonist matches well the type of men of power in your country today—I mean the industrialists—as his mother never could."

A little stiffly I replied, "Victoria abdicated after the loss of her husband, and the sudden retirement of Disraeli two years ago. And as for Edward—"

But her moist lips had formed into a delicious—but mocking—moue. "Oh, have I offended you? . . . Well, I apologize. But Edward is right about one thing: that Albert would have been proud to see this. And even more proud to see the behavior of the craven politicians of your Parliament."

Her perfume filled my head, and I struggled to retain my powers of speech. "What do you mean, mam'selle?"

She brushed her glove through the air. "Françoise, please. Your parliamentarians opposed Albert's first Exhibition; and yet when they saw how well it achieved its principal aim they have fallen over each other to endorse subsequent events." She looked at me quizzically, and two small wrinkles appeared above her button nose. "You do understand the purpose of such fairs, do you not, Mr. Vicars?"

"As His Majesty said, a celebration of—"

Again the glove waved, a little more impatiently. "To promote trade, Mr. Vicars. Your Crystal Cathedral is a vast shop window for your wonderful British goods."

As I trawled my dim brain for a means of continuing the conversation, Françoise's companion touched her arm. "We must not detain your new friend, my dear." His accent was clumsy, and he fixed me with a fish-like stare. "I am sure he has duties."

We introduced ourselves formally—he turned out to be one Frédéric Bourne, an aristocratic young Frenchman of no discernible occupation—and we shook hands even more stiffly.

Françoise watched this with a clinical amusement.

The music was done; the stewards dismantled the rope barriers, and the rows of dignitaries broke ranks. I turned to Françoise once more. "I have been pleased to meet you."

"And I you," she said rapidly in French. "At least, I was pleased to find that you were not one of that party of German pigs."

These words shocked me. "Mam'selle," I protested in her language, "you hold powerful views."

"Does that surprise you?" She raised a perfect eyebrow. "You are a diplomat, sir; surely you understand the significance of the Ems telegram?"

This document was indeed the talk of Europe at that time. A dispute between France and Prussia had flared over King William's proposal of his relative, Prince Leopold Hohenzollern, as candidate for the throne of Spain (which had been vacated by the scandalously promiscuous Queen Isabella). France, of course, had protested strongly; but representations made directly to William by the French ambassador had fallen on deaf ears. Now these representations had been portrayed insultingly by the Prussians in the famous Ems telegram.

"The document," said the girl, "is an affront to France."

I smiled, I hoped indulgently. "My dear mam'selle, such antique issues as the Spanish succession are scarcely of significance in the modern world." I waved my hand at the marvels all around us. "And this, mam'selle, is the modern world!"

She frowned. "Really. Pray do not patronize me, sir. It is obvious to all but the most naïve—" I reddened "—that the Spanish candidature is indeed of little intrinsic interest, but it is the issue which the devious Bismarck is exploiting in order to provoke a war with France."

I leaned toward her and quietly expressed the view of the British diplomatic corps. "To be honest, mam'selle, the Prussians are a bit of a joke, for all their posturing." I ticked points on my fingers. "First, France possesses the finest army in Europe. Second, we live in an era of Rationality. There is a Balance of Power which has endured since the Congress of Vienna, which followed Bonaparte's fall more than fifty years ago; and—"

She silenced me with a wave. "Bismarck is an opportunist. He cares nothing for your Balance; his motivation is his own ambition."

I shook my head. "But how would a war with France serve him?"

"You must ask him that, Mr. Vicars. As for France, you are surely aware that we have already mobilized."

I felt my mouth drop open, like some fish's. "But—"

But the swarthy Bourne was touching her sleeve once more, and she terminated our conversation gracefully. I steadily cursed myself. To have allowed my conversation with this vision to meander into the obscurities of the Hohenzollern candidature! What had I been thinking of?

I called after her, "Perhaps I will see you later in the day . . . ?"

But she was gone in the dissolving throng.

Exhibits were laid out around the Cathedral floor—and the balcony which circled the walls—under massive signs identifying their countries of origin. These signs were constructed from tubes glowing with electric light. Bismarck and his entourage toured the displays with patience and humor. They were particularly drawn by the stand from the United States of America. Among the Colt revolvers, tubs of chewing tobacco and other expressions of the American character, there was a reaping machine provided by the McCormick company; its steam stack and boiler looked large enough for a battleship, and the Prussians gathered in an awed group beneath six-feet-tall cutting blades.

A stranger, a short man with a round, mocking face, now leaned close to me. "Interesting juxtaposition, don't you think?"

"Excuse me?"

"Here, before the fruits of modern, Anglo-Saxon inventiveness, we have the aging generals of the Old World; and even as their armies maneuver toward France they no doubt speculate about how this great American plowshare could be beaten into some mechanical sword."

I laughed. "Having got to know these Prussians, I suspect you are right, sir."

He held out his hand; I shook it. "My name is George Holden," he said. He studied me, looking up into my face with a frank, clear stare; I judged him to be about forty, with ruddy, rather coarse features set out beneath a shock of black hair. An Albert watch-chain like a rope crossed an ample belly.

I introduced myself.

Holden said, "I am pleased to meet you. I feel fortunate to mingle with such company; I am a mere journalist, reporting on these festivities for the *Manchester Guardian.*"

The Prussians had now strolled to the Canadian exhibit. Bismarck picked up a Swiss knife the size of a small book which, a sign proclaimed proudly, bore no less than five hundred blades. A look of wonder on his face, the Iron Chancellor pulled out one outlandish blade after another. "Look at that," said Holden sourly. "Like blessed children, aren't they?"

Actually I thought Bismarck's boyish enjoyment rather endearing; but I said nothing.

The party moved on at length to the largest stand—the British. My pulse quickened with anticipation as we approached; but the Germans, no doubt keen to score some obscure point, stalked past the spectacular exhibits quite rapidly, their graying military heads held erect. However, I saw more than one rheumy eye flicker involuntarily sideways; and as for myself, I stared hungrily, anxious to drink in every detail of these marvels.

The exhibit was dominated by large, gleaming machines which, with their brooding pistons and tall stacks, looked like caged animals in this delicate Cathedral. There was a new form of Light Rail train, with the locomotive shaped rather like a bullet with its stack mouth set flush with its hull. The locomotive looked light and graceful enough to fly, and was mounted on a length of the narrow single rail characteristic of the Light Rail. The novel bullet shape, my new acquaintance Holden told me, was designed to allow the air to slip past the bulk of the locomotive more easily, and so to enable the Light Rail to attain higher speeds. "But," he explained, "it is the enormous concentration of heat energy provided by anti-ice—and the consequently high mechanical efficiency—which enables the construction of compact marvels like this."

A single coach was attached to the locomotive (though a caption informed us that as many as fifty coaches could be hauled safely by this model). Through large picture windows I inspected comfortable couches upholstered in a rich velvet, and the gleam of brass and polished leather made the coach seem as inviting as the finest club lounge.

Another device which caught my eye was a novel form of digging machine. An enclosed carriage no larger than a gurney was fronted by a disc of hardened steel. This disc was some ten feet across and its face glittered with blades and scoops of all sizes. "This will revolutionize our extraction of coal and other minerals," Holden said. "Here is another invention impossible without anti-ice; without the compact, clean boilers made feasible by anti-ice a machine like this would require a boiler and stack the size of a railway locomotive, and within the confines of a mine would choke on its own emissions in half an hour."

We went on past models of new designs of steam presses and cotton mills. My boy's imagination was caught by a model of the new King Edward Dock at Liverpool, complete with a shallow pool of water to represent the Mersey, and toy clippers and hauliers which actually floated!

Now the party paused; and, peering past the Prussians' ramrod-stiff backs, I could see Bismarck being introduced to a tall, spare man of about seventy. This gentleman wore a battered stovepipe hat of the style of some thirty or forty years previously, and his face, framed by handsome, gray-speckled muttonchops, was a wrinkled mask of scars and burn marks, at the center of which rested an artificial nose sculpted from platinum.

Blue eyes glittered down at Bismarck, and the Chancellor's hand was held as if it were month-dead meat.

I turned to Holden, agitated. "That's—that's—"

He was amused at my excitement. "Sir Josiah Traveller;

the great engineer, and the inheritor of the mantle of Brunel—in person."

"I didn't know Traveller was to attend. He is rumored to be something of a recluse."

"Perhaps the lure of Presidents and Chancellors has coaxed the great man out of his shyness."

I studied Holden briefly; although his tone was world-weary and dismissive, I saw how his eyes were fixed on Traveller with a kind of hunger. Teasing him, I said, "Of course, you journalists tell us that Sir Josiah is overestimated. It is only his virtually exclusive access to that marvelous substance anti-ice which has provided his fame."

Holden snorted. "You won't find this journalist spouting such nonsense. Traveller is a genius, my boy. Yes, anti-ice has made his visions into reality; but those visions could have been conceived by no other man. Traveller's anti-ice devices thread silver paths over and under the skin of the globe. Josiah Traveller is the Leonardo of our age . . ." He rubbed his round jaw speculatively. "That's not to say, of course, that he is a genius in all fields. Financial and commercial affairs do seem to baffle him; much as they did his famous mentor, Brunel. You're aware that the launch of the land liner, the *Prince Albert,* is in doubt?"

I shook my head.

"Its fitting-out is virtually complete, but capital to support its operating costs has yet to be obtained by Traveller's company. I hear a new share issue is planned; and Traveller has also, I understand, approached the Cabinet." Holden sniffed and tugged at his watch-chain. "Perhaps that explains his presence here. Are you to attend the launch, Mr. Vicars?"

"I fear I cannot," I replied gloomily. "Much as I would

enjoy it . . . for several reasons,'' I said, thinking of Françoise.

Holden looked at me quizzically, but did not inquire further.

I studied the distaste in Traveller's battered, rather noble face, and imagined his impatience to be done with this and return to his workshops and drafting-tables. ''How unfortunate it is,'' I remarked to Holden, ''that we expect our engineers to be diplomats as well.''

Holden grinned. ''Perhaps it is just as well that we do not also require our diplomats to be engineers.''

Now the Prussians, ever eager to show how unimpressed they were, turned languidly to a further exhibit, a stand of photographs. Traveller stood alone, his gaunt face blank; and I, on an impulse, approached the engineer. ''Sir Josiah,'' I said—and then lapsed in confusion, for the gaze which swiveled down from beyond that beak of platinum was at once scornful and searching. ''Forgive me, sir,'' I went on, and introduced myself.

He nodded curtly. ''So, sir diplomat,'' he said, ''and what is the diplomatic view of these toys I have presented?'' His voice was like the rumble of some vast steam engine, and I wondered if his throat and lungs had been as scorched as his face in the accidents which had left him so marked.

''Toys, sir?'' I indicated the graceful lines of the Light Rail machine, which lay bathed in the blue light of the Cathedral. ''But these are achievements of modern rational mechanics, coupled with the potentialities of anti-ice—''

He leaned down close to me. ''Toys, my boy,'' he said. ''Toys for such as these Prussians of yours. As long as they are distracted it might not occur to them to exploit my anti-ice for other, darker purposes.''

I thought I understood. "You refer to the Crimea, sir."

"I do." He looked at me with a fragment of curiosity. "Most lads your age are as blissfully ignorant of that ghastly campaign as they are of the Gallic expeditions of Caesar."

"Not I." I described to him the experiences of my brother Hedley. I told him how, on his return to England scarred but hale, Hedley had moved back into my parents' home, *Sylvan,* and now worked quietly as an accountant. He had at last married the lady—formerly a kitchen maid—with whom he had once formed an indiscreet liaison and so become impelled to leave home for the Russian war. Hedley had told me of his impressions of Traveller's reactions to the deployment of anti-ice. Traveller listened carefully. "And so," I concluded, "since Sebastopol you have determined that the sole application of anti-ice should be to peaceful projects."

He nodded, his blue eyes like diamonds.

"But," I went on, "Sir Josiah, this is England, not Prussia. You surely need not fear that the British government would again request the application of anti-ice to such a purpose—"

"I think," he interrupted me, his gaze sliding away from me, "that your Prussians have finished their sightseeing here. Perhaps you should join them."

Indeed, Bismarck and his companions were moving regally away from the bank of photographs. Seeking something to say as envoi to Traveller, I essayed, "An intriguing photographic display." In fact it was rather baffling; I peered at a series of curved, shining surfaces set against black backgrounds.

Traveller leaned close to me again. "Intriguing indeed. Do you know what they show?"

I indicated my ignorance.

"Planet Earth," whispered Traveller, "from five hundred miles above the air."

My mouth dropped open, and I tried to frame a question; but already Traveller had turned away, and I could only watch his stiff back recede into the throng.

The Prussians stood in a proud row before the exhibits donated by their homeland, and a photographer ducked under his hood of black velvet. Bismarck beckoned to me. "So, Herr Ned Vicars," he said, "you are not impressed by what we Germans have to offer the world?"

I stammered an answer. "Sir, your exhibits show a high degree of craftsmanship."

He inclined his head and sighed mockingly. "We poor Germans do not have your anti-ice to play with; and so we must make do with better engineers, better craftsmen, and better production techniques. Eh, Herr Vicars?"

Reddening helplessly I sought a response to this teasing—but then an aide touched Bismarck's sleeve. The Chancellor listened closely. At length he straightened up, his eyes bright and hard. "You must excuse me." He clapped his hands once, twice; and the orderly row of Prussians broke up. The photographer came out from under his hood, every sign of exasperation on his face.

Soon the Prussians had formed into an almost military formation, and off they marched with a great air of urgency toward the exit. My superior for the day, one Roderick McAllister, made to hurry after them; I caught his arm. "McAllister, what's happening?"

"Party's over, I'm afraid, Vicars. The Prussians are cutting short their visit; I'll have to go and rearrange their transport—"

"But what about me? What shall I do?"

He called over his shoulder. "You're relieved! Take a

holiday—" And then he was gone; the Prussians had cut a clear path through the surprised throngs of dignitaries; and poor Roderick hurried like a poodle after them.

"Decisive lot, aren't they?"

I scratched my head. "Quite a turn-up, Mr. Holden. Do you know what's happened?"

He looked at me with some surprise, and flattened greased black hair over his scalp. "They don't tell you diplomatic types anything, do they? The rest of this Exhibition's alive with the news."

"What news?"

"France has declared war."

"Well, I'll be— On what pretext?"

He fingered his watch-chain. "That wretched telegram, I shouldn't wonder. Of course the timing is no coincidence. Trust the bloody French to go to war just when our Exhibition is opened; they'll go to any lengths to hog the limelight, won't they?" He studied me. "Still, it's an ill wind, Mr. Vicars; it sounds as if you have an unexpected holiday. I imagine there is still time to get a place at the launch of the *Prince Albert;* I'm traveling out that way myself, if you're interested . . ."

At first, distracted, I shook my head. "I think I should report back to work, holiday or no . . ."

Then I remembered Françoise.

I slapped Holden on the back. "On second thoughts, Mr. Holden, what a jolly good idea that is. Will you let me buy you tea, while we discuss the prospect?"

We made our way across an Exhibition floor that was alive with the talk of war.

[2]

A CHANNEL CROSSING

The *Prince Albert* was not due to slip its moorings for another three weeks, and Holden and I resolved to wait before journeying to Ostend. It was a period I spent kicking my heels in and around my lodgings in Bayswater. The company of my friends, as we haunted the coffee shops, restaurants and music-halls, seemed suddenly callow and unworthy; more than once I found myself gloomily nursing a whiskey and soda water in the corner of a club lounge, watching my chums make giddy idiots of themselves—and considering how the elegant Françoise would regard such behavior.

I returned to the Exhibition, but I did not meet Françoise again. Nor did I find any trace of her in the society columns, assiduously though I searched.

Thus was I foolishly infatuated after our briefest of encounters . . .

But I was twenty-three years old, and doubt that I will

ever regard my younger self with anything other than a mildly embarrassed affection.

At last, on the first of August, I threw together a small carpet-bag and made my way to Dover International Station. Mist still lingered around the docks as I emerged, bleary-eyed, from the mail Light from Waterloo—but there was George Holden, round and bright as a button; he shook my hand and offered me a celebratory nip of brandy from a silver hipflask. At first I demurred; but the hot liquid quickly worked its fiery magic. Our train gleamed on its elevated rail like some aerial fish of wood and brass, and as I stared up at it my prospects seemed tinged with adventure, excitement, and—perhaps—romance.

. . . But we were delayed.

The sun crossed the sky, hot and white. Holden and I drank endless cups of tea and nibbled candied orange peel, and, as that early-morning brandy turned sour in my stomach, we stalked around the confines of the station.

The trouble was centered around one of the pylons which soared out of the tarmacadam platform to support the Light Rail a hundred feet above our heads. This pylon was cordoned off by a length of greasy rope while police officers inspected every accessible inch. These unfortunate constables, sweating in their thick serge tunics, looked rather comical as they crawled up precarious ladders. One of them thumped his head on a cross-beam and his helmet went flying to the macadam, to a great cheer from watching members of the public. The officer rubbed his balding head and uttered something most unworthy.

A stout, aging Peeler had been posted to maintain the cordon; his face was a round pool of sweat and his voice was stained with the thick burr of rural Kent. "We suspect the presence of an explosive device," he said in response to our questions.

"Do you mean a bomb?" I asked, incredulous. "But a bomb of sufficient strength could wreck the Rail. Dozens—hundreds could die!"

The policeman looked somber.

"Who would do such a thing?"

"Ah." He tipped his helmet back. "The world is full of Anarchists, Socialists and other lunatics, sir; not everyone is as sensible as you or I."

Holden touched my sleeve and drew me away. "Maybe," he murmured, "your hay-covered friend is right. But I fear there are plenty of other suspects for such an atrocity, any one of whom might seem quite as rational as you or I—or even as Constable Corn-dolly over there."

I laughed. "But who?"

Holden shrugged. "The Rail is a beautiful artifact, is it not? But there are many who will regard it as a threat. Anything new is a danger to the Old Order, you see, my young friend. Anything new demands new ways of seeing things, new ways of thinking—and, in some parts of our Continent—such revolutions simply will not do."

I rubbed my chin and peered up; the gleaming arc of the Rail swept out over the Channel, oblivious of my confusion.

It was after nine of the evening when at last we boarded the Mechanical Staircase which drew us high into the air and to our train. I looked out over the harbor. The sun was close to the water now and the Moon hung high in the sky, a perfect crescent; the Little Moon was a potato-shaped blur that climbed like a cloud into the darkling sky.

From the Staircase we queued to cross a short bridge. I glanced up the length of the train to the locomotive. The great device lay along its single rail like some great iron panther, its gleaming linkage arms wreathed in condensation. The locomotive was generally cylindrical in layout, like the older coal-fueled designs—although its stack was a mere sketch, a ring of iron barely two inches high. I understood that this locomotive would not expel great volumes of coal smoke; indeed, the mist I saw was not smoke or steam, but condensation gathering around the great Dewar flask which lay at the heart of the locomotive, maintaining its few precious ounces of anti-ice at Arctic temperatures.

A brass plate riveted to the cylinder bore the engine's number and a name: *Dover Flyer.* I smiled at this quaintness.

I handed my carpet-bag to a porter, who carried it along a terrifyingly narrow footpath to a baggage car, and then I followed Holden into our carriage. The carriage itself was more than comfortable, with broad, well-cushioned couches upholstered with leather dyed the rich purple color of the International Light Rail Company. A steward, a small chap with a face rather like a monkey's perched incongruously above his clean white coat, brought us drinks—I had a scotch and water, Holden a brandy—and, as we waited for the rest of the passengers to board, we settled into a couch by a broad picture window in order to smoke and talk.

I remarked to Holden how taken I had been with the quaintness of our locomotive's design, contrasting it unfavorably with the new bullet-profiled devices on display at the Exhibition. Perhaps, I reflected, the advances wrought by anti-ice were not without their cost. At some comfortable length we debated this point, and our talk broadened out into the role and impact of anti-ice technology in general; and finally Holden, becoming more expansive as he relaxed, settled down to relate to me the intriguing tale of the discovery of anti-ice itself . . .

The story of anti-ice (Holden said) began with obscure legends of the aboriginal Australians. According to these savage fellows, at the time the Little Moon first appeared in the European heavens (around 1720), "fire locked in ice" fell from the Australian sky. This ice was tinged with yellow and red, and any man who cupped his hands around the ice would liberate the daemonic fire, to his ultimate doom.

The British explorer Ross, en route to the Antarctic, was intrigued by these legends, overheard in a low bar. He resolved to track them to their source.

His quest brought him to Cape Adare, an Antarctic peninsula south of the Australian continent. Ross and his party spent some days scouting the ice-locked plains. At length they approached a range of low, toothlike mountains and unexpectedly came across a plain strewn with massive boulders. As his dog team threaded its way between these jagged, ice-coated fragments, Ross reflected (he reported in his journal) that it was as if a mountain had exploded and now lay strewn in pieces across the ice. And, oddly enough, there was a gap in the mountain range; it was rather as if a tooth were missing from an otherwise healthy jaw.

As Ross neared the heart of this strange plain he found that the size of the boulders diminished, until the runners of his sled crunched over gravel-like pebbles. The ice hereabouts was also very strange; it was glassy-smooth and, if the top couple of inches were brushed away, quite clear; and there were pebbles and boulders embedded within, as if in amber.

"It seemed to Ross," said Holden, "as if a great explosion had taken place here. A mountain had been shattered, with great boulders hurled miles through the air; in an instant the ice had been flashed to steam which had risen in great clouds into the freezing Polar air. The ice had re-frozen rapidly, embedding the debris." Holden knocked dottle from his pipe, his gnomish features alive with the impetus of his narrative.

With growing excitement Ross pressed on (Holden said).

And at last he reached the very center of the great explosion.

A dome of some yellow substance, perhaps ten feet high, protruded from the ice.

At first Ross thought this was some form of building, and he wondered if he was to discover an unsuspected tribe of Antarctic aboriginals. But he quickly realized that this was no human construction; nor, indeed, was the dome hollow. This was some strange new ice. Ross pressed his face to the chill surface, wiped away a few inches of fresh snow, and peered into the enigmatic interior.

Sheets of a pinkish-red substance hung like veils within the yellow mass.

The party made camp in the lee of the ice dome. Ross was aware that his safest course would be to take back samples of the ice to his ship—or even to England—for thorough analysis. But he remained fascinated by the aboriginals' tales.

He was an inquisitive man; he was, after all, an explorer.

So, when the brief Antarctic night was over, Ross had one of his men scrape away enough of the stuff to fill a tin drinking mug; and this mug was fixed over a small stove.

Most of Ross's party gathered around the stove.

"The resulting explosion," Holden said somberly, "killed three men outright, and left the rest grievously wounded, their dogs dead or terrified and their sleds overturned. Ross himself was to lose an arm and an eye from the incident, and he describes finding, at the site of the stove, a crater a full six feet wide melted into the ice." Holden smiled. "His journal entry for that day became famous. 'Left in a parlous state by this yellow ice. Of the stove, and Ben's mug, we could find no trace.' "

I felt tears prickling my eyes at the simple courage of these words—so typically British, I thought!

Ross and his companions—those surviving—returned to their vessel and made for the nearest civilized port.

"When the news of the discovery reached England the Royal Society dispatched a fresh expedition, fully equipped with the latest scientific apparatus, to Cape Adare; and now that Cape supports a veritable town of Scientists and Engineers. Traveller himself calls the Godforsaken place his second home. And there is a whole new profession—the Cryosynthesists—worthy gentlemen who devise ways, using vast Dewar flasks and so forth, of transporting anti-ice from the Cape and around the globe in a safely chilly condition."

A whistle informed us that at last the train was loaded and ready to depart; and with the slightest of jolts—barely sufficient to jiggle the ice in my whiskey—we set off. The Rail swept past harbor buildings and then out over the English Channel. The last of the sunlight made the water glitter like a field of diamonds beneath our coach, and I felt a surge of exhilaration and pride.

One of that season's sensations had been the fitting out of major Light routes with American-style dining cars; and so our monkey-faced steward now called by to inform us that our dinner would be served in fifteen minutes—and to refresh our glasses.

I said to Holden, "So anti-ice is only available in that one place on Earth, Cape Adare?"

"It is logical that only the polar regions could support the survival of the substance," Holden said, "for if the stuff is brought into warmer climes it rapidly destroys itself—and a good deal of its surroundings. The Antarctic regions have been scoured by our explorers—it is interesting that the British flag was fluttering over the South Pole by the year 1860; who knows when, if not for the incentive of anti-ice, the will would have been found to mount such an expedition?—but no more anti-ice has ever been found."

"So the cache of ice found by Ross is all there is."

"Evidently. Its mass has been estimated as a thousand tons; and, as far as we know, that is all there is to be found in the globe. It really does seem as if the old aboriginal tales were true—that the anti-ice fell from the sky, hurtling across Australia to land at Adare."

I rubbed my chin. "When one considers the fundamental importance of the stuff to Britain's role in the world, that seems a precious small amount."

Holden nodded. "Fortunately, with anti-ice, a little goes a long way. No more than a few ounces a month, for instance, would be needed to power this train . . . Nevertheless, you are right. And we are finding more and more ingenious ways of using up the stuff.

"And this," he went on, "is an argument used by those who oppose the renewed use of anti-ice as a weapon of war. Britain's enemies would have no defense against anti-ice artillery . . . save one: *time.* When we have squandered our precious lode of ice, they can fall on us like wolves."

Holden and I finished our drinks and made our way toward the dining car. As I walked with the glow of my whiskeys inside me, I became aware of a rhythmic unevenness in the train's motion. It felt rather like traveling in a cable car. Glancing out of the windows I saw how the rail as it crossed the sea was suspended from pylons, and as the carriage met each pylon there was the smallest of judders. The pylons were pillars of iron cagework which appeared to sprout directly from the darkening surface of the Channel—but, I knew, the pylons were in fact attached to huge pontoons suspended below the surface. The buoyancy of the pontoons thrust them upwards against the constraint of their anchoring cables, and the result was a platform which was quite rigid and robust in the face of the Channel's notorious currents.

All three Channel bridges had been constructed in that way, I understood, the reasons being the lightness of the Rail itself and the inability of the Channel seabed to take sound foundations.

We took our seats in the restaurant car and soon were bathed in familiar, soothing sounds: the clinking of cutlery against plates ornate with Light Rail livery, the murmur of civilized conversation, the rich aromas of good English cooking and, later, of port, brandy, coffee and fine cigars. Holden and I said little as we ate; but once the meal was done I pushed back my chair, stretched my legs, and raised my brandy glass to Holden. "Let's drink to anti-ice," I said, perhaps a little thickly, "and its progeny, the various wonders of the Age!"

"I'll drink to that," Holden smiled. He leaned back and hitched his plump thumbs into his watch-chain. "But I would not advise you to celebrate the toast by dropping a cube of anti-ice into your next whiskey. Anti-ice, you see, has been so christened because of its remarkable antipathy for any 'normal' substance—in this case, the whiskey and the glass. The anti-ice, and an equal mass of glass and whiskey, would disappear—and be replaced by an enormous quantity of heat energy, in an explosive fashion. Rather interrupting your enjoyment."

"So ordinary whiskey—or anything—can be turned into a substance as destructive as, say, dynamite?"

He smiled indulgently and drew a hand through his shock of unruly hair. "Far more so, young Vicars. But we don't know how. James Maxwell has hypothesized that perhaps the anti-ice reacts in some chemical fashion with normal matter, much as oxygen reacts with other elements, to liberate energy in the form of heat and light." He studied my face, which, I fear, was blank. He said kindly, "I am describing the normal processes of combustion. Fire, Ned."

". . . Ah. Well, there's the answer, then! Anti-ice is a new type of oxygen, and what we have here is a new fire."

"Perhaps. But Joule, following his experiments with Thomson, points out that the energy density of anti-ice reactions is many orders of magnitude greater than that associated with any known chemical reaction. Perhaps we are dealing with forces associated with some deeper structure of matter, below and beyond the known forces involved in chemical reactions. It may be the next century, Ned, before we can probe deeply enough into the heart of matter—with huge microscopes, perhaps—to understand the secrets that lie at its core."

I called for another brandy. "That's all very well," I said expansively, "but what do these famous chaps, Maxwell and—"

"Joule."

"Joule, yes; what do they have to say about what strikes me as the greatest mystery of all—the fact that the stuff is perfectly safe to handle at polar temperatures, and it is only when you heat the stuff up that it becomes explosive—as poor old Ross found to his cost?"

"Ah." Holden knocked out his pipe, thumbed in more tobacco from his leather pouch, and lit it. "Careful—and dangerous—experiments conducted at Adare have shown that, within the substance of anti-ice, intensely strong magnetic currents flow. These currents encase the antipathetical substance, insulating it from normal matter. But when the temperature is raised the magnetic fields break down—with explosive consequences."

I frowned, trying to understand. "And what causes the magnetism? Tiny lodestones, scattered through the stuff?"

He shook his head. "The truth is a little more difficult to grasp—"

"I feared it might be."

Holden described how the experiments of Michael Faraday had shown that a magnetic field can be induced by the presence of a strong electrical current. In the substance of anti-ice, it seems, powerful electrical currents circulate endlessly, so generating the required magnetism. Holden said, "But there is no tiny dynamo stored in the stuff; it seems that the electrical currents simply flow around and around within the ice, like a river in an enclosed channel; without beginning and without end, and without a First Cause; rather as the Persians say the worm Ourobouros survives by endlessly consuming its own tail."

"Do they, by Jove? But look here, Holden: a river simply wouldn't run around and around; it would sooner or later come to rest, for you can't have a circular channel which runs forever downhill—can you?" I added with sudden doubt.

He inclined his head in approval. "Indeed not. But if your circular canal was walled with some marvelous glass, utterly without friction, the water would flow on indefinitely."

I struggled to imagine all this. "And how does this canal help to explain the electrical phenomenon?"

"Faraday has traced invisible paths through samples of anti-ice—and along these paths, there is no resistance to the passage of electricity. Just like the glass channels I describe, you see. Faraday has dubbed this phenomenon 'Enhanced Conductance.' It is precisely this Conductance which breaks down when the temperature of anti-ice is raised. The electrical currents stop circulating, you see; and so the magnetic fields fail."

"It rather sounds as if some commercial interest may be obtained from this matter," I mused. "Although I can't offhand think quite what—"

"Absolutely!" Holden sat back in his chair once more, his head wreathed in smoke. "Imagine if we could replace our cables under the Atlantic with channels of Enhanced Conductance. Then the smallest current, the weakest of signals, could cross the ocean without the slightest loss! And again, if power transmission lines were made of Enhanced material, electrical energy could be scattered throughout the continents, with distance no object!" He thumped his free hand on the table, making the remaining cutlery dance, and one or two heads were turned curiously in our direction. "I tell you, Vicars, such a transformation would make the treasures delivered so far by anti-ice seem like mere baubles. It would change the world, man!"

I laughed, rising to his enthusiasm. "Are the savants confident of delivering such wires and cables?"

He sighed, as if deflating. "I believe Josiah Traveller has constructed prototype devices which exploit Enhanced paths within blocks of anti-ice itself. But it has not proved possible to isolate that component of anti-ice which provides Enhanced Conductance."

I nodded sympathetically, seeing in his rather odd, round little face the soul of a man whose dream—of a transformed Europe—seemed almost attainable, but remained out of reach.

Now he cocked an eye at me, and at my empty brandy glass. "Are you in the mood to hear of other advantages of anti-ice? Such as the high temperatures it generates, which leads to an impressive Carnot efficiency, proportional to the difference in working temperatures between—"

I waved my glass in the air. "By Jove, good fellow, I am impressed by your erudition, but more so by your perspicacity. You are correct!—I am indeed in no mood to dwell further on such scientific ramifications. But, look there!" Rather dramatically I flung my hand toward the picture window.

It was very late now, and—through reflections of the carriage's reduced gas-mantles—I could see how the starry sky bore that rich luminescence, the not-quite-darkness of midsummer. And, like a raft of stars fallen from the sky, the lights of some huge ship were passing beneath our metal viaduct. We craned our heads as the train's motion carried us away from the vessel; with perspective the lights could be seen more clearly to delineate the contours of the ship. The whole tableau was framed by winking hazard lanterns mounted on the Light Rail pylons. "Good Lord," Holden said, "what a marvelous sight."

I had to turn my head from side to side to capture the full length of the craft. "Why, it must be a half-mile long! Surely such a leviathan must be muscled by anti-ice."

Holden sat back in his chair and called for more drink. "Indeed. That monster can only be the *Great Eastern."*

"Brunel's famous design?"

"No, no; I mean the craft designed by Josiah Traveller some five years back, and so named in honor of the great engineer." Holden smiled over his refilled glass. "It is ironic that Traveller suffered similar financial troubles to Brunel in funding his *Eastern.* But then Brunel's vessel was neither fish nor fowl: a passenger liner too ugly and dirty to offer much beyond novelty value. At least Traveller determined from the start that his ship should be primarily a freighter. And so, powered by its anti-ice turbine, large enough to be virtually immune to the weather, and—thanks to the Cryosynthesists—preserving and transporting the most perishable of cargoes, it circles the world without even stopping to refuel!"

I raised my snifter and said, a little more loudly than I might have hoped, "Then here's to Traveller, and all his works!"

Holden raised his glass—his round body, with short arms protruding, put me at that giddy moment in mind of an animated balloon. "Josiah Traveller," Holden mused. "A complex man. At least as fine an engineer as Brunel, and yet scarcely better equipped to deal with the complexities of the world. Perhaps less so. At least Brunel got out and about, and worked with his peers. Traveller, I understand, labors in seclusion in his laboratory at Farnham. He does not work by blueprint or drafting-table; rather, he constructs prototypes of novel inventions which lesser men must translate into operable mechanisms."

"And yet the vision remains his."

"Indeed."

I sat forward eagerly. "And is it true, Holden, that Traveller has journeyed above the air? Those photographs on display in Manchester—"

He waved a hand, a little over-dismissive. "Who knows? With Traveller it is difficult to separate legend from truth. Perhaps the mix of fantasy in him—while a source of creative strength—is also his flaw. Look at his *Prince Albert* project. Does Europe really need a land liner? That, I am afraid, is the sort of hard-nosed question asked by your average investor, who would rather sink money into cotton-mills and lathes; not much fantasy in those souls, I fear."

I sipped my brandy. "No, and I suspect such stay-at-home moneypots will not be the only ones pleased if the *Albert* project were to collapse in financial ignominy."

"Ah." Holden nodded, his eyes narrowing to give him a crafty look. "Quite so. Not every Frenchman will welcome the sight of such a leviathan trailing Union flags to the gates of Paris. Envy is an emotion quite common among your continentals."

I laughed. "Some diplomat you would make, sir!"

"Well, consider them in turn!" he went on confidently. "You have your French under Louis Napoleon, the so-called nephew of Bonaparte, forever conjuring up the bloody days of old. The Russians are a medieval mass dreaming of the future. Austria is little more than a husk—look at the way she folded up in the Seven Weeks War with her German cousin! No wonder they all cast envious eyes at Britain, home of initiative and enterprise—home of the future!"

Caught up by his vigor and lively humor I said, "Perhaps you are right. And as for the Prussians, we can expect the attention of Herr Bismarck to be fully occupied with thoughts of France. Hah! He will soon find he has bitten off more than he can chew, I fear."

Holden looked sharper, more thoughtful. "What a combustible, volatile mixture Europe is . . . Ned, have you come across the pamphlets of the Sons of Gascony? 'Once More Unto Calais' . . . a stirring title. The Sons believe it is a British duty to impose order on the muddled foreigners."

"Sir," I said carefully, a little disturbed by the hard light emerging from beneath Holden's good humor, "remember that Britain is a constitutional monarchy. That is the great difference between us and our continental neighbors; in Britain power is soundly lodged, not in the hands of an individual, but in the fabric of ancient institutions and conventions."

"Quite so," Holden said, nodding. "And yet our Emperor-King—and his mother—advocate the restoration of the Bourbons to the throne of France! What do you think of that? How constitutional is that? Eh?"

I frowned, trying to frame an answer; then I looked into my glass for inspiration, only to find it had emptied itself again; and when I looked up into Holden's pugnacious face I found I had forgotten his question. "I think," I said, "that it is time to retire."

"Retire!" He sounded shocked. "My boy, look yonder: those are the lights of Ostend. You forget you live in the

Age of Miracles, Ned; we have arrived! Come now; I think we should down fresh coffees before we land and begin our forlorn search for a hansom . . ."

With the softest of sighs the train began to slow.

[3]

THE LAND LINER

We spent a few days in Ostend. Then we traveled on to the landlocked construction site of the *Prince Albert,* which lay some eleven miles south of Brussels.

En route our Light Rail arced from north to south over the Belgian capital, following the line of the land railway. We peered down at the Domaine Royale's sylvan expanse and swept over the bristling roof of the Gare du Nord, the main rail station. Brussels, in the bright sunlight, had something of the look of a medieval painting: elegant, golden and ornate, and full of color and life.

At last we slid over the Parc du Bruxelles, a pocket handkerchief of green and white spread out over the breast of the city, and moved on south away from the city.

The countryside to the south was green, quaint and almost English—amid which the *Prince Albert* graving-yard, which soon came sliding over the horizon, was a startling splash of cobbles, rusty iron and oil.

At about six in the evening we arrived at the land dock

terminus. The velvet-clad girths of a party of matrons preceded us down the Mechanical Staircase to the ground, and Holden and I were amused to observe these ladies picking their way through the mud and rust of a dockyard, their hems swishing through oily puddles.

The launch of the *Albert* was scheduled for noon of the next day, and Holden and I summoned a hansom to take us to our inn. The hansom jolted over roughly cobbled roads, and we peered out, bemused. A veritable makeshift city had grown up around the graving-yard—a city constructed of untarred timber, corrugated iron and cardboard, but a city nonetheless. The lanes were lined with pubs and gin houses, already doing a roaring trade despite the earliness of the evening. The ale being quaffed in great quantities was clearly of the heavy, dark English kind. There was something of the atmosphere of a county fair: tumblers rolled endlessly across our path, and we noticed a Punch and Judy stand that might have been brought nail by nail from the East End entrancing a group of children well-dressed enough for nobility; there were notices for exhibitions of such novelties as the Six-Legged Sheep and the Human Arithmometer; and everywhere there was the smell of hot chestnuts, toffee apples and sweetmeats, the bray of the hurdy-gurdy and the roundabout, and the discordant piping of penny whistlers.

"Good Lord, Holden," I said, exhilarated by it all, "it's scarcely like Belgium at all. It's more like the blessed Isle of Dogs."

His small eyes twinkled. "There speaks the cosmopolitan diplomat. And what would you be seeking in the Isle of Dogs, young Ned, eh?" I fear I blushed, but he held up a pudgy hand. "Never mind, lad; I was young once too. But you should scarcely be surprised. The *Prince Albert* is the first land cruiser, intended to sail the plains of northern Europe, but she is an English ship—designed by English naval architects, fitted out by English engineers, and built by English shipwrights. And so a square mile of Belgian soil has become an annex of the East End of London. This is an English colony, lad; a symbol, perhaps, of our technological dominance of Europe."

Now we came to the center of this bustling community. Here, the taverns and boarding-houses clustered thick around a strange hillock. This grass-covered cone of earth, clearly artificial, rose some 150 feet high. At the peak of the mound rested a stone lion, his paw resting on the globe of Earth, his gaze fixed on the distance.

Again there was a faintly disturbing edge to Holden's voice. "And here is the Butte du Lion, Ned; the Lion Mound. Built of soil carried from the battlefield in baskets and sacks by the grateful natives, so that our famous victory could be marked for all time." He gazed up at the noble stone beast, his lower lip working.

And I, too, studied the lion with some awe and tried to imagine that June day a half-century earlier when, not yards from this spot, Wellington had at last faced down the Corsican . . .

For this was, of course, the village of Waterloo; and what more fitting place could there be to build this new symbol of British triumph? (Even though, I reflected, the English army had that day needed the bold intervention of the Prussians to beat off the rampant French. I forbore to mention this to Holden, however.)

Now Holden leaned forward and pointed with the stem of his pipe. "Look there . . ."

That new monument, the land liner, bulked on the western horizon, silhouetted against the setting sun. It was a carcass which loomed out of a sea of shanty dwellings, and it bristled with scaffolding and tarpaulin. Electric arcs illuminated the scaffolding; by their light workmen swarmed like ants.

Holden's voice was gruff, almost as if he were close to tears. "What a sight, Ned. What must these continentals think of such projects? They are like the peasants of the Middle Ages who gazed, straw dangling from their slack jaws, at the soaring lines of the great Gothic cathedrals."

I was about to remark that if we could find a Belgian in this collection of Cockneys then we could perhaps consult him on the issue—when a sound descended from the sky, a roar so powerful it felt as if the palm of God's hand were pressing down on the roof of the hansom. Our horses bucked and whinnied, jolting the cab.

A light passed slowly over us, white and fiercely bright, drawing knife-sharp shadows across the makeshift landscape.

Silence spread among the revelers. The light passed beyond the bulk of the *Albert* and settled behind it, eclipsing the sunset.

"Dear God, Holden," I breathed. "What was that?"

He grinned. "Sir Josiah Traveller, Fellow of the Royal Society, aboard his air-brougham the *Phaeton,"* he said with a flourish.

I stared at the fading glow.

Around us the noise of the city flowed back as water scooped away returns to its container, and our hansom jolted into life once more.

Our hostel was run by a native Belgian. The place was small and shabbily furnished, but it was clean, and the food was plain, wholesome—in the English style—and plentiful.

We had an early night and, at eight on the morning of the launch day, the eighth of August, we set off in our finery for the *Prince.* Our hostel was perhaps two miles from the ship itself, and I made to call a hansom; but Holden advised against it, pointing out that it was a fine morning and a walk might clear our heads.

And so we picked our way through the oily, litter-strewn streets of the *Prince Albert* land dock. Ale-fueled revelry was already in earnest, despite the earliness of the hour—or perhaps, Holden said, it had not ceased since the previous night. It was like a large, impromptu party; we saw well-dressed city gentlemen pushing shillings across bars to buy beer for grimy shipwrights, while ladies of all classes mingled with astonishing abandon. As we walked through streets lined with laughing faces the blood pumped through my veins and my spirits rapidly picked up.

We turned a corner, and the ship hove into view.

I gasped. Holden drew to a halt and hitched his thumbs in the bright cummerbund around his waist. "Now, there's a sight. Would you have wanted to come upon such a spectacle from the poky confines of a hansom, Ned?"

The great land cruiser had been shorn of its restraining tarpaulins and scaffolding, and now it rested on the flat Belgian landscape like some huge, unlikely beast, hedged about by cranes and gantries.

We approached from one flank. In form the ship was something like its ocean-going cousins, with a sharp prow and a rounded keel, but there was little evidence of streamlining, and the white-painted flanks were encrusted with windows, glass-coated companionways and viewing galleries. Three pairs of funnels thrust into the air; they were bright red and each tipped by a copper band and a black cap. People swarmed around in great colorful throngs, staring up in awe at the six great iron wheels on which the ship rested.

A plume of white steam arose already from each of the six funnels, but the ship remained at rest. As we neared I could see how the ship was restrained by great cables leading to scoop-like devices, each taller than a man, which clung to the ground—land anchors, Holden explained, a precaution against the effects of slope—and *Albert* was pinned further to the earth, Gulliver-like, by various gangways and loading ramps.

The Promenade Deck which adorned the upper surface bristled with parasols and glass summer houses, and I made out a bandstand; a small orchestra pumped out tunes which floated out through the still air.

Now we approached one of the wheels; I peered up at a central boss wider than my torso, with spokes fixed by fist-sized iron bolts. "Why, Holden," I marveled, "each of those wheels must be the height of four men!"

"You're correct," he said. "The ship is more than seven hundred feet from prow to stern, eighty feet at her widest point, and over sixty feet from keel to promenade deck. In size and tonnage—eighteen thousand—the craft compares with the great sea-going liners of Brunel . . . Why, the wheels alone weigh in at thirty-six tons each!"

"It's a wonder she doesn't sink into the earth, like an overladen cart on a muddy road."

"Indeed. But as you can see an ingenious device has been fixed around the wheels in order to distribute the weight of the craft." And I saw how three wide paddles of iron had been fixed around each wheel; as the ship moved it would lay these sections of portable roadway ahead of it continually.

We moved through the throng around the vessel. The wheels, the cliff-like hull towering over me, made me feel like an insect beside some huge carriage, and Holden continued to list various engineering marvels. But I admit I was barely listening, nor was I studying Traveller's triumph with the attention it deserved. For my eyes scanned the crowd continually for one face, and one face alone.

At last I saw her.

"Françoise!" I shouted, waving over the heads of those around me.

She was with a small party, strolling slowly up a gangway which led to some dark lower level of the ship. Among the party were a number of mashers and other brightly-dressed young fellows. Now Françoise turned and, spying me, nodded slightly.

I shoved my way through the perfumed throng.

Holden followed, bemused. "What it is to be young," he said, not unkindly.

We reached the ramp. "Mr. Vicars," Françoise said. She raised a lace-gloved hand to hide a smile, and her almond face dipped beneath her parasol. "I suspected we might meet again."

"Really?" I said, breathless and flushed.

"Indeed," Holden said drily. "What an unlikely coincidence it is that the two of you should—ow!"

I had kicked him. Holden was an amusing chap in his way, but there are times and places . . .

Her dress was of blue silk, quite light, and becomingly open at the neck; it showed her waist to be so narrow that

I could imagine encompassing it in one palm. The morning sunlight, diffused by her parasol, nestled in her hair.

For a few seconds I stood there, gawping like a fool. Then Holden kicked me back, and I composed myself.

Now one of the mashers stepped forward and bowed with comic gravity. "Mr. Vicars, we meet again." The fellow wore a short, bright red coat over a yellow and black check waistcoat fixed with heavy brass buttons; his boots were tall and bright yellow, and a nosegay adorned his lapel. This was all fashionable stuff, of course, and quite in keeping with the gaiety of the occasion, but I felt quiet relief that—with Françoise there—I was more soberly costumed. From the midst of all this color a dark, rodent-like face peered at me, and for a moment I struggled for the name. "Ah. Monsieur Bourne. What a pleasure."

He raised his eyebrows mockingly. "Oh, indeed."

Françoise introduced her other companions—personable young men whose faces and names slid past me, unnoticed.

I turned to her. I had rehearsed some light witticisms for her on the season's literary sensation—*The Two Nations,* Disraeli's dystopian fantasy of the future—but I was interrupted by Frédéric Bourne, who said: "I suspect we shall not encounter your Prussian colleagues this day, Mr. Vicars?"

At a loss, I was aware of my mouth opening and closing. "Ah—"

Françoise studied me with a hint of disapproval. "You are surely aware of the progress of the war, Mr. Vicars?"

Holden came to my rescue. "But the news when we left England was favorable. Marshals Bazaine and MacMahon appeared to be putting up a good fight against the Prussians."

"The news has worsened, I fear, sir," Bourne said. "Bazaine has been dislodged from Forbach-Spicheren and is making for Metz, while MacMahon is moving toward Chalons-sur-Marne—"

"You should not hide the gravity of the situation, Frédéric," Françoise said sharply. I watched the fine dusky hairs on the nape of her neck float in the sunlight. She addressed Holden. "MacMahon was defeated at Worth. Twenty thousand men were lost."

Holden whistled. "Mam'selle, I have to say your news is a shock. I imagined that the seasoned armies of France would more than hold their own against the Prussian mobs."

Her elegant face took on a stern frown. "We will not make the mistake again of underestimating them, I imagine."

Holden rubbed his chin. "I suppose the debate in Manchester must rage ever more fiercely, then."

"Debate?" I asked.

"On whether Britain should intervene in this dispute. Put an end to this—this medieval squabbling, and princely posturing."

Françoise bridled; her pretty nostrils flared. "Sir, France would not welcome the intervention of the British. Frenchmen can and will defend France. And this war will not be lost as long as one Frenchman still holds a chassepot before him."

Her words, delivered in a gentle, liquid tone, were hard—not at all, I was abruptly aware through my romantic fug, typical of those of a young society beauty of her class. I had the uneasy feeling that I had much to learn about Mlle. Michelet, and I felt even less confident.

"Well," I said, "are you making for the Grand Saloon, mam'selle? I hear the champagne is already flowing—"

"Good God, no." She stifled a mock yawn with one delicate glove. "If I want to study mirrored walls and arabesques I can stay in Paris. We are making for the engine room and stokehold, Mr. Vicars, under the guide of a ship's engineer."

Holden laughed, apparently pleased.

"It's quite a unique opportunity," Françoise told me coolly. "Would you care to join us, Mr. Vicars?—or is the lure of yet more champagne too strong for you?"

Bourne snickered unattractively.

And so I had no choice. "To the stokehold!" I cried. A doorway cut into the ship's side lay looming open at the top of the gangway, and we made our way—not without some trepidation, at least on my part—into the dark bowels of the vessel.

Our guide was one Jack Dever, an engineer of the James Watt Company which had fitted out the ship's engines. Dever was a thin-faced, gloomy young man clad in oil-stained overalls. His receding hair was slicked back from his forehead and I wondered idly if machine-oil had been applied to his scalp.

With every evidence of impatience and irritation, Dever led us in single file along an iron-walled corridor into the heart of the ship.

We emerged into a vast chamber walled with bare iron. This was the engine room, our guide reluctantly explained; it was one of three—one to each of the craft's axles—and it was as wide as the ship itself. A pair of iron beams the height of two men ran the width of the room, and on these beams rested oscillating-engines—piston-like affairs, now at rest, which leaked gleaming oil. The pistons inclined toward each other in pairs, like mechanical suitors, each pair supporting a huge, T-sectioned metal spindle. The axle itself crossed this stokehold from side to side, piercing through the spindles. Our guide, droning on, told us how these oscillating-engines were keyed to the drive by friction-belts, which could be disengaged on command (relayed by speaking-tube) from the bridge.

I peered up at this mighty metal shaft and envisioned the great wheels borne by the axle, just beyond the hull. In the presence of these idle giants I felt as if I had been reduced to the scale of a mouse. I tried to imagine how this monstrous room would appear when the *Albert* sailed forth. As its tracks chewed the turf of Europe, how these mighty metal limbs would strain and thrash! The room would be a bedlam of shouted orders, grease-covered torsos, running feet.

Holden leaned close to me, a sour amusement in his eyes. "This Dever fellow. Charming chap, eh, Ned?"

I frowned. "Well, perhaps the fellow's busy, Holden. One must make allowances."

"Really? The purpose of today's event is to drum up funding for the operation of the vessel. We should be charmed, wined, welcomed, even here, in the stinking belly of the ship! I'm sure our Mr. Dever knows his stopcocks and bulkheads, but he is a diplomatic disaster. Do our companions look as if they are willing to make allowances for this oaf?"

I peeked at the French, but I disagreed with Holden's gloomy diagnosis; the young continentals, looking like a handful of flowers thrown into the midst of the great machines, peered at the huge engines with every sign of excitement and anticipation. Perhaps the charm and novelty of the vessel itself were outside the scope of Holden's cynical calculations.

I tried to make my way toward the fragrant Françoise, but would have succeeded only at the expense of discretion and good manners. Nevertheless I observed, to my surprise, that she showed no signs of discomfiture in the face of these leviathans of steel. Rather her face was a little flushed, as if she was exhilarated; and she pressed our reluctant guide with a series of baffling questions concerning crank-pins and air pumps.

As I stood admiring that china-delicate profile—oblivious to the competing charms of the greasy machines all around—Holden sidled closer to Françoise. "Rather attractive, all this brute power, mam'selle."

She turned to him. "Quite so, sir."

"Imagine those pistons pumping and thrusting," said Holden in an oily voice, "and the axle gleaming like a sweating limb as it turns—"

Her eyebrows rose by no more than a fraction of an inch and, with the faintest of smiles, she moved away. Holden watched her go, a look of calculation on his round face.

I had not liked his rather obscene tone in this exchange, and as the party moved on through the engine gallery to the stokehold I took the opportunity to draw him to one side and say so.

He frowned and hitched his thumbs in his cummerbund. "I apologize for any offense I've dealt you, Ned," he said, sounding quite insincere, "but I do at least have an object in mind."

"Which is?" I inquired coolly.

"Think about it, lad," Holden murmured. "I know

you're smitten with the delightful Miss Michelet, but you have to admit she's a rum sort of society belle. How many girls her age would take a walk through the smelly heart of some machine? And how many would show such awareness of the ins and outs of the machinery . . . Not to mention the understanding she's shown of the political and military situation? There is more to our Mademoiselle Françoise than meets the eye . . . and it would be nice to know more."

I felt myself drawing away from Holden somewhat during this speech. He had proved an amusing and informative companion, these last few days, and his perceptiveness where people were concerned was clear; but his cynical detachment, his constant probing beneath the surface of events and people—not to mention the rather foreign streak of excessive patriotism which he revealed from time to time—were proving more than a little irritating.

Perhaps it was something to do with the journalistic profession.

I told him that I was not one of those who held that women are not capable of holding rational and informed thoughts in their heads; he laughed, apologized gracefully enough, and the matter was closed.

The stokehold was one of three aboard the *Prince Albert;* there was a stokehold to serve each axle, and each hold contained two boilers.

Each boiler was an iron box taller than two men and wider than three resting end to end; as we approached the nearer I saw how the boiler was encrusted with doors and inspection panels, and that a funnel two feet wide thrust from its upper surface and pierced the ceiling of this chamber, a good thirty feet above us. Yards of entrail-like copper and iron piping wrapped around each funnel and clothed the ceiling and upper walls of the hold, so that, if the contents of the engine room had reminded me of the limbs of gigantic athletes, then this was like being swallowed into the workings of those giants' very bodies.

The heat of the place was remarkable; I felt my collar grow soft and hoped that my appearance would not deteriorate too rapidly. It was beyond me how anyone could work for long periods in such conditions. But, save for a little spilled oil, there was none of the filth and grime one would normally associate with a stokehold; the round bellies of the boilers gleamed with almost autumnal colors, and the polished pipes caught the light in an almost attractive way.

Dever climbed on to a battered wooden stool and opened an inspection hatch perhaps eight feet above the ground; one by one we perched on the stool and peered inside. When it was my turn I made out a nest of more pipes, brass and copper and iron. These pipes carried superheated steam from the boiler to the pistons. If this were an ocean-going craft the water would be supplied by feeds from the sea; but the *Albert* was forced to haul its own supply, in great million-gallon tanks. In fact much of the water was cycled through the ornamental pond on the Promenade Deck!

Dever told us with some relish that if we were to grasp one of the pipes more likely than not our flesh would stick and stay behind, broiled, allowing white bones to slip out like fingers from a glove . . .

Dismissing such revolting nonsense I stood by while Françoise took her turn on the stool. I glared at her companions—and even poor Holden—as if daring them to attempt to glimpse Mlle. Michelet's ankles or lower calves.

When we were done with the pipes, Françoise pressed

Dever. "The anti-ice," she said, her voice deep with enthusiasm. "You must show us the anti-ice."

Dever reached for an inspection door set at about head height in the boiler, and—in an uncharacteristic moment of showmanship—he hurled it wide, so that it clanged against the boiler's iron hide, and watched our reactions with something resembling a grin.

As one we stepped back, startled. For, in the midst of the stokehold's infernal heat, the chamber Dever opened was filled with the frost and ice of winter!

Françoise spoke softly in her native tongue and bent her pretty head to peer into the iced locker. She allowed Dever to murmur his incomprehensible nonsense into her delicate ear, and then she faced the rest of us. "At the heart of this boiler is a Dewar flask," she said crisply. "As you surely know such a flask contains a layer of vacuum trapped between glass walls, and is silvered inside and out, the purpose being to eliminate the transfer of heat into its interior by the processes of conduction, convection and radiation. And the temperature within the flask is lowered to Arctic proportions by refrigerating coils wrapped around the flask."

Holden leaned close to me, his bulbous nose gleaming red in the heat. "An uncommon débutante, indeed."

Françoise went on to explain, fetchingly, how splinters of the anti-ice within the flask were fed by an ingenious system of claws and pistons into a small external chamber, there releasing their pent-up energy in a controlled manner, and so flashing water to steam, hundreds of gallons every minute. "Without such concentrated energy," she concluded, "it would scarcely be possible to drive engines powerful enough to propel this land cruiser."

I applauded and called, "Bravo!—How clear your explanation is. And," I went on, stepping past the Frenchmen and coming close to Françoise, "now I can make sense of the remarkable cleanliness of this place. For the anti-ice stoves eliminate the need for grates banked with burning coal, which are the cause of such grime and dirt."

I was rather proud of that deduction.

Françoise regarded me through a veil of long eyelashes. "Well thought out, Mr. Vicars."

"Ned, please!" I said, glowing.

Now she turned away to follow a conversation between Holden and our guide. Holden's fingers traced the webbing of brass pipes which coated the funnels, and lingered on a stopcock just above the stove itself. Dever nodded gravely and said, "Saving the waste heat from the funnels, that's what those pipes are there for," and launched into a long monologue full of dire prophecies of disaster were the stopcock closed and the pipes allowed to boil dry, and how Traveller had ignored the advice of his engineers about this danger, all to make the engines more efficient . . .

And so on, at dismal and dreary length. The Frenchmen hid yawns behind manicured hands. And I—I only had eyes for Françoise. I watched the gentle curve of her back, the silent movements of her hands over her furled parasol, and I wondered fondly—if a little unscientifically—if, within the Dewar flask of her polite exterior, there might burn a flame of desire which I might kindle!

Our tour concluded at last, to my relief, and we were led back to the exterior hull of the *Albert.* But instead of returning to the ground we found ourselves climbing a spectacular companionway up to the passenger levels of the ship. The steps of the way were iron panels barely a foot wide—finely cast, bearing the name of their manufacturing foundry surrounded by a delicate filigree—and the way was fastened tightly to the white-painted hull. The Belgian countryside opened out all around me, and I could make out as if in miniature the festivities still proceeding in the bars and taverns of the makeshift construction city; when I glanced down I saw faces like so many coins upturned toward us and lit with wonder. But I felt no sense of vertigo, for a glass tube securely encased this precarious companionway, excluding even the wind which must blow so far above the ground.

At the head of the companionway we entered the hull once more. We stepped across a narrow arcade, a bright and airy place lined with light iron columns and floored with panes of thick glass set in lead. And, beyond the arcade, we came to the Grand Saloon of the *Prince Albert.*

This magnificent hall stretched the width of the ship. There was a hubbub of excited conversation from over a thousand people, all brightly dressed and chattering like so many peacocks. I glanced down at my dress jacket a little self-consciously; it had survived in a clean state, if a little heat-crumpled.

A waiter approached us bearing a tray. Holden rubbed his hands and retrieved glasses for both of us. He downed his first glass in one and reached for a second; I followed more sedately, savoring the coolness of the fine champagne. "What a relief," Holden said, stifling a belch behind the back of his hand. "I feel like Odysseus escaped from the forge of the Cyclops."

I thought to look around for Françoise and her party; but she had melted into the throng already. I felt a foolish stab to my heart.

Holden clapped a fatherly hand on my shoulder. "Never mind, Ned," he consoled me. "We're—" he consulted his pocket watch "—a mere thirty minutes from the launch. And here we are quaffing free champagne in the ship's grandest spot! Look around you. Now, there are those who say this Saloon is an Italianate folly inappropriate to a ship—even a land-going ship. What's your view?"

Glasses in hand we wandered through the Grand Saloon. Indeed there was something of an Italian feel to the place. The walls were divided into panels by green pilasters; and the panels bore attractive arabesques depicting the ship's construction, nautical scenes and—incongruously—romping children. The roof was crossed by the ship's beams, which were painted red, blue and gilt; the panels between the beams were done out in gold, giving the ceiling a harmonious and pleasing appearance.

Two mirror-adorned octagonal pillars pierced the Saloon, from floor to ceiling.

More mirrors covered airshafts on the walls of the Saloon. Portières of rich crimson silk hung over the doorways, while sofas of Utrecht velvet, buffets of carved walnut, and leather-topped tables were strewn across a maroon carpet. Chandeliers sparkled with flame, even though the hour was so close to noon.

Holden leaned close to me. "Acetylene lamps. The design showed electric bulbs but they ran out of money."

"You're far too cynical, old man," I said. "The effect is pleasing to the eye. And as for the accusations of decadence I would point to those ship's beams up there; decorated they may be but their robust nature is scarcely concealed."

After collecting more champagne we strolled toward one of the octagonal pillars. Now I realized that its four wider faces had been mirrored to reduce the impression of obstruction while its smaller panels were adorned with arabesques showing emblems of the sea. "And this, no doubt," I said, waving my champagne at the obstruction, "is some structural feature of the vessel, made attractive by the ingenuity of—"

"More than a 'structural feature,' by God," growled a voice behind me. "Those are the funnels from the stokehold, on their way to the fresh air above, lad! Have you never been at sea?"

I jumped, splashing champagne over the leather of my shoes. Bubbles fizzed sadly. I turned.

An imposing figure loomed over me; he was well over six feet tall, even without the stovepipe hat, and dressed in a crumpled black morning suit startlingly out of place amid the plumage of the assembled guests. Eyes of anti-ice blue peered over a platinum nose.

"Good Lord," I stammered. "I mean, ah, Sir Josiah. You remember my companion, Mr. Holden—"

"I barely remember *you,* lad. What was it?—Wickers?—but at least you're a familiar face in this foolish mob. Although if I could have heard you making such dunderheaded remarks about the vessel from across the room, I doubt if I would have sought you out—"

"Well, I'm pleased—"

"Have you met my man?" the great engineer blasted on, utterly ignoring me. I became dimly aware of a slim, hunched chap of about sixty who stood in Sir Josiah's monumental shadow regarding me nervously, silvered hair gleaming in the chandelier light. "Pocket, step up," Traveller said. I shook the fellow's hand—it proved to be dry and surprisingly strong.

"Well, this is a fine business," Traveller said moodily, glaring about him.

Holden consulted his watch and said, "Only ten minutes to the launch, sir."

"Can't stand these bloody affairs," Traveller snorted. "If I didn't need their money I'd kick 'em all over the side." He eyed me quizzically. "And any minute now the band of the Royal bloody Marines is going to strike up, you know."

"Really?" I stammered. "Do—do you like music, sir?"

He ignored that, too. "Come on, Pocket," he said. "I think we've done our bit for the shareholders." He turned and stalked away a few paces, the stained and crumpled tails of his jacket flapping behind him. Then he looked back. "Well?" he boomed. "Care to join me?"

"Ah . . . where, sir?"

"In the *Phaeton,* of course. She's perched on the top deck. Much better view of the Royal Marines from up there, if you like that sort of thing. And you might be amused to inspect her construction." He fixed Holden with a searching stare. "And I daresay I could rustle up some stronger poison for your dissolute companion there, who looks as if he needs it."

Drawing back, I was about to stammer an apology, when Holden kicked me—none too gently—and hissed, "For God's sake, accept! Have you no curiosity? Traveller's flying ship is the wonder of the Age."

"But Françoise—"

Holden ground his teeth. "Françoise will still be here when you get back. Come on, Ned; where's your spirit?"

And so Holden and I hurried through a corridor of curious stares after Traveller.

[4]

PHAETON

Champagne glasses in hand, we climbed a marble staircase to the Promenade Deck of the *Prince Albert,* emerging into strong sunlight.

At the head of the stair I turned back to survey the Saloon's chattering throng. I recognized the young Frenchman Bourne by his absurd masher's costume—he peered up at us with an odd cunning, I thought—but I failed to espy Françoise; and with a stab of regret I turned away to follow the engineer.

Despite myself, Holden's remarks had caused me to reflect. Apart from her quite remarkable looks and figure, what was it about Françoise that attracted me so? . . . After all I knew next to nothing about her. With her unusually broad understanding, not to mention her cutting tongue, she was scarcely comparable to the rather empty-headed young ladies it had been my pleasure to escort up to that point.

Fancy Ned Vicars being attracted to a woman of intelligence!

And then there was that air of mystery which Holden had so bluntly pointed out. Why indeed should a woman, no matter how intelligent, wish to study the finer points of reciprocating arms and steam jackets? And where would she learn such things?

Ah, Françoise! I walked across the Promenade Deck oblivious to the wonders around me. Perhaps it was her very mystery that attracted me so: the sense of the unpredictable, the unfathomable, the wild.

I wondered if I were truly falling in love.

Before Françoise, I would have testified on oath that love on first sight is impossible. If no congress of minds has yet taken place the only attraction is purely glandular in origin.

Surely this was so.

And yet . . .

And yet I had already followed the blessed girl halfway across Europe!

I saw myself then through Françoise's eyes: as a rather vain and shallow young man; one of thousands circling the civilized capitals—although, I allowed, rather more charming and better-looking than the average—

Holden took my arm and shook me. "Good God, Ned; have you no curiosity at all? Look at the wonders you're strolling past!"

As if emerging from a dream I raised my head and gazed about me; and I felt my face, scrutinized by a satisfied Holden, break into a smile.

For the *Albert*'s Promenade Deck was indeed a wonderful, if not magical, place.

The bulk of the deck was laid to lawn, planted here and

there with young trees (firs, of the shallow-rooted kind). We followed a path through the trees, gravel crunching pleasantly beneath our feet. There were shaped bushes and a little statuary, but overall the effect was pleasingly irregular with a hint of the healthy and the natural—just as in the best English gardens, I reflected, which avoid the foppish over-ornate design of, say, the French.

Beyond the trees the ship's funnels soared into the air, copper bands gleaming.

Here we were, perched on the hide of this iron Behemoth sixty feet above the Belgian countryside, and yet it was as if we were strolling through an English country garden!

At length we emerged into a large clear area at the center of the craft. To our left stood a small, ornamented bandstand; the orchestra were vigorously doing their worst to a polka—although the heavier din of the Royal Marines band was now drifting up from the ground in competition. And before us lay a glittering disc of water. This was the *Albert*'s celebrated ornamental pond; it centered on an ornate fountain-figure of Neptune, complete with trident. The sun, glinting from this pool, dazzled me.

I made out the tall, black-frocked figure of Traveller on the far side of the pond and stalking away from us, his stovepipe hat screwed tightly to his head, the man Pocket at his side like a shadow.

Then I looked beyond Traveller and saw for the first time his flying ship *Phaeton.*

To my dazzled eyes it looked for all the world as if, against the backdrop of his wonderful vessel, Traveller was walking on the surface of his portable iron sea; and, just for a brief moment, he acquired in my eyes the aura of the magical.

In overall form the *Phaeton* was rather like a mortar shell, set standing on its base—or rather on three rather fragile-looking legs of wrought iron which raised the body of the vessel some ten feet from the deck. But this shell was tipped by a dome of leaded glass perhaps fifteen feet wide; and the lower hull was marked by what I took to be hatchways and portholes, all set flush with the surface. A hatch near the bottom of the glass dome hung open, and a collapsible staircase of rope and wood hung from it, down the side of the craft and to the deck.

The whole assemblage sat squat on the *Albert*'s deck, perhaps thirty-five feet tall. The hull gleamed silver like a beacon in the sunlight.

A small crowd of sightseers was restrained by a red rope on brass poles. A single British Peeler patroled the interior of this rope circle, hands behind his back and looking uncommonly hot in his heavy black uniform.

We joined Traveller and Pocket within the barrier; Traveller rested rather ostentatiously against one of the *Phaeton*'s three legs, and now I could see how the leg terminated in runners—like a sled's, but mounted on gimbals, no doubt to allow the vessel to rest on uneven surfaces—and how the leg was decorated with ironwork, a delicate filigree. Three nozzles like gaping mouths hung in the craft's noonday shadow, and I noticed now how the deck surface beneath the nozzles showed signs of scorching, even—in one or two places—of melting.

Traveller said, "Enjoy your stroll, did you? I thought your friend was thirstier than that, Wickers." He reached and took our empty champagne glasses. "And you won't be needing these lemonade beakers." He turned and hurled the two glasses as far as he could into the air. Sparkling and turning they flew clean over the side of the

Albert, and I winced as a tinkling crash and cries of protest came floating up from the throng gathered below.

The Peeler stared after the glasses, bemused.

I turned to Traveller once more—to find he had vanished! In some confusion I peered about the filigreed legs, the gaping nozzles—until a voice came drifting down from above. "What are you waiting for? Pocket—help them."

I peered up, squinting in the sun, and there was the engineer already half-way up his portable ladder and climbing with the alacrity of a man half his age.

Holden grinned at me. "I think we're in for an interesting afternoon." With some hesitation, but gamely enough, he clambered aboard the swaying ladder and hauled his spherical bulk into the air.

Traveller's man steadied the base of the ladder for Holden. Despite the warmth of the day he looked as pale as ice; a greasy film of perspiration stood on his brow, and his skinny hand trembled continually.

"Are you all right, Pocket?"

He dipped his small, bony head. "Oh yes, sir; you mustn't mind me." His voice was broad East End overlaid with a tinge of Traveller's gruff Mancunian, telling of years in the engineer's service.

"But you look quite ill."

He leaned toward me and whispered, "It's the heights, sir. I can't stand 'em. I get dizzy stepping on to a curb."

I stared up at the swaying rope staircase. "Good Lord," I breathed. "And yet you will follow us up there?"

He shrugged, smiling faintly. "I wouldn't worry about it, sir; I've seen a lot more terrifying sights than an old rope ladder, thanks to Sir Josiah."

"I'll bet you have."

Holden had scrambled through the hatch; and I grasped the rope handrails and climbed the staircase resolutely.

The hatchway at the base of the dome was a circular orifice lined with a screw thread, no doubt intended to seal the vessel hermetically. I clambered down two steps to a carpeted deck, and found myself inside the domed tip of the *Phaeton.* The centerpiece of this stifling glasshouse was a large wooden table, inset in the fashion of marquetry with map-like designs. On the far side of the circular chamber was a large reclining couch. Arrayed before the couch were a range of instruments, mounted securely on brass plinths; I recognized a telescope and an astrolabe, but the rest left me baffled.

The panes of the glass dome afforded magnified views of the flat Belgian countryside. Sunlight, scattered into spectra and highlights by the panes, filled the chamber with a watery illumination, and there was an agreeable smell of finely-turned metal, of wood and oil.

Through a wheeled hatchway set in the floor the platinum-tipped profile of Traveller peered up at me. "Get along here, young Wickers," he snapped.

I replied gracefully enough but said I preferred to wait a few moments. I leaned against the doorway, studying the various instruments. At length the collapsible staircase began to twitch and jerk, and finally Pocket's face, now the color of aging butter, appeared above the metal jamb.

I proffered my hand. Pocket grasped it gratefully and hauled himself into the comforting interior of the craft. For a few moments he stood hunched over on himself, his hands dangling by his side; then he straightened his shoulders, pulled down his jacket, and was once more the picture of a manservant.

He indicated the hatch to the level below. "If you will proceed, sir," he said smoothly.

I thanked him and did so.

The transatmospheric carriage *Phaeton* was divided into three levels. Uppermost was the Bridge, Traveller's title for the glass-domed chamber by which I had entered the craft. The lowest level, about seven feet in height, was the Engine Chamber which contained the anti-ice Dewars which propelled the craft. And sandwiched between Bridge and Engine Chamber, and occupying the bulk of the craft's volume, was the Smoking Cabin.

From the Bridge I clambered down into this Smoking Cabin via a small wooden ladder. I found myself in a cylindrical chamber perhaps eight feet in height and twelve in diameter. The floor was covered with oil-cloth and topped by Turkish rugs—fixed in place by hooks and eyes, I noticed—while the walls and ceiling were coated with padded pigskin, fixed with brass studs in a diamond pattern. A set of prints of English hunting scenes had been affixed to the walls by more brass studs. Light shafted into the Cabin through several small round portholes; the ports pierced walls perhaps a foot thick. Traveller and Holden stood waiting for me, immense brandy snifters cradled in their hands, looking every bit as comfortable as if they were in the inner snug of some London club. Traveller seemed lost in thought and his eyes wandered sightlessly over the leatherwork. His stovepipe had been suspended from a hook on the wall; only a few graying wisps of hair straggled over his desert-like scalp. But his appearance remained impressive; the shape of his head was fine and powerful, with an unusually large brain-case complementing the refined features of his face.

Holden grinned at me, his round face and body both

seeming to glow with satisfaction. "I say, Vicars. What a marvelous jaunt this is. Eh?"

I could only agree.

It may be imagined that this Smoking Cabin was rather cramped. But it was quite bright and contained only one piece of furniture, a small walnut table fixed to the floor at the center of the room; a glass dome was attached to the table by copper rivets, and within the dome was a fine model of a ship I recognized as Brunel's masterpiece of steam, the *Great Eastern.* Every fixture, every detail of the paddlewheels appeared to have been caught in wood and tin by the modeler.

And so the Cabin seemed quite large and airy, even after Pocket pulled the ceiling hatch closed after him. I remember watching absently as daylight was excluded by this simple action. If I had known how long it would be before I would breathe fresh air again, I would surely have knocked poor Pocket aside and forced open that hatch . . .

Looking around the blank walls of the Cabin I began to wonder where Holden's brandy had appeared from. Perhaps Traveller was after all some sort of conjurer. Holden caught me eyeing his snifter and said brightly, "Don't fret, Vicars; like your belle Mademoiselle Michelet, there is more to this compact little chamber than meets the eye."

Traveller was startled from his reverie by these words. "Who the devil are you?—Oh, yes—Wickers. Well, serve the man, Pocket."

The patient servant approached a wall, tapped gently at a brass stud set some three feet from the floor—and to my amazement a panel two feet square swung open, revealing a well-stocked bar built into the interior of the skin of the ship. Holden grinned, watching my reaction. "Isn't it marvelous? The whole ship's like some wonderful toy, Wickers—er, Vicars."

The bar had its own interior light, a small acetylene lamp. I decided that Traveller's ingenuity would have arranged for this little lamp to be activated by the opening of the panel. I noticed now that there were other acetylene mantles set at intervals around the walls of the Cabin.

Pocket extracted a small tray and another snifter containing a good measure of brandy.

Traveller took a mouthful of liqueur, letting it lie on his palate for some seconds before swallowing. "Stuff of life," he said at length.

I raised the snifter to my nose; rich fumes filled my head before I drew a few drops across my tongue; and I could only agree with our host's assessment.

Pocket closed the little bar-cupboard, and the room was complete once more; then, remarkably, the little servant blended into the background to such an extent that within a few moments I had virtually forgotten he was there.

"So," Holden said, "why the name *Phaeton?*"

"Don't you know your classics, man?" Traveller punched at a wall stud with one fist, and a panel hinged downwards to form a chair upholstered with rich, well-stuffed velvet. Two small legs swiveled downwards from the seat to the floor, and Traveller sat and crossed his legs, seeming quite at ease. Next he extracted a pocket humidor from within his frock coat and drew out a small, shriveled-looking black cigarette. Within moments the Cabin was filled with acrid clouds of blue smoke; wisps curled high into the air, drawn no doubt by some pump mechanism to discreet grilles.

I murmured to Holden, "Turkish, if I'm not mistaken. One would almost envy Sir Josiah his platinum nose."

"Well, Sir Wickers," Traveller boomed, "your schooling may not have been superior to your friend's, but at least it must have been more recent. Tell us who Phaeton was."

The invaluable Pocket was discreetly moving about the Cabin drawing down more concealed chairs, and while he did so I scoured hopefully through my empty memory. "Phaeton? Ah . . . Was he the chap who flew too close to the sun?"

Traveller snorted in disgust, but Holden said smoothly, "Your memory is close, Ned. Phaeton, son of Helios and Clymene, was allowed to drive the Chariot of the Sun for a day. But he was transfixed by a thunderbolt from Jupiter, I'm afraid."

"Poor chap. Whatever for?"

"Because," Traveller said magisterially, "otherwise he would have ignited the planet." He turned to Holden. "So you knew the myth after all, sir. Were you hoping to trip me in my ignorance?"

"Of course not, Sir Josiah. My question concerned the relevance of this myth to your craft. Is it possible," Holden probed, "for this craft to set the world aflame, then? Perhaps its interaction with some stratospheric phenomenon—"

"Stuff and nonsense, man," Traveller burst out, evidently irritated. "Perhaps you are a follower of that French buffoon Fourier, who believes that the temperature of superatmospheric space is never lower than a few degrees below freezing point!—even disputing direct measurements to the contrary."

I thrilled to these mysterious words—what direct measurements?—but Sir Josiah, incensed, charged on. "Perhaps you believe that the Earth is surrounded by a ring of fire! Perhaps you believe—oh, dash it." He took a pull of his brandy and allowed Pocket to refill his glass.

Holden had observed the engineer carefully through this outburst, rather as an angler watches the flutterings of a fly. "So, Sir Josiah—Phaeton?"

"The *Phaeton* is powered by anti-ice," Traveller said. "Obviously. And it is to anti-ice that my chosen name refers."

I inquired seriously, "Then you imply that anti-ice itself might burn the planet, sir?"

He looked at me, and for a moment, beneath the layer of bluster, I caught a glimpse once more of the man I had first met, who had shared with me his memories of the Crimean campaign. "It can do all but, my boy," he said, comparatively softly. "If allowed into the wrong hands."

I frowned. "Do you mean criminals, Sir Josiah?"

"I mean all politicians, Prime Ministers, plutocrats and princes!" And with these words he waved Pocket to recharge our glasses.

I leaned toward Holden. "Is he a Republican, do you think?"

Holden's face was blank and impassive. "Rather more extreme than that, I suspect, Ned."

A clock chimed. I looked about for the timepiece, at last determining that the mechanism must be contained within the finely modeled ship on its plinth.

Holden handed his emptied glass to Pocket. "Well, Sir Josiah, I counted twelve beats; and the moment of launch is on us. I suggest we ascend to your Bridge deck and view the proceedings!"

Traveller, grumbling under his breath, downed the last of his brandy and stood. Then he climbed the first few steps of the ladder which led up to the ceiling hatchway and pushed at the wheeled lid. Pocket circled the Cabin raising the seats to their stowing positions. I remarked, "Perhaps the *Albert* is already in motion, Holden, for I am sure I can feel a vibration through the soles of my feet."

Holden stood four-square, hands behind his back, and said, "Perhaps you are right, Ned." He glanced uneasily at Traveller, who continued to push at the closed hatch.

Traveller said, "This is dashed strange. Pocket, did you—"

And the floor bucked beneath my feet, throwing me like a doll. A roar like a great shout penetrated the Cabin, and it was as if my very skull rattled with the noise; a light as bright as the sun pierced the small portholes.

The sound died. I sat up, winded, and looked around. My companions had been thrown down where they stood. The resourceful Pocket was already on his feet; the rotund journalist was sweating profusely and rubbing his behind, evidently in some distress. I was more concerned for Traveller, though, who, on his ladder, had been some feet from the ground. The distinguished gentleman now lay on his back, legs spreadeagled, staring up at the stuck hatch; coincidentally his stovepipe had been cast from its hook and had landed at his feet.

I hurried to his side. "Are you all right?"

Traveller hauled his thin torso upright and snapped, "Never mind me, boy; we have to get that blessed hatch open . . ."

I tried to restrain him by placing my hands on his shoulders. "Sir, you may be hurt—"

"Ned. Look at this."

I turned to see Holden peering through a small port. Pocket stood at his side, wringing his hands nervously, obviously unsure which way to turn.

Taking advantage of my distraction Traveller shoved me aside with surprising strength, got to his feet, and hauled himself up the ladder once more.

I climbed to my feet—noticing as I did so that the deck continued to vibrate in that odd fashion—and joined Holden at his vantage point.

Where two funnels had stood over the *Albert*'s central stokehold only one remained; a smoking stump no more than six feet tall stood in the site of the other, looking like a smashed tooth, and all around lay fragments of twisted metal, proud painted colors still visible on some forlorn scraps.

The fir trees of the mobile forest lay flattened and scorched. Among the tree splinters crawled something red and torn. My throat tightened and I turned away.

"Dear God, Holden," I said, trying to draw breath from the smoke-laden air, "has the stokehold been destroyed?"

"Surely not," Holden said, his black hair mussed about his red and perspiring brow. "The devastation would be far greater, with the very decks ripped open."

The floor's vibration increased in amplitude to a steady, rhythmic judder, intensifying my feeling of nausea. I reached for the padded wall to steady myself. "Then what has happened?"

"Recall our expedition around the stokehold, in which we studied the heat-saving arrangement of pipes around each funnel? And there was a stopcock—"

"Yes. I remember now. And that rum fellow Dever came out with apocalyptic warnings of the consequences were the stopcock closed."

"I fear that is precisely the chain of events which has occurred," Holden said, his voice uncharacteristically hard.

"Pocket!" Traveller continued to press at the jammed hatch. "In God's name give me a hand here." Pocket joined him and, cramped together at the top of the ladder, they heaved at the wheel which should have opened the hatch.

I watched them absently. "Holden, many people must have been hurt."

He studied me for a moment, his round, pocked face filled with concern, and he reached to the wall and opened a seat. "Ned, sit down."

I let him guide me to the seat; its padding afforded a welcome relief from that odd and continuing vibration. "But how could such an accident occur? Surely the ship's crew would be aware of such elementary hazards."

"This catastrophe was no accident, Ned."

I frowned. "What do you mean?"

"That the stopcock was left closed deliberately. And when the Captain raised steam and engaged his traction, at the precise stroke of noon, steam flooded into the dried and superheated pipe—with the devastating consequences we have witnessed.

"Ned, I believe a saboteur is responsible for this wanton act."

I shook my head; I felt light-headed and numbed by the rapidly unfolding events. I could scarcely comprehend Holden's words. "But why would any saboteur act in such a way?"

"We must suspect the Prussians," Holden said harshly, his mouth a tight little line. "They, after all, initiated the present war with France with their devious conniving over the Ems telegram. Perhaps this incident is an Ems telegram for our King, eh? Well, by God; if they think they can tweak the lion's tail—"

But I was scarcely listening, for some unused deductive bump was beginning to function. "Holden—"

"No time! No time!" Traveller leapt down from his ladder and began pulling out the seats once more. "Sit, all of you! There are restraints beneath the seat cushions; Vicars, I will help you. Pocket, make that fat fellow sit down!"

But Sir Josiah's incomprehensible behavior—even his use of my correct name—went past me in a blur. "Holden, I cannot remember the geography of the ship." I found I was shouting over a rising noise, a rushing like a waterfall from somewhere beneath our feet; Traveller hovered over me, frock coat flapping, as he pulled the patent restraints about my waist and chest. "Holden!" I cried. "Funnels ran through the Grand Saloon, did they not?"

"They did, lad."

Now Traveller and Pocket took their own seats; soon the four of us sat strapped at the four points of the compass in the little Cabin, staring at each other wild-eyed. I called to Holden, "And the funnel which exploded—was it one of those running through that Saloon? It was, wasn't it?"

"Ned, there's nothing you can do now."

The whole of the *Phaeton* rattled around me, but all I could see were those mirrored columns passing through the crowded Saloon. There must be hundreds dead.

And—

"I must go to her." I tried to stand, slumped foolishly as the restraints hauled me back, and fumbled with the buckles at my waist and breastbone.

"Vicars, I beg of you!" Traveller's voice was a roar which drowned out even the supernatural clamor from beneath our feet. "Stay in your seat!"

My straps released, I stood and reached for the ladder.

The floor bucked beneath me again; I caught a glimpse of the Inferno through the nearest port—the Promenade Deck careering wildly, live steam fleeing across the metal, people running from the steam, screaming—and then came a brief sensation of falling, a muffled, thumplike explosion beneath the floor, another lurch sideways.

I slammed into the floor. I felt blood under my face, and a steady pressure which pressed me through the rugs and into the metal beneath.

As if from a great distance I heard the voice of Holden. "May God preserve us," he cried. "The *Phaeton* is aloft!"

With a great effort I lifted my head once more to the port. Now the landscape was curved over on itself, an inverted blue bowl; but still there was the noise, the vibration, the stink of my own blood—

Darkness folded around me.

[5]

ABOVE THE AIR

It was as if I lay in the softest feather-bed in the world. I drifted in silence, content to doze like a child.

". . . Ned? Ned, can you hear my voice?"

The words stirred my awareness. At first I resisted their probing, but the voice persisted, and at last I felt myself bobbing like a cork to the surface of consciousness.

I opened my eyes. The round face of Holden hovered over me, bearing every expression of concern; he had lost his cummerbund, his collar and tie were crumpled and pulled around through a right-angle, and his mussed hair appeared oddly to float around his face, like an oiled, black halo.

"Holden." I found my throat was dry, and the taste of blood lingered in my mouth.

"Are you all right? Can you sit up?"

I lay there for a moment, allowing the sensations of my body, my limbs, to run through my mind. "I certainly feel stiff, as if I have been worked over by a few toughs; and yet

I feel remarkably comfortable." I turned my head, half-expecting to find that I was lying on some form of bunk bed, but only a rug—bloodstained—lay beneath me. "How long have I been out?"

Holden took my shoulder and lifted me to a sitting position; I seemed to bounce oddly on the Turkish rug and my stomach lurched briefly, as if I were falling. I dismissed this as dizziness. "Only a few minutes," Holden said, "but—Ned, our situation has changed. I think you should prepare yourself for a shock."

"A shock?"

I glanced around the craft. Holden himself was crouched on the rug, grasping its edge as if his life depended on it; poor Pocket remained strapped into his chair, his face as clammy as a plucked chicken.

And Traveller?

Sir Josiah stood before a porthole, his stovepipe screwed tightly to his head. In one hand he held a small notebook and pencil, and the other hand he held between his face and the window with fingers outstretched; blue-white light streamed in through the window, casting highlights from the polished platinum fixed to his face. (The other windows were darkened, I noticed, and the Cabin's acetylene lamps had been lit.)

Then I wondered if I were still dreaming.

I have said that Traveller stood before his port, and such was indeed my impression on first glance; but as I studied him more closely I observed that his large shoes were some four inches *above the oilskin.* Indeed, a slight bend in Traveller's knees allowed me to inspect the manufacturer's name imprinted on the soles.

Thus Sir Josiah floated in the air like some illusionist, apparently without support.

I looked up into Holden's face. His hand was on my shoulder. "Steady, now, Ned. Take it one item at a time—"

A wave of panic swept over me. "Holden, am I losing my mind?" I pushed at the rug with my hands, intending to draw my legs under me and stand up. The rug drifted from beneath my fingers, and I sailed into the air as if drawn by an invisible string. I scrabbled at the rug, first with my hands, then with the tips of my boots, but to no avail; and soon I was stranded, adrift in the air, arms and legs outstretched like some flailing starfish.

"Holden! What is happening to me?"

Holden remained seated on the rug, his fingers wrapped around it. "Ned, come down from there."

"If you'll tell me how, I will," I shouted with feeling. Now, with a soft impact, my neck and shoulders collided with the upper, curving hull of the chamber. I reached behind my back with both hands, seeking a purchase, but my fingers slid over the frustratingly sheer leather of the walls, and I succeeded only in pushing myself forward so that I hung upside down in the air. It was as if Holden hung absurdly from the ceiling, and Pocket was suspended from the straps of his chair, while the *Great Eastern* model in its glass case dangled like some nautical chandelier.

My stomach revolved.

A strong hand shot out and grabbed my arm. "In God's name, Wickers, keep your breakfast down; we'd never get the damn place cleaned up."

It was Traveller; with his bony ankles wrapped in chair straps like some frock-coated monkey's he hauled me through a disconcerting 180 degrees and hurled me bodily toward the floor. I landed close to a chair; with relief I grabbed at it, pulled myself down and strapped in.

In the exertion Traveller's hat had become dislodged.

Now it hung in the air, rotating like a dandelion seed; with grunts of irritation Traveller swatted at it until the hat sailed into his arms, and then he jammed it safely back on his head.

With comparative normality restored—save for the disturbing propensity of my legs to hover in mid-air—I remarked to Holden, quite coolly in the circumstances, "I have no doubt this all has a rational explanation."

"Oh, indeed." He brushed a hand over his black hair, plastering it into comparative order. "Although I suspect you will not enjoy the answer."

Traveller floated once more before a blue-lit porthole (a different one, I noted, showing that the mysterious blue light had moved about the ship). I said loudly, "Sir Josiah, since you are responsible for our entrapment within this aerial brougham, I think you owe us some explanation of our condition."

Traveller stood—or rather floated—quite at ease in the air, one hand resting on the sill of the port. From a pocket he extracted his small humidor, opened it and drew out a cigarette and—leaving the humidor dangling in mid-air!—struck a match, and soon the air was filled with tendrils of acrid gas. Traveller then mercifully stowed away the acrobatic humidor. "What is it that makes young men so damnably pompous? Our situation is obvious," he said briskly.

I opened my mouth and would have replied intemperately, but Holden stepped in smoothly. "You must recall our unscientific vocations, sir; events are not always as self-explanatory to us as they are perhaps to you."

"For example," I said frostily, "perhaps you would be good enough to supply an explanation of this damnable mid-air floating. Is it some phenomenon connected with flight above the ground?"

Traveller rubbed the stub of human nose which remained between his eyes. "Good God, what do they teach in the schools these days? Is the work of Sir Isaac Newton a closed book?"

Stubbornly I said, "Please describe how the eminent Sir Isaac is arranging for you to float about in the air like a human dust-mote."

"The *Phaeton*'s engines have been turned off," Traveller said. "Perhaps you noticed a difference in the ambient noise."

I was startled; for, until Sir Josiah pointed it out, I had not noticed the silence of the Cabin.

My heart leapt. "Then we are on the ground. But where?" I gazed out of the darkened windows—noting that the odd blue light had shifted once more, so that it shone through still another port. "It is night-time outside. Have we traveled to a region of darkness?" My mind raced; perhaps we were in North America or some other distant land—or what if we were stranded in some untrodden jungle? "But surely we have nothing to fear," I said rapidly. "All we need do is climb down from the craft and seek out the nearest British Consul; no city on Earth is without representation, and comfort and aid will be provided—"

"Ned." Holden looked at me steadily, although I noticed that his plump hands, still wrapped around the carpet, were trembling. "You must be still and try to understand. We are rather further from any Consulate than you imagine."

Traveller spoke slowly and simply, as if to a child. "Let us take this one step at a time. The engines are still. But we are not on the ground. Surely that is obvious, even to a diplomat. Instead—without the rocket propulsion provided by the engines—the craft is falling freely. And we are falling within it; and so we float, as a marble would seem to float within a dropped box." Sir Josiah continued with a long and complicated expansion of this concept, involving the lack of reaction forces between my backside and the chair I sat in . . .

But I had grasped the essential concept. We were falling.

A wave of panic swept over me and I grabbed at my restraints. "Then we are doomed, for we shall surely be dashed against the ground within moments!"

Traveller groaned theatrically and slapped at his thigh; and Holden said, "Ned, you don't see it yet. We are in no danger of falling to the ground."

I scratched my head. "Then I confess I am utterly at a loss, Holden."

Traveller said slowly, "At the moment of the *Albert*'s launch—and the sabotage—*Phaeton*'s engines ignited. The craft rose into the air—and rose still higher, accelerating—and continued to rise, leaving the Earth far behind."

I felt a chill course through my veins, and abruptly I felt faint, light-headed. "Then are we in the upper atmosphere?"

Traveller extinguished his cigarette in a tray built into the nearest seat, and extended an arm to me. "Ned, I think you should join me. Do you think you can do that?"

The thought of launching myself once more like some trampolinist filled me with dread; but I opened the buckles and pushed off the floating straps. I straightened up so that I floated in the air, and pushed with both hands against my seat. Like a log of wood I crossed the Cabin, fetching up at last against Traveller, whose strong hand propelled me to the porthole frame.

"Thank you, sir."

The blue illumination picked out his battered, predatory profile. "Now if you will consider the view . . ."

I pulled my face close to the port. A globe hung suspended against a backdrop of stars, like some wonderful blue lantern; a third of it was in shadow, and lights twinkled in that darkness. On the bright side of the globe the familiar shapes of continents could be made out through a film of wispy cloud. A small, brilliant point of light came crawling around the globe's far limb, evoking highlights from the ocean below.

This was, of course, the Earth, and the minuscule companion traversing patiently through its ninety-minute month was the Little Moon.

I felt Traveller's hand on my shoulder. "Even the Empire seems diminutive from this distance, eh, Ned?"

"Are we still in the atmosphere?"

"I fear not. Beyond the hull of the *Phaeton* lies only the desert of space: airless, lightless—and some tens of degrees colder than hypothesized by Monsieur Fourier."

"And are we still traveling away from the world?"

"We are." Traveller extracted his notebook with some dexterity, using only the fingers of one hand, and checked calculations. "I have estimated our velocity by triangulating against known points on the globe below. My results are crude, of course, as I lack anything resembling the proper equipment—"

"Nevertheless," Holden prompted.

"Nevertheless I have ascertained that we are falling away from the Earth at some five hundred miles per hour. And this is consistent with the time of some minutes during which the rockets thrust, driving us away from Earth at approximately twice the acceleration due to sea-level gravity."

There was a sobbing behind me; I turned from the image of Earth. Pocket, still strapped into his chair, had buried his face in his hands; his shoulders shook and his thin hair fell about his fingers.

I explored my own feelings. So we were above the air. And it must be true after all that Traveller had journeyed this way before—not once, but many times. My mood of panic dissipated, to be replaced by a boyish sense of wonder.

Earth's image shifted to my right, and I deduced that the ship must be rotating slowly. Through some trick of perspective the planet looked like a vast bowl, constructed of the finest china, but it was a bowl which held all the cities and peoples who had ever lived; and who could have guessed at such bewildering beauty?

I turned to Traveller and said, "I've no idea why, Sir Josiah, but I feel quite calm at present, and will feel calmer still when you ignite the *Phaeton*'s engines once more and return us to the ground."

I could see kindliness and a mean impatience warring across Traveller's scarred brow. "Ned, it was not I who launched the *Phaeton* in the first place."

"It wasn't? Then how—"

"The craft is directed from the Bridge. Do you not recall how I struggled to open the access hatch to the Bridge before the launch?"

I noticed now that the hatch in the ceiling remained locked, although it bore the scars of Traveller's efforts to prize it open.

"Then who is responsible?"

"How can we know?" Traveller said.

"But we can speculate," Holden said from the floor, a trace of anger emerging through his fear. "For this event and the wrecking of the *Prince Albert* are surely not unconnected."

Fear sank deep into my thoughts. "You infer that we are in the hands of a saboteur?"

Holden said grimly, "I fear that a member of the same band of Prussians is at this moment at the controls of this craft."

The full horror of our predicament at last broke over me. "We are trapped in this box, hurtling ever further from the Earth, and at the mercy of a crazed Prussian . . . Then we must gain access to the Bridge at once!"

I would have started for the hatch immediately, but Traveller laid a restraining hand on my arm. "I've spent some time trying that route, Ned. And even if access to the Bridge were somehow acquired, we would face many obstacles before a successful return to Earth."

Holden demanded, "What obstacles, Traveller?"

Traveller smiled. "They will keep. And in the meantime, you are my guests on this craft. What do you say, Pocket?"

The wretched manservant could do nothing but shake his head, his face still buried in his sodden hands.

Traveller pulled at the crumpled lapel of my jacket. "You, for instance, are still encrusted with the blood you spilled during the launch. And what better than a hot bath to relieve the aches of your bruises, eh? Pocket, would you arrange that? And then perhaps we should take a little light supper—"

"Bath? A little light supper?" I could scarcely believe my ears. "Sir Josiah, this is neither the time nor the place. And Pocket is hardly in a fit state to—"

"On the contrary," Traveller said heavily, fixing me with a knowing glare. "There is nothing better the redoubtable Pocket could do now than fix you a hot bath." I stared back at Sir Josiah, and then turned to watch Pocket; and the manservant, despite a distressing clumsiness, displayed a markedly increased composure as he tackled these tasks.

I reflected that Josiah Traveller was perhaps blessed with a greater understanding of his fellow creatures than he cared to affect.

Already I knew that no end of marvels had been hidden within the padded walls of the Smoking Cabin; but I could scarcely have guessed that it would be possible to take a full, hot bath in conditions quite as comfortable as any middle-range English gentlemen's club.

Pocket drew back a section of Turkish rug from the floor to reveal a series of panels; these folded up to form a screen some five feet tall within which I was able to remove my stained clothes in privacy. The section of floor beneath these panels was covered with overlapping rubber sheets, and there were taps laid into recesses in the floor. Pocket turned the taps—finding his body twisting rather comically in response—and from beneath the floor there came the sound of rushing water. At length a pleasant warmth and a few wisps of steam seeped around the rubber sheets, giving the place the atmosphere of a bathhouse.

When the water was ready Pocket bade me slide between the rubber sheets. Leaving only my head protruding into the air, I entered water which was just on the hot side of comfortable. The bath itself—the size and shape of a coffin, I deduced from its feel—lay beneath the rubber, and the overlapping sheets completely restrained the water which would otherwise have drifted about the air of the Cabin. I lay there feeling the aches depart from my bruised flesh. And when the brave Pocket brought me a brandy—sealed into a snifter-sized globe, from which one sucked the liquor through a small rubber nipple—and as the incongruous smells of cooking meat—and the sound of piano music!—drifted over my screen, I closed my eyes and found it quite impossible to believe that I was at that moment suspended in a small metal can and hurtling between the worlds at five hundred miles per hour.

I emerged from the bath and allowed Pocket to assist me with a towel. When I was dry I dressed, again with Pocket's assistance. My clothes had been cleaned and brushed, only superficially, but sufficiently to give me the feeling of freshness and comfort.

"So, Pocket; and how are you now?"

"More myself, thank you, sir," he said, evidently embarrassed.

"What is your view of our situation? Have you shared such adventures with Sir Josiah before?"

Pocket's thin mouth twitched. "We've seen some scrapes, I dare say, sir," he said, "but nothing quite on the scale of this little lot . . . I have two grandchildren, sir," he blurted suddenly.

I straightened my jacket. "Never fear, old chap. I am quite sure it will not be long before Sir Josiah finds a way to reunite you with your family."

"He is a resourceful bloke," Pocket said; and with deft movements—already he seemed to be growing accustomed to our falling conditions—he folded away the privacy screen.

I touched his bony shoulder. "Tell me," I said. "Is Traveller aware of your—infirmity?"

"I suppose you don't know him all that well, sir. I doubt very much he is aware of any such thing."

I was scarcely surprised to see that Traveller had unfolded a small piano from the Cabin wall; he floated before it, one foot locked around a fold-down leg, and played the jolly melodies I had heard earlier. Holden remained sprawled on, or against, his rug; he watched Traveller in a bemused fashion, currently the most ill-at-ease of the four reluctant voyagers.

He turned to me and forced a smile. "So, are your wounds healed?"

"Salved, at least; thank you." I nodded at Traveller. "Will the marvels of the man not cease?"

Holden raised his eyebrows. "What amazes me is not the fact that he's playing the piano in interplanetary space—no such feat could surprise me any more—but what he's playing."

I listened more closely, and was startled to recognize one of the bawdier music-hall melodies popular at the time.

Traveller became aware of our attention and, with an uncharacteristic touch of self-consciousness, abandoned his tune in mid-phrase. "Rather a neat little device," he observed. "I picked it up at the Exhibition of '51. Intended for yachts, I think."

"Really?" Holden replied drily.

A gong sounded softly; I turned to observe Pocket hovering in the air, utterly composed, bearing a small disc of metal. "Supper is served, gentlemen."

"Splendid!" Traveller cried, and he folded his piano with a snap.

And so I took part in one of the strangest repasts, surely, in the tangled story of mankind.

The three of us took our seats. I wore my harness loosely, just sufficiently tight to keep from floating around the place. Pocket spread napkins over our laps and helped us affix wooden trays to our knees with leather straps. The food itself had been wrapped in packets of greased paper which Pocket drew from one of the Cabin's ubiquitous cubbyholes. Another hinged panel hid a small iron stove into which Pocket inserted his packets. The meal, when served, was of astonishingly high quality; we started with a fish mousse of intense but delicate flavor, followed by slices of roast lamb, potatoes and peas embedded in gravy; and concluded with a heavy syrup pudding. We drank—from globes—a satisfactory French vintage with the main course, and concluded with smaller globes of port, and thick, strongly flavored cigars.

The whole was served with silver cutlery and on china decorated with the livery of the Prince Albert company, which centered on a crest depicting the Neptunian sculpture decorating the *Albert*'s Promenade Deck.

It was a meal that would have graced many a high table across dear, distant England, even if some of the circumstances remained a little peculiar. The only constraint on the food seemed to be the necessity to glue it to its plate or bowl in some way. The gravy served with the main roast, for instance, was thus rather more glutinous than I would otherwise have preferred, but it served its purpose—save for one or two peas which bounced away from my fork.

But never before had I been served by a waiter who swam through the air like a fish.

Pocket was allowed to sit with us to eat, as there was no separate galley or kitchen.

When Pocket had cleared away the debris we sat in the silence of the Smoking Cabin, sipping at our port and watching Earthlight slant through the smoky air. Holden said, "I have to congratulate you on your table, Sir Josiah. I refer both to the quality of the provision, and to the ingenuity with which you have arranged your galley."

"Hydraulic presses, that's the secret," Traveller said comfortably, and he stretched his long legs out in the air before him. "The food is prepared in a decent restaurant in London I favor from time to time—and then rapidly dried out, in hot ovens, and compressed into those packets you observed. The result is a small, compact bundle which can be stored for some weeks without spoiling, and which requires the application of only a little heat and water to be reconstituted into a fine meal."

"Remarkable," I observed. "And I would hazard that there are many more such meals stored in the walls of this vessel?"

"Oh, yes," Traveller said. "We have some weeks' provisions."

Holden relit his cigar. (I noticed how oddly match flames behaved in this falling condition; the flame clustered in a little globe around the head of the match, and would extinguish itself rapidly if one did not draw the match gently through the air to new regions of oxygen.) The journalist said, "I am relieved that we are in little danger of starving to death. But perhaps this is the moment at which we should discuss the provisions available to us in general."

The thought of starvation had not entered my limited imagination before that moment; but of course Holden was right. After all we were lost in a cold, desolate void, with only the contents of this fragile vessel available to sustain us. I reflected guiltily now on my enjoyment of the meal; perhaps we should already have entered a regime of rations.

"Very well. As for water," Traveller said, "we carry several gallons." He thumped the floor with one bony foot. "It is contained below, in a series of small tanks. One large tank would be unsuitable, you see, for as the craft flies there would be a danger of the water sloshing about—"

"Several gallons hardly sounds a lot," I said uneasily. "Especially since I've already run a bath."

Traveller smiled. "You need not worry, Wickers; bathing water is passed through a series of filters and pipes which enable it to be used several times over. It is fit to drink, even after four or five filterings." He laughed at our expressions. "But the water we use in the closet—which Pocket will show you later—is vented directly, you will be relieved to hear, from the hull of the craft." Then his expression melted to one of worry and calculation. "Nevertheless water remains our problem. For water is used as our reaction mass, and I very much fear that our Prussian friend may have expended rather too much of it for comfort."

I would have asked for a discourse on this worrying mystery, reaction mass, but Holden was leaning forward urgently. "Sir Josiah, what of air? This is a small vessel. How can four men—or five, counting the Prussian—survive here for more than a few hours?"

Traveller waved a long-fingered hand languidly. "Sir, you need have no concerns. Once more an ingenious—if I may say so—filtering system is in operation. In one hour a healthy man will absorb the oxygen contained in twenty-five gallons of air, and replace it with carbonic acid, useless for respiration. A pump works continuously to draw the air from this Cabin—and the Bridge—through grilles. The air is passed through potassium chlorate, at a temperature several hundred degrees above room temperature; the chlorate decomposes to the chloride salt of potassium and releases oxygen to replenish the stale air. And then a measure of caustic potash is applied, which combines with the carbonic acid, so removing it from the air.

"We have stocks of the relevant chemicals sufficient to sustain life for several weeks."

"Ah." Holden nodded, evidently impressed.

"As for heat and light," Traveller went on, "acetylene burners power the lamps above our heads, and also heat air which is passed through pipes embedded in the hull of the craft. In fact, bathed as we are in relentless sunlight, it is not cold which is our problem but the danger of being cooked. Hence the slow rotation of the craft which you have observed, and which serves to spread the burden of the sun's radiation over all parts of the ship's hull."

"Then," I said, "you see no obstacle to our surviving and returning safely to our home world."

"I did not say that, Ned." His cigar extinguished, Traveller lit up one of his preferred Turkish concoctions. "I designed the *Phaeton* to conduct observations in the upper atmosphere of the Earth. I even hoped one day to bring it into Earth orbit." (This concept, which was new to me, was explained later by Holden; it involves the continual falling, under the influence of gravity, of a body around a planet, much as the Little Moon circles the Earth.) "But," Traveller went on, "the *Phaeton* is not designed for a flight into deep space."

He went on to describe the principles of the marvelous craft's propulsion system. Anti-ice stoves, it seemed, were used to heat steam to monstrous temperatures. But instead of directing the expansion of the hot gas to a piston (as in the design of the land liner's drive system), pipes led the steam to the nozzles I had observed affixed to the base of the craft, whence the steam was expelled. By hurling the superheated steam away from itself, the *Phaeton* drove itself forward. Thus a skater may push away his companion; the companion slides away across the lake, but the skater himself is impelled backwards by the reaction force. This is the principle of the rocket, and the "reaction mass" mentioned earlier by Traveller was the steam hurled away by the rocket.

This steam emerged from its nozzles at many thousands of miles per hour.

But even so, to enable the craft to move forwards with an acceleration of twice that due to Earth's gravity, a full four pounds of water had to be lost to space every second.

Holden nodded gravely. "Then the weight of the completed craft can be no more than two or three tons."

Traveller looked briefly impressed. "The weight of the craft is clearly at a premium," he said. "And that drove my selection of aluminum as the principal construction material of the hull. It is far lighter than any iron alloy, or steel, despite its absurd price—a full nine sovereigns a pound, as compared to two or three pennies for cast iron."

"Good Lord," Holden said.

"My choice of water for the reaction material was driven by its wide availability and cheapness—even if the *Phaeton* were to crash into the sea, a tankful of brine would suffice to get me airborne again."

I gestured to the darkened windows. "But there is no ocean out there."

"No. We have only what remains in our tanks. And, although I cannot be sure without access to the Bridge, there lies our problem. I very much fear that our Prussian host may have exhausted our supply beyond the point at which we can turn the ship around and reverse its flight from Earth—and even if we could, there may be nothing left to work the rockets so that we could land in a controlled fashion, and not plummet like some meteor into the landscape."

I shivered at these words, and crushed the port bulb in my hand.

[6]

EVERYDAY LIFE BETWEEN THE WORLDS

In our interplanetary capsule we were bereft of day and night—or rather of the Earth's diurnal rhythms, which had been replaced by the rotation of the *Phaeton;* if one cared to, one could watch a sunrise every quarter of an hour. But we kept to much the same hours as if we were firmly on English soil. We slept on pallets which folded down from the walls of the Cabin. My bed, into which I bound myself each night with tightly tucked blankets, supported me as if with the softest of mattresses—although, if I worked an arm free in my sleep, it was disconcerting to wake to find it floating before my face, apparently disembodied.

At half past seven each morning we would be awoken by the soft chiming of an alarm mechanism in the *Great Eastern.* Pocket would lift the small blinds from the portholes, ceding entry to twin beams of sun- and Earthlight, and we would take it in turns to slip into the concealed bathtub.

The toilet facilities were necessarily of a rather crude

nature, consisting of an apparatus which unfolded from the padded wall and which could be surrounded by a light but airtight screen, so that privacy and cleanliness were to some degree maintained. As Traveller had assured us, the waste materials were vented directly into space.

It was even possible to shave on board the *Phaeton*! Having loose whiskers floating around the craft would hardly have been pleasant, of course, but, by using an excess of shaving soap, one could trap all but a few stray wisps quite cleanly. And any floating debris and dust was swept up by the invaluable Pocket. He used a flexible hose, attached through a socket in the wall to one of the air-circulation pumps. Daily Pocket scurried around the craft with this device, probing and scooping; at first Holden and I found the sight comical, but as the days wore on we grew to appreciate the value of the invention, for without it our hurtling prison would soon have become as squalid as a Calcutta den.

Traveller maintained a small wardrobe on board the ship, as did Pocket; Traveller loaned Holden and me undergarments and dressing-gowns, and the marvelous Pocket found ways to clean (using soaped sponges and cloths) the worst from our battered launch day finery.

And so it was that we three gentlemen—a little crumpled, perhaps, but more than presentable to polite company—would take our places in our table-seats at around eight-thirty, and allow Pocket to serve us with hot tea, bacon and buttered toast.

Traveller had extensive theories about the hazards of gravity-free living, among which he listed the wasting of unused muscles and bones, and he predicted that on our eventual return to Earth we might be left so weak we would require carrying from the vessel. And so while

Pocket prepared lunch—usually a light, cold snack—we would don our dressing-gowns and take part in a vigorous exercise routine. This included shadow-boxing, a novel form of running which involved pacing around and around the walls of the Cabin rather as a mouse circles its treadmill, and occasionally a little good-humored wrestling.

Holden proved to be over-ample of girth, short of breath and generally unhealthy; Pocket was wasted and rather frail; and Traveller—though willing enough, vigorous and limber—was seven decades old and a mild asthmatic, a condition not aided by the wholesale destruction of his nose and sinuses in some ancient anti-ice accident. So it was I who would work on alone in our exercise bouts, the youngest and healthiest of us all.

The afternoons we would while away with games—the *Phaeton* bore several compendia of games such as chess and drafts, manufactured in a special miniaturized form for ease of storage; and we would also indulge in a few hands of bridge, with Traveller's patent magnetized card decks. Holden was a willing player but rather unadventurous, while Sir Josiah proved imaginative but rash to a fault in his play! Poor Pocket, drafted in to make up the four, knew little more than the rules of the game; and after the first few rubbers the three of us discreetly drew lots to determine who would bear the misfortune of partnering the poor fellow.

Supper was the heaviest meal of the day, served around seven, usually with wine and followed by a globe or two of port with cigars; Pocket drew the blinds at this hour, excluding the unearthly heavens beyond the hull and allowing us the illusion of a comfortable sanctuary. It was quite pleasant to sit in companionable silence, lightly strapped to our wall-chairs, watching cigar smoke curl toward the hidden air filters.

The evening would close, more often than not, with a rendition by Traveller on his collapsible piano of a few hymns, or, more likely, of some of the rowdy variety-palace numbers of which he appeared to hold an encyclopedic knowledge. With the port settling inside us we would float at all angles around the engineer, his coat tails floating in the air as he played, bawling out ditties that would have made our mothers blush!

And so for the next several days our ship traveled on, a tiny bubble of warmth, air and English civilization, adrift on a river of celestial darkness.

Once the vertiginous fear generated by our state of continual falling was passed—and also, in poor Holden's case, a severe physical sickness reminiscent of *mal de mer*—we found the sensation of continual drifting more than pleasant. The novelties of floating, the endless ingenuity of Traveller's marvelous gadgets, and the sheer peculiarity of our position all combined to make our predicament at first fascinating and even enjoyable.

But the darker side of our situation was never far beneath the surface of my thoughts, and—as time wore on—the dangers and uncertainty confronting us emerged ever more clearly in my mind, as sand blows steadily away to reveal buried ruins.

My dreams centered on Françoise.

I passed idle hours envisioning the love which might one day blossom between us—and my dreams were so intense that sometimes it was as if I knew already that feeling of companionship, of relief that one is no longer alone, that comes from true love. And, even beyond that: as I meditated further, Françoise's sweet and distant face became transformed in my mind into a symbol of the human world from which I had been torn.

Each morning I would watch eagerly as Pocket folded back the blinds, hoping beyond hope that somehow our situation might have changed during the night, that our flight might have been reversed by our unseen pilot (though Traveller impatiently explained more than once that were the engines engaged again we should hardly sleep through the experience). But each morning I was disappointed; each morning Earth shriveled a little more, demonstrating that we continued to recede from the planet of our birth by hundreds more miles every minute.

So we four strangers, thrown so suddenly into this aerial jail together, waited out the days. We were tolerant of each other—wary even. Holden and Traveller bore their plight with stoicism and fortitude, broken only by Traveller's impatience to return to his various engineering projects on Earth. (Personally I found my work, and Spiers's malevolent little face, easy to forget.) And Pocket—though the most vertigo-prone of us all—seemed as happy in his domestic routine as if he were on solid ground.

But as time went on without change, boredom, resentment and claustrophobic irritation grew within me like weeds; and on the fifth morning, as I sat in my chair facing Pocket's bacon and toast breakfast and listening to Traveller and Holden discuss the vagaries of the Stock Exchange, something broke inside me.

I rose from my chair and dashed away my breakfast tray. "I can no longer listen to this!" I hovered in the air like some avenging angel, an effect spoilt only by fragments of orbiting toast.

Traveller looked up, a blob of marmalade perched

comically on his platinum nose. "Good God, Wickers. Restrain yourself, sir."

I felt my anger shine through the trembling of my voice. "Sir Josiah, for the hundredth and last time my name is Vicars, Edward Vicars; and as for restraint, I have had quite enough of that over the last several days."

Holden said gloomily, "This will do no good, Ned."

I turned on him. "Holden, we remain trapped in this ridiculous padded box which hurtles ever more deeply into the untracked void! And yet you sit and debate hypothetical stock movements—"

Traveller took another bite of toast. "What alternative do you propose?"

I thumped my fist into my palm. "That we abandon this game of normality; that we sit down and discuss ways of wresting back control of this vessel from the deranged Hun who has occupied the Bridge."

Holden said, "Ned—"

But Traveller nodded. "We will converse on any subject you nominate," he said with a rasp. "But, sir, you will allow me to finish my breakfast in good order."

I spluttered, "Breakfast? How can you swallow toast in a situation unparalleled in the experience of man—when, indeed, our very lives are at peril . . ."

I continued in this vein at some length, but the old gentleman would have none of it; and I was forced to subside, fuming, and wait until breakfast was over and cleared away.

Traveller, utterly composed, wiped his long fingers on a napkin.

"Now then, Ned, I sympathize with your sentiments, and even admire your resolve which, while founded on ignorance and hotheadedness, nevertheless contains elements of courage. However, Ned, you are not as stupid as you appear, and you know very well that the connecting hatchway between this compartment and the Bridge is jammed from above. And we are bereft of tools by means of which we might effect a forced entry."

I found myself grinding my teeth together. "And your conclusion?"

"That there is nothing we can do to improve our prospects—although there are many actions we can take which would make things worse."

Holden had blanched, but steepled his fat fingers together in a composed manner. "Then what do you recommend?"

"We must accept that which we cannot change. We must hope that our Teutonic pilot sees fit to reverse the course of this vessel—if indeed he can. Then we must pray that the craft retains the ability to return us safely to our native world."

I leapt from my chair and cannonaded from the padded ceiling. "Hope? Pray? You counsel us with inactivity, Sir Josiah. Will you continue to press this advice when the marmalade supply dwindles to naught?"

Traveller barked laughter.

I said, "I for one am not prepared to face my death without a fight."

Holden sat straighter in his chair and faced me grimly. "I hope you will face your death with resolution, as an Englishman should, Ned."

That evoked a sunburst of shame inside my anger, but I went on regardless: "Holden, there is nothing English about lying down to die."

Traveller rested his hands on his lap. "Gentlemen, it can certainly do no harm to talk. Provided," he said to me severely, "we conduct our conversation in a civilized fashion."

I climbed back into my chair; but my fingers danced restlessly on the chair's arms throughout the ensuing discussion.

"So," said Traveller, "what would you like to talk about, Ned?"

"It's obvious. We must find a way to open that hatch to the Bridge."

"And I have already explained that such a course of action is impossible. What else do you suggest?"

Baffled and angry, I looked to Holden, who said smoothly, "Sir Josiah, I fear that without the advantage of your deep knowledge of the *Phaeton* and its construction, young Ned is likely to lack ideas. Perhaps we could explore the nature of the craft's design, in the hope of some notion evolving. For example, how thick are these walls?"

Traveller's eyebrows rose. "The walls? Perhaps, you speculate, a heroic figure could slip between the inner and outer hulls, slither like a ferret up to the Bridge, and burst upon our German friend? Alas, the space between the hulls is only nine inches deep—a little too narrow even for our young companion, let alone one with such ample girth as yours—and in any event is occupied by pipes for heating, water and air, by springs which cushion the inner compartment from impact—the inner chamber is gimballed, you know—and the various beds, chairs and other devices of which you both make such extensive use. And anyway the double hull terminates at the joint with the Bridge; the Bridge and Smoking Cabin are separate, airtight compartments.

"To save you time, let me say that the only access to the Bridge—other than the blocked hatch above us—is through the hatch set in the Bridge's outer glass wall. And that, of course, could only be opened were one positioned outside the vessel."

Holden shook his head. "I cannot understand how you allowed a design in which access to the vessel's controls can be blocked so easily!"

Sir Josiah smiled. "In my youthful naïvety, I did not anticipate sabotage. I never envisaged the situation which pertains today."

Traveller's use of the word "airtight" had given me an idea. "Sir, where is the air supply which feeds the Bridge?"

"Bridge and Smoking Cabin are both fed by the same network of air pipes, which climb through the hull from pumps and filter sets in the Engine Chamber beneath our feet."

I nodded. "To which we have access."

"Ned, what's in your mind?" Holden asked.

"Suppose we were to block the air pipes which feed the Bridge? Then our Hunnish companion would surely expire in his own stink within a few hours."

Traveller nodded gravely. "Elegantly put. But while such a course of action would be satisfyingly vengeful, I fear it would leave us only worse off. We would still have no access to the Bridge, and would have replaced a German pilot with a dead one!"

The engineer's calm, condescending dissection of my proposals, all delivered in the flat, nasal tones of the Mancunian, enraged me. "Then let us continue," I said, endeavoring to keep my voice steady. "The air pumps lie within the Engine Chamber. What else is to be found there?"

"You can see for yourself," said Traveller. "Pocket, would you raise the maintenance covers?"

The patient servant, with scarcely a nod, pushed himself from his seat and floated down toward the floor. There he tugged at the Turkish rug and oilskin which covered the bulkhead; the carpets were affixed by hooks and eyes which disengaged readily enough, but the poor man had a deal of trouble rolling up the loosened carpets in our floating condition. Pocket steadily refused all our offers of help, the only request he made of us being to raise our feet from time to time.

I never knew a man who knew his place so well, and filled it to such perfection.

At last the carpets were rolled up and stuffed into a crevice near the top of the Cabin wall. The bulkhead so revealed bore the sheen of aluminum, but it was not a solid slab; instead the bulkhead, some fifteen feet wide, was little more than a framework into which great holes had been cut, and these holes were covered by large rectangular plates held in place by wingnuts. One portion of the bulkhead was covered by overlapping sheets of rubber; this, I recalled, concealed the enclosed bath we used daily.

Now Traveller braced his feet against the ridged aluminum surface and twisted away the wingnuts restraining one of the plates. He stored the nuts neatly in a row—in thin air—while he worked, finally stowing them in a waistcoat pocket. "You need not fear a loss of air," he said. "This bulkhead is not airtight, and the lower compartment is held at the same pressure as the Cabin."

Holden and I peered inside the hole. The compartment revealed was some seven feet deep, and directly below the hole was a sphere perhaps four feet in diameter, held in place by a stout framework; this sphere was coated with silver plate, so that our reflections, and those of the acetylene lamps above and behind us, danced in its curving belly. This, Traveller explained, was one of the *Phaeton*'s three anti-ice Dewar flasks. I considered the flask with something approaching awe, and I touched its silvered epidermis. But I felt only a smooth, pleasantly warm surface; there was no hint of the layer of vacuum which lay beneath the vessel's outer shell, nor of the handful of primordial violence which lay at its heart.

Traveller showed us an elaborate system of rods which, he said, led through the hull to levers set in the Bridge. The rods penetrated the Dewar, said Traveller, thereby forming the basis of the system by which—under direction from the Bridge—controlled portions of anti-ice could be moved from the central Arctic compartment of the Dewar, allowed to melt and so release their heat.

Traveller told us how the anti-ice energy was used to heat water in a series of fire-tube boilers. These were metal boxes surrounding water-bearing pipes. Super-heated steam was piped out of the boilers and then back through channels cut through the anti-ice Dewars themselves.

Now, to improve the performance of his motors, Traveller ingeniously exploited that other marvelous property of anti-ice, its Enhanced Conductance.

Powerful electrical currents circulated endlessly through the anti-ice slabs. These currents generated strong magnetic fields which accelerated further the superhot steam before it was expelled from the ship's three nozzles, which were situated beneath the Dewars. By this elaborate arrangement, Traveller said, it was possible to raise the steam's "exit velocity" to extraordinary levels without further contact with the ship's pipes and plates, which would otherwise surely have melted. This high velocity enabled a design requiring a comparatively small "reaction mass."

Traveller raised another plate, and we were confronted by a jumble of piping, slim tanks each about the size of a bookcase, globes of brass, and various other pieces of machinery. The bookcase tanks contained the water which served so many of the ship's systems, Traveller explained. Acetylene gas and air were stored in compressed conditions in the spherical reservoirs. Pumps drove fluids and gases continuously around the hull and interior of the craft, much as human organs maintain the flow of vital fluids around the body; and the pumps worked exclusively off the heat generated by the anti-ice boilers. There was also a robust hypocaust which heated the supply of bathing water.

I stared gloomily into the craft's bowels. The machinery was markedly less pristine than the stokehold of the *Prince Albert,* for example; the metalwork was roughly finished and patched, and scorched by crude welds, demonstrating—to my discomfort—that *Phaeton* was, after all, nothing more than an engineering prototype.

And, even more depressing, I could see no opportunity to change our trapped situation, save by wrecking the very systems on which our lives depended.

"Sir Josiah," I said, "the purpose of these removable panels must be to allow access to the equipment here, so that any repairs necessary can be effected in flight."

"Correct."

"Where, then, is your tool kit?"

For the first time the engineer, floating above the disassembled bulkhead, looked a little chagrined. "The tools I carry are not stored in this compartment, nor in the Cabin, as perhaps they should be. They are on the Bridge."

I slapped my forehead with frustration. "Then there is a perfectly good tool kit aboard, which might be used to force access to the Bridge, and it is stored not ten feet from here—but it is sealed with that deranged Hun behind the upper hatch!"

Holden floated with his arms folded, his several chins resting on his vest, and his legs stuck straight out before him. "Sir Josiah, you have shown us the anti-ice propulsive system and the water supply. What else is stored in this Engine Chamber?"

Traveller clapped his hands together. "Pocket?" As the manservant moved to unscrew the wingnuts restraining the cover of another subcompartment, Traveller said, "What I will show you now is an experiment of mine, yet to be made fully functional. You can see that I have designed for access to the engine section in case of some internal breakdown during a flight. But I have also imagined the circumstance in which some damage is done to the ship's exterior, by an untoward event."

I was mystified by this. "But we travel through empty space, sir—a vacuum, if your ideas are correct. What agent is available to do such injury?"

Traveller frowned, and his face, with its platinum centerpiece, became a mask of intimidating grimness. "Outer space is far from unoccupied, young Ned; for meteors lance constantly through its darkness."

"Meteors?"

Holden interjected, "Fragments of rock or dust, Ned; they travel at several hundreds of miles an hour, and, when they encounter Earth's atmosphere, they burn up, forming the phenomenon of shooting stars with which you are familiar. According to the newest theories several tons of this interplanetary dust—both meteors and their heavier kin, meteorites, which can cause impacts large enough to leave craters—fall to Earth every week!"

Traveller locked his hands behind his head and leaned back in mid-air, quite at ease. "The subject is fascinating. Traces of carbon have been detected in meteorite fragments; and carbon, of course, owes its origin solely to the action of living organisms, proving that the domain of life must extend beyond the limits of Earth. For example, the French have—"

"Sir Josiah, please! Can we return to the point? The scientific interest of these meteor objects is no doubt enormous, but I'd just as soon do without the blighters, for they sound more than a little dangerous to me!"

The aluminum walls suddenly seemed as frail as the canvas of a tent, and I pictured hundreds of rock fragments traveling with the speed of bullets. I reflected ruefully that perhaps the Lord had thought I had not had enough to worry about already.

Traveller's subsequent words, though, reassured me to some extent. "One should not worry unduly," he said, "for space is large, and the chances of such a collision are vanishingly small. But it seemed to me that I should essay preparations for such an eventuality—or for other disasters which might affect the exterior of the craft."

The newly exposed sector of the Engine Chamber contained an aluminum box set flat against the lower floor of the compartment; the box was about the size and shape of a coffin and it was sealed by a lid held in place by a wheel lock. Traveller explained that this "air cupboard" was airtight, and that on its far side was another door which led to the exterior of the craft—to space! This second door could be opened by a man within the box by means of another wheel. "The air in the box would puff out to space, of course," Traveller said blithely, "but—as long as the upper door were sealed shut—no harm would come to the inhabitants of the Cabin. Thus access to the exterior can be gained without breach of the airtight shell."

Holden frowned as he studied this device. "Most ingenious," he said quietly, "except for the fate of the poor chap inside that coffin, who would surely die for lack of air within minutes of opening that second door."

"Not at all," said Traveller, "for inside the cupboard is a special suit. The suit is completely sealed, and is fed with air by a hose arrangement from within the ship. Thus a man could live and work in the vacuum of space for several minutes without ill effect."

I found this difficult to envisage, but—after some minutes of questioning—I grasped the essentials of the arrangement.

And my destiny lay before me, as clear as a road marked on a map.

A kind of calmness settled over me, and I said quietly, "Traveler, how long is this connecting air hose?"

"Over forty feet, when fully extended. It was my intention that the intrepid engineer could reach any section of the ship."

I nodded. "In particular," I said slowly, "he could make his way to the Bridge area, and to the hatchway which admits entry to the Bridge from the outside."

Holden's face filled with wonder and a kind of hope. "Ah. And the suited man could thereby gain access to the Bridge itself."

Traveller glared thunderously. "Young man, are you suggesting that such an adventure should actually be undertaken?"

I shrugged, still quite calm. "It seems to me to offer a chance, if a slim one, of surviving; while to stay here and do nothing promises only a slow and uncomfortable death."

"But this is an experimental system!" His arms flapped like the wings of some absurd bird. "I have worn that suit for only a few seconds at a time, and that on the surface of the Earth; I have yet to solve the problems of airflow, of heat loss—"

"What of all that?" I asked. "Let this be the ultimate test, Sir Josiah, the test to destruction. Surely the lessons learned in such a jaunt would be invaluable in the construction of new and better suits in the future."

That tempted the scientist buried within the old fellow, and I saw naked curiosity surface for a moment in his eyes, but he said, "My young friend, I would not survive such a trip long enough to put any such lessons into practice. Now let us close this compartment up and—"

"I too am sure you would not survive such a trip, sir," I said frankly. "For you are of advanced years and—forgive me—an asthmatic." I surveyed the rest of the ship's company. "Holden is far too rotund to squeeze into this device—and, if he will pardon, is hardly in the physical state to undertake such a strenuous jaunt. And Pocket—" The servant's eyes were fixed on mine, and were filled with imploring; I only said gently, "Of course we could not ask our faithful friend to undertake such a voyage. Gentlemen, the course is clear."

"Ned, you can't mean—"

"Vicars, I absolutely forbid it. This is suicide!"

I let their words cascade around my ears, hardly hearing, for my mind was quite made up. My eyes saw past my shipmates to the hull of the vessel—and then, as if the wall were turned to glass, I seemed to see into the void itself; a place of infinite cold, of vacuum, riddled by speeding bullets of rock . . .

And a place into which, I knew now, I must soon step.

[7]

ALONE

I was all for plunging straight on with my adventure, for it was still early in the morning; but Traveller insisted that to propel myself out of the ship without making adequate preparations would reduce my slight chances of success to zero.

So it was that Traveller determined that a full two days should elapse before I was to enter the coffin-shaped air cupboard. Although I was unsure as to the effect of this delay on my fragile courage and mental state, I ceded the position.

Traveller went to work on my physical preparedness. "You are entering an unexplored realm, and it is impossible to be sure what effect the environment of space will have on your body, clothed in its protective suit as it will be," he said. So he put me on an intensive diet of light meals, with plenty of bread and soup. Traveller insisted on—and enforced—a slow chewing of every mouthful, so as to avoid the possibility of swallowing air. At first I railed against this regime, but Traveller curtly pointed out that a stomach filled with gas is like a balloon; and in the airless vacuum of space there would be no atmosphere to constrain the unlimited expansion of such a balloon under pressure from the air contained within . . .

He extended this analogy in brutal terms; and I chewed my bread with renewed enthusiasm.

I was fed cod liver oil and various other iron solutions, whose purpose was to enhance my strength, and from a small pharmacy Traveller maintained, doses of senna pods and syrup of figs, in order that I might be cleansed internally of all unwanted baggage. As I strained under the agony of these medicaments I wondered if I had entered a sort of Purgatory, an anteroom to the airless Hell I would face beyond the hull.

Finally Traveller mixed a solution of a bromide salt in my tea. This puzzled me, although I had heard of such potions being fed to infantrymen in the field. At length Traveller took me to one side and explained that the purpose of the bromide was to restrain what he called certain impulses common to young men of my age and temperament, which might have unfortunate consequences for a body locked into an air suit. I was bewildered by this; for, although I thought often of Françoise during those dark days, my thoughts were more in the form of silent prayers for her safety and our eventual reunion than any more excitable speculation; and it was difficult to envisage any such notions distracting me at my moment of greatest peril!

Still, I took Traveller's bromide with good humor.

The first night was difficult to face, for Traveller expressly forbade any alcohol with my meals; and as I lay in my pallet within the darkened Cabin my heart pounded and sleep seemed impossibly far away. After perhaps an hour of this I rose and complained to Traveller. With many muttered protests he rose—the bobble on his nightcap floated behind him as he glided through the air—and prepared for me a powerful sleeping draft. With this inside me I slept a dreamless sleep; and Traveller repeated the dose on the next evening.

So it was that I awoke on 15 August 1870, somewhere beyond the atmosphere of Earth, with my body purged, cleansed and relaxed, ready to journey alone into the endless void beyond the hull of the *Phaeton.*

Traveller had me strip naked save for a brief pair of shorts, and he gave me a greasy, sour-smelling oil which he bade me smear over all my skin below my neck. "This is an extract of whale blubber," he said. "It has three purposes: the first is to nourish the skin; the second is to retain the heat of the body; and the third, and most important, is to provide a seal between your skin and the material of the air suit."

Holden looked puzzled by this. "Then the air suit will not provide a shell of air around Ned's body?"

"Such a shell would swell up instantly, like a balloon, under the pressure of the air it contained," Traveller said. "It would become quite rigid, trapping the space voyager as if crucified in an immovable box." He held out his arms and legs in the air and waggled his fingers helplessly, miming such a predicament.

I had had no idea that air—invisible, intangible—could exert such forces.

Once I was greased up, Pocket opened up the air cupboard and extracted Traveller's patent air suit. The suit consisted of undergarments and an outer coverall; the undergarments—combinations, gloves and boot-like stockings—were of india rubber. I was made to squeeze any stray air bubbles out of the space between the rubber and my skin. I was fortunate that my physique was at least roughly comparable to that of Traveller for whom the suit had been tailored, and the undergarments fitted well enough, chafing only around the armpits and knees.

Next a stout band of rubber and leather was affixed around my chest. This corset-like affair was uncomfortably tight, but Traveller explained how the device would assist my chest muscles as I labored to breathe without the assistance of external air pressure.

Now I donned the outer layer, which was a one-piece combination affair with attached mittens and overboots. This coverall was of resined leather. Leather was used, explained Traveller, because of the tendency of india rubber to dry out and become fragile in a vacuum. The most striking aspect of the coverall was that it was silvered; an ingenious process had permitted its soaking in silver plate so that it looked as if it were woven from spun mercury. This was intended to exclude the direct rays of the sun, Traveller said, and I began to understand the paradoxical complications facing the space engineer; direct sunlight, without the blanket of atmosphere, is violent and must be guarded against, but simultaneously heat leaks from any shadowed area since, again, there is no layer of air to trap it.

The outer suit opened at the front and I clambered awkwardly into it. The suit was fitted at the neck with a collar of copper just wide enough to admit my head. This collar fitted to the inner rubber suit, forming an airtight seal; air was smoothed out of the interface between the outer and inner suits and the outer was sealed up by flaps and straps.

I raised my silvered, mittened hand. "I feel odd.

Greased up and encased in this garment, with its mittens and booties, I am like some grotesque infant!"

Traveller grunted impatiently. "Wickers, the outfit is not designed for comic effect. What need do you have, for example, of an infantryman's heavy boots, since your feet do not have to bear any weight? Now if you've quite finished your prattle let us fit the helmet."

The topping-off of the air suit consisted of a globular helmet of copper; circular windows of thick optical glass were fitted in the metal, and a pair of hoses, bound together, was fitted to the crown of the helmet. These pipes led, Traveller explained, to a pump located inside the air cupboard itself. Traveller floated before me holding this intimidating cage in his long fingers, and said, "Well, Ned, once you are sealed up in this case it will be difficult for us to talk to you." He clapped one hand on my suited shoulder and said, "I wish you Godspeed, my boy. You were, of course, right; it is no virtue to go down into darkness without a fight."

I found I had to swallow before I could speak. "Thank you, sir."

Pocket leaned toward me. "You take my prayers as well, Mr. Vicars."

"Ned." Holden's face was grim, and his deep-sunk eyes appeared on the verge of tears. "I wish I were twenty years younger, and able to take your place."

"I know you do, George." As I hovered there encased in my bizarre integuments, I found the steady gaze of all three of my colleagues most distressing. I said, struggling to maintain the composure of my face, "I see no point in further delay, Sir Josiah. The helmet?"

Pocket and Traveller lifted the globe over my head carefully, chafing my ears on its rim only slightly. The rim engaged the copper collar at my neck, and the two gentlemen turned the helmet about. The low grinding of screw threads filled the echoing helmet, and there was a smell of burnished copper, of rubber, resin and the incongruous stink of whale blubber. The four windows of the helmet turned around me, and glimpses of the Cabin slid past my gaze as if I were at the center of some unusual magic lantern.

At last the helmet was fitted into its seat, and one of the windows had come to rest before my face. I was encased in a silence broken only by a steady hissing from above my head—the reassuring signature of the air pipes which circulated air through my helmet, delivering me fresh oxygen and extracting the carbonic acid I expelled.

Traveller loomed before my face window, his features creased with concern and curiosity. His voice came to me only as a distant muffle. "Are you all right? Can you breathe comfortably?"

My breathing was shallow, but as much, I suspected, from my nervousness as from the air supply, and I seemed capable—given the corset around my chest—of drawing quite deep breaths in perfect comfort. The only disadvantage of the piped supply was a slightly metallic flavor to the air. And so, at length, I made a "thumbs up" sign to Traveller, and indicated by mittened gestures my impatience to enter the air cupboard and get on with it.

Traveller and Pocket now guided me, one arm each, to the aperture in the lower bulkhead and thence into the air cupboard. They laid me face down, directly over the wheel arrangement which would permit me to open the hull, and sealed closed the hatch behind me. As the light of the Cabin was excluded, and I was encased in copper-tinged darkness with only the sound of my own breathing for company, my heart began to hammer as if it would burst.

I reached through the dark for the wheel before my chest, grasped it with my mittened hands, and twisted it firmly.

At first there was only the grind of metal on metal—and then, with a sudden, shocking explosion, the hatch flew back on its hinges and out of my hands. Sound died with a soft sigh, and a moment of gale pushed me in the back and propelled me forward; I grabbed at the doorframe but my mittened fingers slithered across the metal, and I tumbled helplessly out of the *Phaeton* and into empty space!

Suddenly there was nothing above, around, below me; and for the next few moments I lost control of my reactions. I cried for help—unheard, of course, in the soundless vacuum of space—and I scrabbled at my suit and air hoses like some animal.

This first reaction passed, however, and by force of will I restored a semblance of rationality.

I closed my eyes and tried to steady my breathing, frightened of overtaxing my supply. I was merely floating, after all, a sensation which was hardly novel after so many days, and I calmed myself with the illusion that I was safe within the aluminum walls of the *Phaeton.*

I flexed my elbows and knees cautiously. Thanks to trapped air the suit joints were a good deal stiffer than inside the craft, and my fingers and feet tingled, warning me of constrictions in my circulation. But on the whole Traveller's elaborate precautions had proved successful.

With courage grasped in both hands, I opened my eyes—and found I had been rendered virtually blind by a condensation which had gathered over my helmet windows. Beyond this homely mist there were blurs of white and blue that must be the sun and Earth; and I decided I must be floating in the vacuum some yards from the vessel. I raised my mittens and dabbed at the face plate, but the mist, of course, had gathered inside the helmet. And, I abruptly realized, I had no way of reaching inside the helmet to attend to this matter; my own face was as inaccessible to me as the mountains of the Moon!

Of course, on this realization, I was plagued with a series of itches in nose, ears and eyes; I determinedly put these aside. But my sightlessness was a more serious problem, and I felt baffled. After some moments, though, I suspected the mist was clearing slightly, and I wondered if the pumped air was causing the panes to clear. I resolved to wait for several minutes, a time during which I would control my breathing as far as I could, to see if matters improved.

At length the panes did clear enough for me to see out, but they never cleared entirely, and I grew convinced that this problem of condensation, which had been utterly unanticipated even by the genius of Traveller, would form a major obstacle to the future colonization of space. But the steady breathing which I maintained for some minutes did coincidentally have a calming effect on me.

As soon as my visor had cleared, then, I gazed fearfully out into my new domain.

I floated in a sky that was utterly black; not even stars shone, for the sun—a sphere too bright to study, hanging to my left hand side—rendered other objects invisible. There were no clouds, of course, and, in the absence of atmosphere, not even the faint azure tinge of a dark Earth night.

Ahead of me the Moon hung cold and austere, her seas and mountains picked out in sharp gray tones. I turned to the Earth, which was a wonderful sculpture in blue and white; the Little Moon was a speck of light which crawled low across the sunlit face of the globe. The outlines of the continents could clearly be seen—it was, I saw, noon in North America—and it was as if the planet were some vast timepiece, arranged for my amusement.

It was difficult to believe, from my astonishing height, that even now, as dawn broke over Europe, the armies of France and Prussia were preparing to launch at each other once more. How absurd such horror, such squalor, seemed from this lofty height! Perhaps, I thought with a touch of terrifying pride, I had acquired the perspective of the gods; perhaps when all men had the chance to study the world from this vantage, war, envy and greed would be banished from our hearts.

I remembered Françoise, and I prayed silently that she, and all the millions of others trapped in that bowl of light, would remain safe through this day.

Ahead of me, hanging before the face of the Moon, was the *Phaeton* herself. The craft was about thirty feet from me and appeared to lie on her side; her three stubby legs jutted from her base, useless, and in that base I saw the open port through which I had emerged. The whole effect was of some rather absurd, fragile toy, the shadows of the legs and other features as sharp as stencils across her hull; and I had a sudden shock of dislocation as I recalled the last time I had seen the ship from the outside, perched proudly atop the *Prince Albert* in the soft Belgian sunshine.

The twin hoses looped across space, connecting me to the air cupboard; and I decided that I must have fallen to the full extent of the pipes and then bounced back by some yards.

I reached above my head to the hose which was fixed there and, using both mittened hands, began to haul myself awkwardly along the tubes to the brougham. The exertion caused my breathing to speed up and my face-window steamed over once more; but I was still able to see the vessel and so proceeded. At last I fetched up against the air cupboard hatch; I clung securely to one leg of the craft and waited for some minutes for my faceplate to clear.

I imagined Holden, Pocket and Traveller not ten feet above my head, resting as warm and comfortable as in any living-room.

I pulled my way up the leg and reached the lower skirt of the main hull of the craft. On to the vessel's curving aluminum skin, Traveller had instructed me, had been fastened many small handles, designed to assist repairmen and other engineers. These and other protuberances made the task of pulling myself along the *Phaeton*'s hull toward the Bridge quite easy. I proceeded slowly, taking care that my air hoses did not snag. As I worked silver flaked from my leather suit, so that I became surrounded by a cloud of sparkling fragments.

After a few minutes I was clinging like some silvered insect to the hull just below the dome which covered the Bridge. A few feet above me was the wheeled hatch through which I would enter the vessel.

I had gone over the required sequence of events from this point with Holden and Traveller, and, we had concluded rather grimly, I had only one possible course of action. All trace of my celestial mood of a few minutes earlier dissipated. I closed my eyes and listened to the rush of blood in my ears. I had never before killed a man; nor had I seriously contemplated the possibility of such an action.

But, I told myself resolutely, the inhabitant of that Bridge was no civilized man; he was a Hun, an animal who had attempted to take the lives of four men, and who had also, in all probability, joined in the conspiracy to wreck the *Prince Albert.*

He had shown no mercy, and deserved none.

So, with my resolve renewed, I pulled myself above the sill of the windowed dome.

I braced my feet against handles set in the lower hull and turned the wheel which would open the hatch. Speed was of the essence. The Bridge occupant was no experienced space voyager, of course, any more than the rest of us; and would, perhaps, understand little of the deadly implications of this grotesquely suited figure appearing outside his window. So we had hoped.

As I worked I made out the interior of the Bridge. Amid the banks of elaborate instruments a lone figure drifted forward, gazing up at me with more curiosity than fear. He wore a bright red jacket. He made no move to stop me—but, I realized with a sinking heart, he held an advantage which we should have foreseen.

In his hand was a pistol, pointed squarely at my chest.

I considered abandoning my quest and ducking back to safety—but what would that avail me? If ever I were to enter the Bridge by this route, this was surely my best chance. In any event, if he were to take a shot at me he would surely blast a hole in one or more glass panes, thereby allowing his air to escape and so destroying himself as well as me!

. . . But would our saboteur understand this?

And then again, whatever the state of our pilot's thoughts, what of my own? Now that I saw this "monstrous Hun" as a real human figure with a life and past of his own, did I have the resolve to kill him in this way?

All this passed through my feverish soul in a few seconds. Abruptly I concluded that I would sooner die from a clean bullet through the heart than suffocate slowly; and if I should destroy the saboteur, well, it was no more than he had intended for me, Françoise, Traveller, and thousands of others at the launch of the *Prince Albert!*

So, with renewed vigor, I turned the wheel.

The saboteur moved away from the windows, and the fist which held the pistol wavered.

In an instant, the seal broke. The hatch flapped up, narrowly missing my faceplate, and a gale thrust at my chest. I kept firm hold of my wheel with both hands; I was pulled aside and driven against the Bridge windowglass. Papers and other fragments billowed around me, and I saw the sparkle of ice crystals on the breeze.

The saboteur was prepared for none of this.

He was bowled through the air toward the hatchway; as he tumbled through the frame his pistol fell harmlessly from his shocked fingers and disappeared into the blackness, and with his fingertips the saboteur clung to the lip of the hatch, hanging there on the very rim of infinity! One yellow boot fell from his dangling leg and tumbled away into space; long black hair flapped across his brow, and he turned an agonized face to mine, tongue blue and protruding, eyes frozen over.

But, despite these grotesqueries, and despite the ultimate peril of that moment, I recognized the man and found room for a fresh shock. For this was no Prussian saboteur; this was Frédéric Bourne, companion of Françoise!

The last vestiges of air had escaped now; Bourne's head lolled back, and his fingers loosened on the hatchway rim.

Without further thought I grabbed at his wrist. Then, using my one free hand rather awkwardly, I hauled my way into the Bridge. My airhoses and the unfortunate Bourne came dangling after me, Bourne bumping hard against the frame. Once inside I shoved Bourne deeper into the interior of the craft, and dragged in a few more feet of hose.

I grabbed at the hatch and slammed it closed, trapping my hoses, and labored to turn the wheel.

As soon as my hose was blocked the comforting susurrus of piped air, my constant companion through this jaunt, died away. Traveller had estimated that I should have sufficient seconds of air in my helmet and the remaining few feet of hose to allow me to open the way to my colleagues in the Smoking Cabin. But these calculations seemed remote as I labored in a suit that grew as tight and constricting as any iron maiden, and as my helmet turned at last into an impenetrable fog of condensation.

I pushed myself to the floor and groped blindly across it, staring through my panes of mist in the vain hope of espying the hatchway. My head began to pound and my chest to ache, and I imagined the carbonic acid expelled by my lungs clustering about my face like some poison—

My feet, scrabbling over the floor, encountered a wheel set on a raised hatch. I grabbed it with both hands, uttering a fervent prayer of thanks, and hauled at the wheel with what strength I had left . . . but to no avail. Exploration by touch informed me that a crowbar had been jammed into the spokes of the wheel, completely restricting its movement.

It was the work of a moment to remove the bar, and then the wheel turned easily.

The helmet grew darker, and I wondered if my senses were failing; the ache in my lungs seemed now to have spread to all parts of my neck and chest, and my arms felt as if all energy had been drained from them.

The wheel turned in my hands, mysteriously; a final fragment of rationality told me that Holden and Traveller must be working at their side of the hatch also. I released the wheel and floated into darkness.

The pain evaporated, and a soft illumination began to break through my darkness, a blue-white light like that of Earth.

I fell into the light.

When I opened my eyes again I fully expected to see the inside of my hellish copper helmet-prison once more. But my head was free; the furnishings of the Smoking Cabin were all about me. Holden's face hovered over me, a round pool of concern. "Ned? Ned, can you hear me?"

I tried to speak, but found that my throat was as sore as if it had been scoured, and I could only whisper, "Holden? I have succeeded, then?"

His lips were pressed together, and he nodded gravely. "You have indeed, my lad. Although I fear we are not out of the woods yet."

He offered me a globe of brandy; the hot liquid coursed through my wounded throat. I raised my head. Holden pushed me back, saying I should not try to move yet; but I saw that I still wore the air suit, save for the helmet, and was lightly bound by a blanket into my bunk. "Bourne?" I gasped. "Did he survive?"

"Indeed he did, thanks to your generosity," Holden said. "Although if it were up to me I would have pitched the Frenchie out of the hatch . . ."

"Where is he?"

"The far bunk, being tended by Pocket. He went without air for perhaps a minute—but Traveller feels he will suffer no permanent damage. Sadly."

I rested my head back on my pillow. Through the storm of the recent events my surprise at the identity of our saboteur still shone like a clear ray.

"And Traveller?" I asked. "Where is he?"

"On the Bridge." He smiled. "Ned, while Pocket and I worked at the two of you—unscrewing your helmet and so on—our host made directly for the various instruments of the Bridge, like a child reunited with lost toys!"

I found the strength to laugh. "Well, that's Traveller. Holden, you said we were not out of the wood; has Traveller reached some verdict already from his instrumentation?"

Holden nodded and bit at his nail. "It appears our French friend has indeed used too much water for our return to Earth to be possible. But that's not the worst of it, Ned."

Still stunned, I suppose, by my recent experiences, I absorbed this news with equanimity, and said, "But what could be worse than such a sentence of doom?"

"Traveller has changed. It's as if he has been galvanized by your example of determination and action; he has now resolved, he says, that we should return to Earth. But, Ned—" Holden's eyes were wide with fear"—In order to save us, Traveller intends to take us to the surface of the Moon, and search for water there!"

I closed my eyes, wondering if I were trapped within some dream induced by carbonic acid.

[8]

A DEBATE

The days that followed were a blur. My perambulation through space had left my systems drained. And the strange environment of the *Phaeton*—the floating conditions, the rhythm of day and night marked only by the habitual routines of Pocket and Holden (Traveller, buried in his Bridge, was never to be seen now in the Smoking Cabin), the smoky, still air that made one long to hurl open a window—all of this combined to immerse me in a dreamlike state. Perhaps our isolation from the natural conditions of Earth had something to do with my distracted mental state; perhaps our human bodies are more bound than we know to the diurnal rhythms of our mother world.

I was disturbed several times, however, by a roaring sound, a gentle pressure that pushed me deeper into my cot. At such times I vaguely wondered if I had traveled through time as well as through the vacuum and had somehow been returned to those nightmare moments of the launch of the *Phaeton* into space. But each disturbance faded after a few seconds; and each time I relapsed into my unnatural slumber. I learned later that my connection of these events with the launch was not unfounded, for the sound I heard was indeed that of the vessel's main rockets. Traveller, installed in his pilot's couch, worked his motors so that we blazed through space; once more—however briefly—we were masters of our own destiny.

But this time we were not simply hauling away from Earth; this time Traveller was guiding us to a destination far stranger . . .

Apart from gentle washings, feedings of soup and warm tea, and other ministrations performed by the gentle Pocket, the others made no attempt to wake me, believing that it was better to let Nature take her course. And I had no wish to emerge rapidly from this womblike half-sleep; for what should I find on awakening?—only the same grisly parade of doom-laden alternatives which had driven me to my desperate jaunt through vacuum.

But at last my strange sac of sleep dissolved, and I was expelled, as reluctantly as any mewling infant, into a hostile world.

Finding myself loosely bound up in a blanket cocoon, and too weak even to extricate myself, I called feebly for Pocket.

The manservant was able to lift me from my bed as if I were an infant . . . although the rather mysterious Law of Equal and Opposite Reactions, as expounded by the great Sir Isaac Newton, caused him to lurch adversely through the air. He dressed me in a gown belonging to Traveller, fed me once more, and even shaved me.

The face I saw in the shaving mirror was gaunt-cheeked, with eyes red and rimmed with darkness. I was, I feared, scarcely recognizable as the young man who had joined the launch of the *Prince Albert* in such fine humor only days before. "Good Lord, Pocket, I should hardly sweep la belle Françoise from her feet in this condition."

The good chap rested a hand on my shoulder. "Don't you bother with any such considerations, sir. Once I've fed you up you'll be in as fine fettle as you ever were."

His cheery, homely voice, with its base of genuine warmth, was immensely comforting. "Thank you for your care, Pocket."

"It's you who wants thanking, Mr. Vicars."

Now George Holden hove into view from the Bridge; with a kind of featherlight clumsiness he lowered his girth through the famous ceiling hatch—now jammed open—and floated across the air. "My dear Ned," he said. "How are you?"

"Quite well," I said, rather embarrassed by his effusiveness.

"You may have saved all our lives, thanks to your extraordinary courage—I could never have faced that stroll in the dark! Even the thought of immersing my head in that copper cage causes me to shudder—"

I shivered. "Don't remind me. In any event, I have scarcely rescued us; we are still lost in space, are we not, dependent for salvation on Traveller's eccentric plans?"

"Perhaps, but at least we can now put such plans into operation; without your courage we would still be trapped, falling out of control into the darkness, our lives maintained at the whim of a French swine. As you lay unconscious for so long, we began to fear that the carbonic acid in that suit had done for you after all, lad; and I could have broken the throat of the Frenchie with my own hands, these hands which have held nothing more cruel than a pen for thirty years."

I frowned, a little taken aback by this torrent of anger. "Holden, how long have I been asleep? What is today's date?"

"According to Traveller's instruments today is the twenty-second of August. You have slept, therefore, for a full seven days."

"I . . . Good Lord." In my still rather dazed state I tried vainly to work out how much further I had traveled from the Earth in that time, but—unable, in my fuddled condition, to recall if there were twenty-four or sixty hours in a day—I abandoned the project. "And the saboteur, Holden; the man Bourne. What of him? Has he recovered consciousness?"

Holden snorted. "Yes. Would that he had been killed. In fact he emerged from his airlessness-induced torpor rather more rapidly than you." He turned and pointed to the bunk folded out from the wall opposite me, and I made out a shapeless bundle of rather soiled blankets. "There the wretch still lies," Holden said bitterly, "surviving in a ship he would have turned into an aluminum coffin for us all."

Holden kept me company for a while, but then tiredness crept over me once more and, with apologies to the journalist, I had Pocket assist me to a prone position in my bunk and closed my eyes for some hours.

When I awoke the Smoking Cabin was empty, save for Pocket, myself—and the shapeless bundle in the far bunk. I asked Pocket for some tea; then, refreshed, I emerged from my bunk. After so long in bed I feared that my legs would buckle under me, and had we been on Earth perhaps they would have; but here in the comfortable floating conditions of space I felt as strong as I had ever done, and I pulled my way confidently across the Cabin.

I hovered over Bourne. The Frenchman lay facing the wall—I could see his eyes were open—and when my shadow touched him he turned and stared up at me. He was scarcely recognizable as Françoise Michelet's haughty, even arrogant companion of a few days earlier. His face, always thin, had been reduced to the skeletal—his cheekbones jutted like shelves—and his lower chin was coated with a tangle of unruly beard. The remains of his masher's costume—the red jacket and checked waist-coat—were now stained and crumpled, their gaudy colors only adding to the fellow's pathetic aspect.

We stared at each other for several seconds. Then he said, "I suppose now you will finish the job you started, Monsieur Vicars."

"What do you mean?"

"That you intend to kill me." He said this quite without emotion, as one will describe the state of the weather, and continued to regard me.

I frowned and probed at my feelings. Here, I reminded myself, was a man who had stolen Traveller's prototype craft; who had imprisoned myself and my three companions and hurled us into interplanetary space, quite probably to our deaths; who had directly caused the deaths of many innocent spectators at the launch of the *Phaeton;* and who had, no doubt, also been implicated in the plot to sabotage the *Prince Albert* itself, thereby taking the lives of perhaps hundreds more—including, possibly, that of Françoise Michelet, the girl on whom my foolish heart had fastened. I said quietly, "I have every reason to kill you. I have every reason to hate you."

He regarded me quite without fear. "And do you?"

I looked within my heart, and at Bourne's thin, suffering face. "I don't know," I said honestly. "I need to think about it."

He nodded. "Well," he said drily, "I suspect your companion does not share your calmness.

"Which one? Traveller?"

"The engineer? No. The other; the fat one."

"Holden? He has threatened you?"

Bourne laughed and turned his face to the wall; when next he spoke his voice was muffled. "Since the engineer restrained him from strangling me in my weakened condition your Monsieur Holden has decided to starve me to death; or perhaps to dry me out like a leaf in autumn."

"What do you mean?" I turned to the manservant, who had been watching us circumspectly. "Pocket? Is this true?"

Pocket nodded, but tapped his thin nose. "He was already half-starved after all those days on the Bridge without food or water, sir. But I wasn't going to let anybody starve to death; I've been feeding him scraps and leavings when no one's looking."

I felt a great relief that Holden's systematic cruelty had been subverted. "Good for you, Pocket; you were quite right. What did Sir Josiah have to say about all this?"

Pocket shrugged philosophically. "After he calmed Mr. Holden down, the day when you did your great deed—well, sir, you know how Sir Josiah is. I expect he's forgotten all about this Frenchie; he's scarcely been down here since."

I smiled. "That I can well imagine."

"I did not ask for the charity of a servant," Bourne said coldly.

"And charity you're not receiving, my lad," said Pocket.

"But if you think I'm about to spend my last few days sharing a tin box with the body of a Frenchie you've another think coming." He spoke sternly, but rather in the manner of a parent admonishing a child; and I realized then that there was no malice in any corner of this remarkable chap's character.

I turned once more to the Frenchman. "Why, Bourne?"

He twisted his head, his face distorted by the movement. "Why what?"

"Why did you steal this craft, cause so much damage and suffering?"

He turned his head away without reply.

With a strength that surprised me I grabbed his shoulder and twisted him around. "I think you owe me an answer," I hissed at him.

"There is no point. You British would never understand."

I pressed my lips together, suppressing my anger. "Tell me anyway."

"Because of the tricolore," he snapped. "The tricolore!"

He twisted out of my grasp and, no matter how I persisted, refused to say any more.

I found, to my horror, that Bourne had been held in restraints improvised from trouser-belts and fragments of airhose; at my insistence—and on the proviso that he remain in his couch, and that one of us watch him at all times—the next day he was released and sat up gingerly, rubbing at wrists and ankles which were quite blue.

Feeling stronger, I climbed, with Holden, up through the ceiling hatchway.

When I had forced entry to the Bridge several days earlier my impressions had been blurred and fragmentary, after the manner of a nightmare; now, though, I saw that the place in flight was a basin of mechanical marvels. Devices whirred and clicked incessantly, so that one had the impression of a veritable artificial mind conducting operations aboard the craft; and the whole was lidded over by the glass latticework of the *Phaeton*'s nose. This dome now admitted a flood of silver light from a Moon which hung huge—ominously huge—at the crown of the ship.

"Ah, Wickers!" The voice boomed from somewhere above me; I turned and made out, in sharp moonlight shadows, the great throne fastened against one wall of the chamber. The throne, which was of purple, plumply stuffed damask finished with ropes of velvet, loomed over the Bridge like the couch of a Caesar. Traveller settled back in this throne; he sat with feet up, a loose restraint about his waist, lacking only a servant girl peeling grapes to complete the picture of the potentate at ease. "Rather an easier entry to the Bridge than last time, eh?"

"Indeed."

I pushed off from the deck and floated up into the glass-lined dome, grasped one white-painted strut and hovered there, quite comfortably. Holden stayed close to the deck, among the clusters of instruments. From my new vantage point I saw how a pair of levers, connected to pivots fixed to the adjacent wall, were fixed to either side of Traveller's couch; to the top of each lever was affixed a smaller steel handle which could be squeezed by the pilot's fist. Later I was to learn how the smaller handles controlled the thrust of the *Phaeton*'s rockets while the levers themselves directed the swivelling of the nozzles, so steering the ship through space.

This couch, no doubt, was where the wretched Bourne had sat on a hot August afternoon, his forehead slick with a terrified sweat, in order to rip the craft from Earth.

Above Traveller's head was suspended a long, black-painted tube which terminated in an angled eyepiece. I saw how this device could be pushed through seals beyond the hull, affording the pilot a wide angle of vision. Thus, thanks to this periscope and the optical glass of the dome, Traveller had a panoramic view of the universe beyond the walls of his ship—as well as of the metal landscape formed by his banks of devices. The centerpiece of this array of instruments was a table-like affair I recalled from my earlier visit, a wooden disc five feet across with a circular map inlaid in its center. Smaller instruments were gathered around this table, the dial-face of each illuminated by a small, steady light; the lights formed little yellow islands of illumination in a sea of moonshadow darkness. These dials, I saw now, were turned to face the throne (as I thought of it); the intention was clearly to allow the pilot from his couch to form an instant assessment of the state of the *Phaeton*—but the effect was rather of a crowd of mechanical pilgrims, each bearing a steady candle before his chest, faces turned in supplication to their lord.

I complimented Traveller on the admirable clarity of his design, but added that much of the detail left me baffled.

To my dismay Traveller took that as a cue for a lecture.

"Where to start—where to start . . . To begin with you will no doubt recognize the Ruhmkorff devices."

". . . I beg your pardon?"

"The electrical coils which provide light for the instruments." These coils, Traveller explained, provided a steadier and more secure light than that afforded by acetylene lamps, and were less prone to coat the dials of the instruments with soot. He then went on to describe each instrument, with its manufacturer, function, limitations, and even, in some cases, its price, in the loving detail which other folk apply to describing their children. Holden, floating down in the depths of the instrument banks, instantly sensed my bafflement, and began to play up; he would indicate each instrument in turn with a flourish like a conjurer's assistant, and I had to cram my fist into my mouth to avoid bursting into laughter.

Traveler, of course, lectured on oblivious.

There were chronometers, manometers, Eigel Centigrade thermometers. There was a bank of compasses set in a three-dimensional array, so that their faces lay at all angles to each other. Traveller sighed over this arrangement. "I had hoped to use the direction of magnetic flux to navigate through space," he said, "but I am disappointed to find that the effect fades away more than a few tens of miles from the surface of the Earth."

"Damned inconvenient!" Holden called drily.

"Instead you rely on a sextant," I said, indicating a large, intricate brass device consisting of a tube mounted on a toothed wheel. "Surely," I went on, "the Carthaginians themselves would have recognized such a device . . . but could never have imagined it placed in such a setting."

"Carthaginians in space," Traveller mused. "Now there is an idea for a romance . . . But, of course, one could never make such a tale plausible enough to convince the modern public. It would be even more controversial than Disraeli's fashionable fable . . ." I noticed that Holden looked up from his clowning with interest at that whimsical suggestion. Traveller went on, "You're quite right, Wickers; between planets, the principles of navigation by the stars are exactly the same as those which guide mariners across the surface of Earth's seas. But the practice is somewhat more difficult, requiring as it does the determination of the position of a vessel in three co-ordinates." Traveller went on to explain an elaborate system—using graphs, tables and charts—which he had devised of plotting the locus of a craft which looped like a fly through the emptiness of space. The mathematical calculations involved were facilitated by means of a mechanical device Traveller called an arithmometer. This was a box stuffed with brass gears, cogs and dials; it featured two large cylinders on which were fixed rolls of digits, and Traveller had Holden demonstrate how, by turning various wheels and handles, one could induce the arithmometer to simulate the processes of addition, subtraction, multiplication and division.

Since he had never before ventured more than a few hundred miles from the surface of the Earth—so that the features of the home world had always been at hand, like a vast, illuminated map—Traveller had never previously been forced to rely on his patent navigation systems. I fancied he rather enjoyed the challenge. "And in any event," he went on, "navigation by the stars is not our primary means of guidance."

I asked politely, "And that is?"

For answer he threw aside his waist restraint and launched himself from the throne, coming to rest balanced on his fingertips, upside down over the circular table at the center of the Bridge, his sidewhiskers wafting gently. "This!" he cried. "Here is my mechanical pride and joy."

I drifted down to join him, and I inspected the surface of the table more carefully. It was, as I had noted earlier, inlaid with a map; now I saw that this map showed the Earth as it might be viewed from a rocket craft far above the North Pole, with the ice-locked north centered in the disc-shaped map, and the equatorial countries of Africa and South America smeared around the rim. Traveller showed us how, by turning a lever, he could invert this disc and display a similar view of the South Polar regions. The map was painted, a little clumsily, with natural colors—shades of blue for the oceans, and brown and green for the land. Traveller explained proudly that the coloring was based on his own observation of the planet from his aerial platform *Phaeton.*

Holden asked why national boundaries were not shown.

Traveller said, "And of what value would a display of political allegiance be to the aerial voyager? Sir, take a look through the window and inspect Earth—if you can find it in the moonglow. From this height, even our glorious Empire is less dramatic than the shadings of the empty oceans."

Holden bridled at this. "Sir Josiah, I must take exception. A dominion like His Majesty's is an enduring monument."

Traveller's first word of reply was straight from the threepenny stalls at the music-halls. He went on, "Good God, man; look out of the window! From here, the wanderings of Marco Polo are no more significant than the trail of a fly on the glass; the empires of Caesar, Kublai Khan, Boney—and of the blessed Edward—all rolled up and added together make less difference than the imperfections of a single pane of glass!

"Holden, from our vantage point the affairs of great men are reduced to their true status: to stuff and nonsense; and the pompous fantasies of our deranged and incompetent leaders are revealed for what they are."

Holden drew himself up to his full height, pulling his barrel-shaped stomach toward his chest; but since he floated in the air above the navigation table like the rest of us, and he was besides upside down compared to me and Traveller, the effect was less impressive than he might have hoped. "Sir Josiah, I suggest you explain to our French saboteur how political affairs are irrelevant in this celestial prison. It was politics that brought us here, remember."

Traveller shrugged. "Which only serves to prove that there is nothing so small as the imagination of a man."

"And, like Bourne, sir," Holden hissed, "you sound like a damned Anarchist."

I had been seeking ways to defuse this argument, and now I felt compelled to say, "Steady on, Holden; I think you should take that back."

But Traveller laid a restraining hand on my arm. "Holden, have you actually read the thoughts of such Anarchist luminaries as Proudhon?"

Holden sniffed. "I have read of the actions of such as Bakunin; that is enough for me."

Traveller laughed, his face lit from above by the electric lights embedded in his navigation table. "If you had studied beyond the end of your nose, sir, you would know that your Anarchist has rather a fine view of his fellow human. The nobility of the free man—"

"Rubbish," said Holden sternly.

Traveller turned to me. "Ned, the Anarchist does not believe in lawlessness, or outlawed behavior. Rather he believes that man is capable of living in harmony with his brother, without the restraint of law at all!—that all men are essentially decent chaps, no more desirous of destroying each other, on the whole, than the average Englishman is desirous of murdering his wife, child and dog. And in his natural state man lived as an Anarchist in Eden, unlawed and uncaring!"

Holden muttered something about blasphemy, but I pondered these puzzling concepts. "But how would we order ourselves, without laws? How could we run our great industrial concerns? How would we distribute the posts of society? Would not the poor man envy the rich man's castle, and, without the disincentive of the law, be disposed to break in at once and carry off the furniture?"

"In all probability, such discrepancies would never arise," said Traveller, "and if they did they would be resolved in an amicable fashion. Each man would know his place, and assume it without comment or complaint for the common good."

"Pious nonsense," Holden snapped, by now quite red-faced; and I found myself forced to agree with him for once.

"And," I went on, "if we once lived in a naturally lawless state, like animals—"

"Not animals, Ned," Traveller corrected me. "As free men."

"But if this is so, then why do we have laws now?"

Traveller smiled, and the light of ancient lunar seas shone from his platinum nose. "Perhaps you should be a philosopher, Ned. These, of course, are the questions with which right-thinking men have wrestled for many years. We have laws because there are certain individuals—I would include all politicians and princes—who require laws to subjugate their brothers, in order to achieve their own vainglorious ends."

I considered these remarkable sentiments. The England I knew was a rational, Christian country, a society informed by industrial principles and confident of its own power and rightness—a confidence fueled largely by the industries to which Traveller's anti-ice inventions had contributed so significantly.

But here was a man at the very heart of all this technological achievement, espousing the ideas of an idealistic Russian! I wondered, not for the first time, at the power of the experiences—in the Crimea and elsewhere—which had led Traveller to such conclusions. And I wondered how such experiences might have modulated the views of one such as George Holden . . .

Meanwhile Holden had pulled himself closer to us. His fury showed in the beetroot color of his round face, and in the way his chest strained against the buttons of his waistcoat. "You sail close to treason, sir."

Again I urged him to apologize; again Traveller waved me down. He said calmly, "I will forget you said that, Holden."

Holden's fleshy jowls trembled. "And have you forgotten the bombs thrown by your Anarchist companions? Only the rule of law stands between the freedoms enjoyed by a British gentleman and the actions of one such as Bourne, who would kill for a flag, a piece of colored cloth!"

"Perhaps," Traveller said—and then he shouted back, "But so would you, sir, murder for such a reason!—For it was you who had to be physically restrained from throwing the poor chap straight out through the air cupboard—"

"Is everything all right, gentlemen?"

The cool, rational voice of Pocket, who had pushed his head and shoulders through the open hatchway, caused us to stop. Suddenly we became selfconscious; Traveller and

Holden were arranged like two tin soldiers in a box, upside down compared to each other and roaring abuse at each other's toecaps; while I hung in the air at an indeterminate angle between them, ineffectually trying to calm the situation.

We moved away from each other, pulling down our waistcoats and harumphing selfconsciously. Traveller reassured Pocket that everything was in order, and suggested that perhaps some tea might knit together our troubled community. Pocket, imperturbable, said he would proceed with this straightaway, and popped his head back through the hatch. Holden was still purple with rage, but he was making a visible effort to control himself; Traveller was quite unmoved. "Well, gentlemen," he said, "a fine impression we have given of the Island Race to our Gallic friend below. Perhaps we should stick to uncontroversial subjects in future?"

"I think that would be a very good idea, sir," I said fervently.

"Now then, Ned," Traveller said, turning once more to his navigation device, "where were we?"

I studied the map of Earth once more. "You were saying that this is a navigation table."

"Exactly."

Now I pressed my nose close to the tabletop. Around the central map, I saw, the table was perforated by an array of small holes, so that the surface was like a coarse wooden sieve. A line of tiny metal flags, gaily colored, protruded from some of the holes; the trail they marked emerged from the surface of the Earth and swept off along a graceful curve. The meaning of this was not hard to deduce; it was a representation, on a flat surface, of our path through space. "But how is this maintained?" I asked Traveller. "From your maps and charts?"

Traveller smiled. "Watch for a few minutes."

We hovered over the table—Holden included, his breathing still rapid but his color fading fast—and were at last rewarded with the sight of a new flag popping spontaneously through a hole. At the same time, I became aware that the disc-map was also turning, slower than the hour-hand of a clock. "So," I said, "the table maintains itself automatically. The map turns with the Earth—once every day, I should judge—and the flags emerge from the surface as we surge forward into space."

"Correct," Traveller said briskly.

"But how is it done?"

"There is a clockwork mechanism to drive the orrery—the turning Earth. In fact the whole device was constructed, to great precision, by the younger Boisonnas, clockmaker of Geneva. But the secret of the navigation tracking device is an arrangement of gyroscopes, suspended within the body of the table."

As usual I was baffled. "Gyroscopes?"

Traveller sighed. "Little spinning tops, Ned. Spinning objects retain their orientation in space, as you may know—that is another reason the rocket engines are designed to impart a spin to the whole of the *Phaeton*—and so the table is able to 'sense' the turnings of the ship's path. This, coupled with springloaded devices to measure acceleration, is sufficient to determine the position of the ship at any time, without reference to the stars at all; one could black out the windows of this Bridge and still be confident of one's navigation to within a few miles, thanks to my ingenious arrangement."

Holden was tapping the table with a forefinger, close to

the surface of the model Earth; he was indicating, I saw, the representation of England, and in particular a heavy black line which passed from the central Pole, through London, and on beyond the boundary of the world by several thousand miles. "And this?"

"The Greenwich Meridian, of course," Traveller said impatiently.

Holden nodded, calmly enough, but caught my eye; and we both pondered the unconscious symbolism provided by this surprising gentleman-Anarchist: for here was the worldwide symbol of British rationality and science, sweeping beyond the surface of the Earth and on to the stars.

I traced the line of position flags as it swept depressingly far from Earth's surface; soon, I saw, we would leave the boundary of the navigation table altogether. I mentioned this to Traveller. "I admit I had not envisaged traveling quite so far in this untried craft," he said. "But the table will not be without its uses." So saying he popped his head below the table and rummaged through a cupboard set into the deck; he emerged holding rolls of paper some four feet wide, which he proceeded to unroll and lay flat against the table. He revealed a map designed in four sheets and marked with the imprint of Beer and Moedler. "From this rather fine Mappa Selenographica," Traveller said, "which I carry to facilitate telescopic observations from above the atmosphere, I intend to improvise an analogue of the table's polar-view Earth maps. A little adjustment of the gearings and the table should serve us in as good stead as we arrive at our destination . . ."

Traveller beamed at this further exhibition of his own inventiveness, his eyes fixed on the chart; but Holden and I exchanged despairing glances, and then looked down at the chart in silence. At that moment the cares and struggles of Earth did indeed seem distant and remote; for this "Mappa" showed the dead seas and airless mountains of the world to which we were, it seemed, irrevocably headed: it was a map of the Moon.

[9]

IN THE SHADOW OF THE MOON

Traveling at several hundred miles each hour, it took the *Phaeton* twenty days to journey from the Earth to the environs of the Moon.

On the eighteenth day I joined Traveller on his Bridge. The Moon lay dead ahead of the craft, so that it was poised directly above the glass dome of the Bridge. We were already so close to the sister world that it was barely possible to make out the edges of her glowing round face, and the closer we approached the more it seemed that the Moon was flattening into a landscape above us. But it was a strange, inverted landscape. Razor-edged lunar mountains hung above me like stalactites, or unlikely chandeliers which poured ghostly reflected sunlight into our Bridge. My Earth-trained perspective refused to allow me to perceive myself as hanging upside-down above the Moon; it was as if those mountains, those bowls of dust which were the lunar seas, those plains pocked by craters and laced by white rays, were about to tumble down about my defenseless ears.

I looked down at the navigation table, reconfigured now by Traveller to show the Moon. The path of the hapless *Phaeton,* delineated by little flags, had been heading past the limb of the satellite; now it curved gracefully toward the Moon, so that, if undisturbed, the ship would pass around the lunar perimeter. At first I had imagined that these changes in our path had been due to the firing of our rocket engines, but Traveller explained that the rockets had done little but tweak our path in the required direction; far from the influence of Earth, we were now being pulled across the sky by the gravity of the lunar rocks themselves.

"So, Ned," Traveller called, and I turned to see him in his throne-chair, bathed in harsh, sharp radiance. "What an adventure awaits us."

"Sir Josiah, I understand that gravity is pulling us into this orbit toward the Moon. But will gravity pull us all the way down to the surface?"

"No, Ned; if we do not fire the rockets again we will follow a hyperbolic path around the hidden hemisphere of the Moon and be flung away from her."

"Then let us be flung away, if it is anywhere in the direction of our homeworld! Sir, the Moon is indeed magnificent, but it was surely never designed to sustain human life. Is it truly necessary for us to descend to its surface?"

Traveller sighed and, to my discomfiture, he reached up and removed the platinum nose from his face; with one thumb he rubbed the rim of the dark cavity so revealed, and then replaced the nose into his skull. "Ned, every time I discern some glimmering of intelligence in that bullet-shaped cranium of yours I am disappointed by a crass remark. I have explained this to you at least twice."

"Then I apologize, sir, for the point is still unclear to me."

"Is specific impulse such a difficult concept? Dear God . . . Very well, Ned. To enable the *Phaeton* to come so far our Monsieur Bourne has severely depleted our supply of reaction mass—of water. Even if we could somehow bend our trajectory to return to Earth, we should surely burn like toast as we hurtled uncontrolled through the atmosphere, with our remnants smashing into oblivion in the ground. So we need more water."

"A cheerful prospect. But if it is so impossible to land on Earth, how can we hope to land safely on the Moon?"

Traveller's face was turned up to the Moon, and I imagined him struggling for patience. "Because the pull of gravity is only one-sixth that at Earth's surface. And so our enfeebled rockets can bring us safely out of orbit and to a soft landing on the lunar plains long before we run out of water."

I turned my face up to the Moon; I let its pale light fill my eyes, and I voiced my darkest fear. "Sir Josiah, let us face the truth. The Moon is a desolate, airless planet; we are no more likely to find water down there, frozen or otherwise, than we are to find a Cockney urchin selling hot chestnuts."

Traveller snorted laughter, his nose giving the sound a disconcerting metallic ring. "Forgive me, Professor Lord Ned; I did not realize you were such an expert on lunar and planetary theories."

"I am not, sir," I said with some dignity, "but nor am I a fool; and I am capable of following the newspapers."

"Very well. There are three counters to your objections

to my plan. First, that we have no alternative! There is nowhere else accessible to us which offers even the prospect of water, or any other suitable liquid. So it is the Moon or nothing, Ned.

"Second, the opinion of the savants on the composition of the lunar surface is not as united as you appear to believe."

"But surely the accepted wisdom is that the Moon is barren, inert, lifeless, and without atmosphere."

"Pah!" Traveller snorted. "And what observations are such theories based on? For every sighting of a sharp occultation of a star by the limb of the Moon—'demonstrating' by the absence of dimming or refraction, you see, that there is no air—I can quote another in direct contradiction. Only twenty years ago the Frenchman Laussedat noted a refraction of the solar disc during an eclipse." Traveller, lying prone in his couch, held out his arms as if to embrace the lunar goddess above him. "I accept that our own eyes show us now that the Moon cannot have a blanket of atmosphere as thick as that of Earth; for surely if she did, her mountains and valleys would be hidden by a swirling layer of clouds and haze. And the lighter gravity, so advantageous to us in other ways, does not lend itself to the retention of a heavy atmosphere. But it is surely not beyond the bounds of possibility that we may find pockets of air in the deeper valleys, or even that a rarefied air might linger over the entire surface?

"And besides, recall that we have only observed one side of the Moon. The satellite dances about the Earth, keeping one face modestly turned away. Even from this vantage point we have not yet seen the hidden face, Ned! Who knows what we may find?"

"Craters, and mountains, and seas of dust."

"Mr. Wickers, your mind is like a shriveled prune, dry and incapable of surprise. What if the theories of Hansen are verified? Eh?" Hansen, it emerged, was a Danish astronomer who had suggested that the Moon had been pulled, by Earth's gravity, into an egg-shape, and circled the Earth with the fatter end averted; and that a layer of thick atmosphere had accumulated over this heavier hemisphere, conveniently hidden from the view of inquisitive astronomers.

"Well, Sir Josiah," I said, "we must wait and see."

He snorted again. "Spoken like a feeble scientist, lad. You must learn to think like an engineer! To a scientist nothing is proven until it is demonstrated, every way up, before the eyes of a dozen of his sober-suited peers. But an engineer seeks what is possible. I don't care if this theory is right or wrong; I ask instead what I can do with it."

"Sir Josiah, you listed three counters to my objection. What is the third?"

Now he twisted in his chair and craned his neck; his deformed face, half-silhouetted by the moonlight, was alive with excitement. "Ah, Ned, the third counter is simply this: whether we live or die, what fun it will be to walk among the mountains of the Moon!"

I peered up at the forbidding world rotating slowly above me and wished I could find it in my young heart to share Traveller's enthusiasm for the exotic and the spectacular; but, at that moment, I would have given all my astonishing experiences to be safely back in the snug bar of a Manchester club.

After the excitement of the reclaiming of the Bridge we had returned to our settled routine—with the exception that poor Bourne sat in his chair in the Cabin now, a silent, resentful specter—and the remaining hours of our voyage wore away rapidly.

But at last I awoke, as usual with the homely smell of Pocket's toast and tea in my nostrils, knowing instantly that this was the twentieth day of our flight—the day on which Sir Josiah Traveller would land us on the surface of the Moon itself, or else take us to our deaths!

Traveller had assured us that we would land at around eight in the morning; and so Pocket awoke us a little earlier than usual, at five. We washed quickly and ate a healthy breakfast. Traveller insisted on this, even though I for one could scarcely swallow a mouthful. I fed Bourne and allowed him to wash sketchily. Pocket climbed through the hatch to bring Traveller this last breakfast at his station on the Bridge.

With the meal completed and the debris hastily stowed away, we prepared for our descent. Traveller had explained to us that at ten minutes past seven his engines would fire one almighty burst, designed to knock us into a path which must inevitably meet the lunar surface.

I ensured that Bourne was correctly restrained by his safety straps. The Frenchman's feet and hands were also knotted together by leather belts; pale, obviously frightened, he averted his eyes with a trace of defiance. I pushed away from him, reached my own seat, and began to haul the straps around me—and then, with an oath, pulled myself across the Cabin once more and, with fingers stiffened by anger, loosened the bindings around Bourne's wrists. Bourne neither aided nor abetted me.

Holden, already in his place, shouted angrily, "Ned! What in God's name are you doing? Will you loose that animal amongst us, at such a moment?"

I turned on him, feeling my face flush with fury. "He is not an animal, George. He is a human being, a brother to any of us here. We may be going to our deaths today. Whatever his crimes, Bourne deserves to meet his fate with dignity."

Holden made to protest further, but Pocket, strapped tightly in his own chair, called out, "Please postpone your debate, sirs, for I fear that the engines are about to ignite, and the young gentleman will be injured if he does not resume his seat forthwith."

A glance at Traveller's *Great Eastern* clock, still sitting proudly in its case at the center of the Cabin after all our adventures, showed me that it was already eight minutes past the hour. So with haste I returned to my chair and strapped myself in. We sat for long seconds; I avoided the others' eyes for fear of finding only the reflections of my own terror . . .

Then the great engines spoke once more.

I was pressed deep into my seat, and I envisaged our precious water being thrust as freezing steam into space. The rockets fired for perhaps two minutes—and then, as suddenly as they had awoken, they fell silent. An ominous quiet descended on the Cabin, and we stared at each other wildly.

From the Bridge there was no sound.

"Holden, what has happened?" I hissed. "Do you think it worked? Are we heading to the Moon?"

Holden bit his lip, his round face red and moist with fear. "The engines fired on cue, at any rate," he said. "But as to the rest, I am scarcely qualified to judge. As with so much of this horrible adventure, we are reduced to waiting and seeing."

The minutes stretched out without event, and my fear

became supplemented by boredom and irritation. "I say, Holden, I know Traveller is a great man—and that one must expect such chaps to display the odd eccentricity—but all the same, it seems inhuman to keep us sitting down here in suspense like this."

Holden turned to the servant. "Pocket? Do you think we should check if Sir Josiah is well?"

Pocket shook his thin head, and I saw how sweat beaded over the bristles of hair at his neck. The manservant, restrained by circumstance from his customary round of chores, seemed the most nervous of all of us. "Sir Josiah doesn't like to be disturbed at his work, sir."

I ground my fist into the palm of my hand. "But this is scarcely a normal time, damn it."

Holden said, "I think we had best let Traveller get on with his work, Ned, and try to be patient."

"Perhaps you're right." I cast about the Cabin, seeking diversion from my own thoughts, and lit on the unhappy figure of Bourne; the Frenchman sat with his head lolling against his chest, a prisoner even within this prison. I said, "I have to say again, Holden, it's damn heartless of you to have wanted to keep this poor chap restrained still. What further damage can the fellow do?"

Holden glared at Bourne. "He is an Anarchist, Ned; and as such cannot be trusted."

Now Bourne looked up with some defiance; in his heavily accented English he said, "I am no Anarchist. I am a Frenchman."

I studied his thin, proud features. "You told me you took the *Phaeton* because of the tricolore. What did you mean?"

He fixed me with a condescending stare. "That you need to ask such a question, English, is sufficient answer."

I felt angry that my overtures, friendly enough in the circumstances, should be treated in this way. "What the devil is that supposed to mean? Look here—"

"You won't get any civility out of that one, Ned," Holden said wearily. "The tricolore—the flag of their Revolution in which the rabble murdered their anointed rulers, and then turned on each other; the tricolore—which the upstart Corsican carried all over Europe; the tricolore—symbol of blood, chaos and murder—"

"Yes, but what's it got to do with the *Phaeton?*"

"Think about it, Ned; try to see the last few decades from your Frenchie's point of view. His famous Emperor is thrashed by Wellington and carted off to exile. The Congress of Vienna, which has settled the Balance of Power in Europe for all time, and which seems such a noble achievement to us, is invidious to him; for no more can he count on the division of his foes in order to spread his creed of lawlessness and riot across Europe—"

Bourne laughed softly. "I point out that we are now ruled by an Emperor, not by a Robespierre."

"Yes," said Holden with disdain, "by Louis Napoleon, who calls himself the bastard son of Bonaparte—"

"The nephew," interjected Bourne. "But—despite the legitimacy of Louis' original election to power—your King would have the Emperor replaced, would he not, by a restoration of the old monarchy?" He laughed again.

Holden ignored this. "Ned, your Frenchman has, this century, been thwarted in his ambitions of greed and lawlessness. He has been forced to witness the influence of Britain extend still further across the Continent—and the world—buttressed by the robust nature of our constitutional settlement, and the power of our industrial economy. And his resentment has grown."

Bourne continued to laugh quietly.

Holden snapped, "Do you deny this?"

Bourne became still. "I do not deny your hegemony in Europe," he said. "But it is based on one thing, and one thing alone: anti-ice, and your monopoly on the substance. Thus you lay your anti-ice Rails across our fields, and build your stations with English names into which English goods are brought for sale.

"And worse—worse than all this—is your hidden threat to use anti-ice as a final weapon of war. Where is your Balance of Power now, Mr. Holden?"

"There is no such intention," Holden said stiffly.

"But you have deployed such weapons of terror already," Bourne said, "against the Russians in the Crimea. We know what you are capable of. You British talk, and act, as if anti-ice was some supernatural outcropping of your racial superiority. It is not; your possession of it is no more than a historical accident, and yet you use this transient superiority to impose your ways, your policies, your very thinking, on the rest of mankind."

Now it was Holden's turn to laugh, but I sat quietly, thinking over Bourne's words. I will admit that even a month earlier I would instinctively have sided with Holden in this debate, but now, hearing the cold, precise words of this Frenchie—no, of this man, a man about my own age—I found my old certitudes more fragile than I had supposed. "But," I asked Bourne, "what if this is true? Is the British way so bad? Holden has described the Congress of Vienna; Britain's diplomats have striven for a just peace—"

"I am French, not British," he said. "We want to find our own destiny, not follow you to yours. The Prussians, and the rest of the Germans, too; if history says that fragmented nation is to unify, who is Britain to stand in the way? And even—even if our nations wish to go to war, then it is not for you to say 'no.' " His face was pale, but his eyes were clear and steady.

"Then your taking of the *Phaeton*—perhaps ultimately at the expense of your own life—"

"—was an act designed to waste a few more pounds of the wretched anti-ice. To remove the reckless genius-criminal Traveller. It is known already that your stock of the substance is running low. There is no nobler way for a Frenchman to spend his life than to speed this process."

Despite the starkness of this statement, I was irresistibly reminded of Traveller's remarks to the effect that his purpose in building such great devices as the *Albert* was to distract the politicians and generals from the military exploitation of anti-ice! Was Bourne's analysis of the situation really so different from that of the great Englishman?

I frowned. "Holden thinks you are a saboteur."

He shook his head, smiling thinly. "No. I am a franc-tireur."

"A what?"

"A free-shooter. A new type of soldier; a soldier in a gentleman's clothes, who fights to free his homeland with any tools available."

"Damn pretty sentiments," Holden said with loathing and contempt. "And when the anti-ice is all gone—wasted by such acts as this—then what? Will you rise and murder us in our beds?"

Bourne's smile widened. "You are so afraid, aren't you, English? You fear even your own mobs, who perhaps might become infected by ours. And you understand so little.

"I heard Sir Josiah call himself an Anarchist." He spat. "And in the same breath describe how each man will know his 'place.' Traveller and his like do not know the meaning of the words 'free man.' Was it not the industrialists who, in 1849, overturned Shaftesbury's working conditions reforms of a few years earlier?"

I looked blankly at Holden, who raised a hand dismissively. "He means some aberrant pieces of legislation, Ned, long since thrown out and forgotten. Shaftesbury introduced a ten-hour working day limit, for example. Conditions on the use of women in the mines. That sort of thing."

I was puzzled. "But industry could not function under such restraints. Could it?"

"Of course not! And so the 'reforms' were discarded."

"But," said Bourne, "at what cost to your British souls. Eh? Vicars, do you remember an English writer called Dickens?"

"Who?"

Again Holden explained, impatiently. Charles Dickens had turned out pot-boilers in the 1840s, achieving a brief popularity. Holden sighed briefly. "Do you remember Little Nell, Pocket?"

The manservant's face creased to a smile. "Ah, yes, sir. Everyone followed the serials then, didn't they? And when Nell died there was scarce a dry eye in the country, I dare say."

"Dickens. I never heard of the fellow," I admitted. "What happened to him?"

"About 1850 he began a new serial," Holden remembered. "*David Copperfield.* Another heavy, weepy work. It flopped completely, being utterly removed from the mood of the day. Ned, it was in that same year of 1850 that the first Light Rail, between Liverpool and Manchester, was opened! People were excited by the future—by change, enterprise, possibilities. They didn't want to read this dreary stuff about the plight of the shiftless."

"So," said Bourne, "Dickens left Britain for good. He lived and worked in America, where his social awareness had long been appreciated; he campaigned on a variety of reform issues right up to his recent death."

"What is your point?" I demanded coolly.

"That your British hearts are riven by internal contradiction—the same contradiction which expelled such a good man as Dickens from your body politic, leaving you the colder and the poorer. The contradiction which allows Traveller to believe that his Anarchism can be validly founded on a heap of laboring, disenfranchised poor. A contradiction which, in the end, will tear you apart—and a contradiction which now drives you to meddle in the affairs of other nations. Do you not fear that nationalism will erupt out of France and across Europe, disrupting your Balance of Power for ever—and do your mothers still frighten you as children with tales of how 'Boney' will get you if you misbehave?"

I laughed—for my own mother had done precisely that—but Bourne, excited, continued now in a harsher voice. "Ned, there is a strain of modern Englishmen called the Sons of Gascony. Are you familiar with their theories?"

"I have heard of them," I admitted stiffly.

"The Sons are the distillation of your national character, in some ways; for, constantly aware of the past, they live in constant fear of it—and constantly plan revenge. After the Norman Conquest a series of forts, each twenty or so miles apart, was built across England and Wales, the purpose being to subdue the conquered English. These forts have now been absorbed into your great castles—Windsor, the London Tower. And the north of England was razed."

I frowned. "But that's eight centuries ago. Who cares about such matters now?"

Bourne laughed. "To the Sons it is as yesterday. The tides of history since, with all their flotsam of ancient victories and defeats, only add to their fears. They brood on Gascony, which was an English domain from the Conquest to the sixteenth century, when the final fragment—Calais—was lost by Mary Tudor.

"Vicars, the Sons plan a final solution to the ancient 'problem' of the French. Again boats will cross the Channel; again there will be a Conquest—and again, every few miles, the terrible forts will be thrown up. But this time guns powered by anti-ice will loom from their turrets; and this time it will be the regions of France which will be ground underfoot."

"But that's monstrous," I said, stunned.

"Ask Holden," Bourne snapped. "Well, sir? Do you deny the existence of such a movement? And do you deny your own sympathy for its aims?"

Holden opened his mouth to reply—but he was not given the chance; for at that moment a terrible cry emanated from the open hatchway above our heads.

We looked at each other in horror; for it had been Traveller, our only pilot as we hurtled toward the Moon, and he had sounded in mortal distress!

Strapped helplessly into my seat, I looked up at the open hatchway to the Bridge. A shaft of Moonlight raked down through the hatch and shone in the smoky air of the Cabin. I felt oddly resentful at this turn of events; if only, I reflected, I had been allowed to sit in this cozy Cabin and debate politics until it was all over . . . one way or the other.

But, it seemed, I could no longer hide from events.

I looked at Holden. "What do you think we should do, George?"

Holden chewed at his nail. "I've no idea."

"But he must be in some sort of difficulty up there. Why else would he cry out so? . . . But in that case, wouldn't he call for help?"

Pocket said, "That wouldn't be Sir Josiah's way, sir. He's not one to admit weakness."

Holden snorted. "Well, in a situation like this that's a damned irresponsible attitude."

"Unless," I breathed, "he's been disabled completely. Perhaps he is lying up there unconscious—or even dead! In which case the *Phaeton* is without a pilot—"

Only Bourne, slumped within himself, appeared unmoved by this lurid speculation.

"Now, Ned, we shouldn't get carried away," Holden said, his voice tight with tension.

"I think one of us should go up there," I said.

Pocket said, "I wouldn't advise it, sir. Sir Josiah wouldn't like—"

"Damn his likes and dislikes. I'm talking about saving all our lives, man!"

"Ned, think on," Holden said nervously. "What if Traveller ignites the motors while you are between decks? You could be dashed against the bulkhead, hurt or killed. No, I think we should sit and wait."

I shook my head. If Holden had lost his nerve—well, he had my sympathy, and I did not remark on the fact. Instead I opened up my restraints and pushed my way out of the chair. I said, "Gentlemen, I propose to ascend. If all is well with Traveller, then the worst that will happen is that I will be the target of a few ripe insults. And if something amiss has occurred—well, perhaps I will be able to offer assistance.

"I think you should stay strapped into your seats."

And with those words, and feeling their helpless eyes on my back, I launched myself into the air and pulled through the hatch to the Bridge.

The Moon hung over the *Phaeton* like the battered underside of the sky. The rotation of the ship had been stilled now, and the Sun lay somewhere to our left-hand side, so that the shadows of the lunar features were long and sharp, like splashes of ink over a glowing white surface. The ragged peaks and crater rims slid from right to left past the Bridge windows, showing that we were already traveling close around the curve of this world, toward its night side.

I stared in fascination. I knew that no man, even armed with the mightiest telescope on Earth, had before seen the sister world in such dazzling detail.

I observed with interest how the larger craters, which looked from this angle more like circular walled encampments, appeared to contain a central peak, while the smaller craters were smooth within; and I saw too how craters overlaid craters, so that it was as if the Moon had been bombarded by a hail of meteors or other objects not once, in some wild remote past of the Solar System, but many times, again and again. And the sharpness of the smaller craters' rims attested to their newness, implying that this bombardment continued even in the present day.

Now a new feature hove into view, a mountainous ridge very like a crater wall—except that, in this world of circles, this wall was virtually straight, traveling from top to bottom of our window. The area beyond the wall appeared oddly free of craters, although the ground was very broken up. I pushed myself away from the deck and floated up to the nose of the Bridge dome. As I looked across the surface of the Moon and deeper into the dark side, I could make out no limit to this strange craterless region. The delimiting wall was now receding behind the ship, and I was startled to see that the wall was not straight after all: it curved inwards around the shattered region in a mighty sweep, and I realized of a sudden that we were flying over the interior of an immense crater; so immense indeed that the curve of its walls almost dwarfed the curve of the satellite itself!

Now I knew that we must have reached the side of the Moon hidden from Earth, for this monstrous crater must cover most of a hemisphere, overshadowing by far the great walled plains of the Earth-facing side such as Copernicus and Ptolemaeus.

Soon the boundary wall of the giant crater had receded from view behind the curve of the planet, but the far wall was still nowhere to be seen, and I peered up in wonder at hundreds of square miles of desolation—desolation, that is, even by lunar standards.

There was a soft groan behind me.

I turned in the air, suddenly mindful of my mission. Poor Traveller lay strapped to his throne-couch with his face buried in his huge hands; his stovepipe hat floated in the air beside him, and wisps of white hair orbited his cranium. A fat notebook was strapped, open, to his right thigh; into this, I knew, he had over the last few days been entering painstaking details of the schedule—the maneuvers, the rocket bursts—which would deliver us safely to the surface.

I did a graceful somersault, kicked against the windows, and settled gently to the deck at Traveller's side. I took his arm and shook it urgently. "Sir Josiah, what is troubling you?"

He lifted his face from his hands. His expression was a mixture of anger and despair, and his eyes were pinpoints of blue in Moon shadows. "Ned, we are done for. Done for! To have come so far, to have endured so much, only to be betrayed by the folly of that pompous Danish idiot!"

". . . To which Dane do you refer?" I asked cautiously.

"Hansen, of course, and his absurd breakfast-egg theory of the lunar shape. Look at it!" He shook a fist at the shattered landscape which loomed over us. "It's as clear as day that the Moon is a perfect sphere after all, that the mass must be uniformly distributed, that the backside of the wretched world must be as devoid of air as the face!"

I stared up at the lunar desolation. There were sparkles and glints deep in the shadow of the fragments of the shattered land, showing the possibility of granite, perhaps, or quartz. Traveller's sudden loss of spirit, I decided, stemmed not from despair or fear, but from a feeling of betrayal—by the Moon itself, by the Creator for having the temerity to design a world so unsuited to Traveller's purposes, and even by this poor chap Hansen, who, of the three, was surely the most blameless!

Traveller lay back in his couch and stared up at the Moon, muttering.

I was bewildered. Even if the lunar landing was a fruitless exercise, I reflected, we had no choice but to continue with it; and only Traveller could bring our journey to a successful conclusion. But it was clear that Traveller had retreated into himself, and was, at this moment, quite incapable of piloting the craft.

I had to do something, or we should all be killed after all.

With some hesitation I reached out and touched his arm. "Sir Josiah, not long ago you accused me of lacking imagination. Now I feel obliged to identify the same fault in yourself. Was it not you who explained that, come success or failure, life or death, we should be in for some terrific fun?"

His face was heavily scored by Moon shadows, and for the first time since I had met him he looked his true age. He said quietly, "I had banked on Hansen's crackpot theories, Ned. With the banishment of my hopes of finding water, I find little fun in the prospect of a certain death."

He sounded old, frail, frightened and surprisingly vulnerable; I felt privileged to see behind the bluff mask to the true man. But at this moment I needed the old Traveller, the wild, the supremely confident, the arrogant!

I pointed above my head. "Then, sir, at least you have surely not lost your wonder! Look at that crater floor above us. We have discovered the mightiest feature on the Moon—a fitting monument to your achievements—and, if our story is ever told by future generations, they shall surely name it after the great Josiah Traveller!"

He looked vaguely interested at that, and he raised his beak of a platinum nose to the silver landscape. "Traveller Crater. Perhaps. No doubt some bastardized Latin version will be used."

"And," I said, "think of the impact which must have caused such a monstrous scar. It must have come close to splitting the damn Moon in two."

He stroked his chin and inspected the huge crater with an appraising eye. "And yet it is scarcely possible to envisage a meteorite impact of such a magnitude . . . No, Ned; I suspect the explanation for that vast feature is still more exotic."

"What do you mean?"

"Anti-ice! Ned, if that remarkable compound has been discovered on the surface of the Earth, what is to stop it being available on other planets and satellites?

"I envisage a comet-like body falling in to the Solar System, perhaps from the stars, largely or wholly composed of anti-ice. As the Sun's heat touches it I imagine little pockets of the ice exploding, and the wretched body being twisted and spun this way and that.

"At last, though, blazing and glowing, it falls close to the Earth—only to find the inert form of Earth's patient companion in its way.

"The detonation is astounding—as you say, almost enough to split the Moon in two. Crater walls roll across the tortured surface like waves across a sea. And one must imagine millions of tons of pulverized lunar rock and dust being hurled into space—with fragments of the original anti-ice comet embedded within it. And so, perhaps, some fragments reached even the surface of the Earth itself."

I stared up at that desolate craterscape and shivered, imagining it superimposed on a map of Europe. "Then we must be grateful to the Moon that the comet never reached Earth, Sir Josiah."

"Indeed."

"And do you suppose the wretched Professor Hansen could have been right after all? Could there have been an air-covered area of the Moon—perhaps inhabited, but now laid waste by the anti-ice explosion?"

He shook his head, a little wistfully. "No, lad; I fear the good Dane was wrong all the way; for the geometry of the Moon itself does not support his egg-shape theory. Our chances of finding the water we need to save our lives remain negligible."

In desperation I turned my face up to the darkling landscape over which we flew, inverted. So my diplomatic skills had succeeded in bringing Traveller out of his funk—but not to the extent that he might lift a finger to save our lives.

. . . And then I noticed once more, twinkling like a hundred Bethlehem stars, bright, glassy sparkles amid the tumbled lunar mountains. I cried out and pointed. "Traveller! Before you sink completely into despair, look above you. What do you see, shining in the last of the Sun's rays?"

Again he rubbed his chin, but he looked closely. "It could be nothing, lad," he said gently. "Outcroppings of quartz or feldspar—"

"But it could be water, frozen pools of it shining in the sunlight!"

He turned to me almost kindly, and I sensed he was about to launch into an extended lecture on the source of my latest misapprehension—and then, like the reappearance of the Sun from a cloudbank, his face lit up with determination. "By God, Ned, you could be right. Who knows? And it's certain we will never find out if we let ourselves fall helplessly to that tumbled surface. Enough of this! We have a world to conquer." And he grabbed his stovepipe hat out of the air and screwed it down over his cranium.

I was filled with elation. I said, "Will you resume the plan you have written in your little book?"

He looked down at the notebook still tied to his knee. "What, this? I have moped my way into too great a deviance from the schedule, I fear." He tore the book from his knee and hurled it, spinning, into the shadows of the

Bridge. "It is too late for calculation. Now we must pilot the *Phaeton* as she was meant to be piloted—with our hands, our minds, our eyes. Hold on, Ned!"

And he hauled back his levers; the anti-ice rockets roared, and I was hurled bodily to the deck.

The next several minutes were a nightmarish blur. Traveller kept the rockets shouting, and the deck of the Bridge—an uneven series of riveted plates—pressed into my face and chest. I could do nothing but cling to whatever purchase I could find—like the iron pillars which supported Traveller's couch—and reflect that it was typical of Traveller to neglect utterly the well-being of those he was trying to save. Surely a delay of a few seconds to allow me to regain my seat in the Cabin would not have mattered one way or the other.

After some minutes the quality of the Moonlight seemed to change. The shadow of my head shifted and lengthened across the deck; and at last I was plunged into a darkness broken only by the dim glow of Traveller's Ruhmkorff coils. I surmised that the ship had been turned around, so that our nose now pointed away from the Moon.

Then, blessed relief!—the motors reduced. Though the rockets continued to fire at a subdued level, it was as if a vast weight had been lifted from my shoulders. I cautiously pushed my face away from the floor, got to my hands and knees, and then to my feet—and surprised myself to find I was standing!

"Sir Josiah! We are no longer floating . . ."

He lay in his couch, lightly playing his control levers. "Oh, hullo, Ned; I'd quite forgotten you were there. No, we are no longer in free fall. I decided that boldness was the best course of action. So I launched us directly at the lunar surface, from which we were in any event a mere few thousand miles—"

"I was quite crushed against the plates."

He looked at me in some surprise. "Were you? But the thrust was only a little more than a terrestrial gravity." His look turned to sternness. "You have become weakened by the floating condition," he said. "I warned you that you should maintain your exercise regime, as I have done; it is a wonder your bones, reduced to brittleness, did not crumble to dust."

I framed a reply, which would have touched on the reasons for my abandonment of his routine—namely the several days I had spent as an invalid following my supposedly heroic jaunt into space—but I forbore. I said, "And then you turned the ship around."

"Yes; now we are falling backside first toward the Moon," he confirmed cheerfully. "The thrust you feel is about the gravitational acceleration we should experience on the surface of the Moon, which has been computed to be a sixth part of Earth's. I have reduced our speed to an acceptably low level, and now I am firing the rockets in order to keep our speed constant." He fixed me with a quizzical eye. "I presume you understand the dynamics of our situation?—that the equality of lunar gravity and the rocket thrust is no coincidence?"

"Perhaps we could go over the theory later," I said drily. I raised myself to my toes and bounced up and down on the deck; in my enfeebled state even this fractional gravity felt significant, but I was able to jump easily into the air. "So this is how it would feel if one could walk around on the Moon?"

"Quite so." Now he craned back his neck and peered

into his periscope. "Now I must fix on our landing site. We will land amid lunar mountains, during a sunset."

Clinging to the couch I turned to look through the windows. The sky above, away from the Sun, was utterly dark; and as we were descending toward the Moon's hidden face Earth herself was concealed from us now. All around us gaunt fingers of rock, shattered in that ancient explosion, reached serrated edges toward us, and shadows pooled like spilt blood.

I asked, "Why not land in a daylit area? Those shadows must make a choice of a safe landing spot virtually impossible."

With some impatience Traveller replied, "But the *Phaeton* has not been designed for extended jaunts on the lunar surface, Ned! Recall that while she is in space the craft must rotate continually to avoid one side or the other overheating in the Sun's rays. Here, such rotation will not be possible—yet the solar rays will be just as intense as between worlds. I would hope that our stay here, if the Lord allows us to survive our landing, will not encompass more than a few hours; but even that length of time in the pitiless glare of the Sun would rapidly cause our fragile vessel to burn up. And in the lunar night we would freeze solid. No; our best hope is that I can place us with some fraction of our surface in shadow, and the rest in the sunlight, so that we attain some balance between fire and ice."

We sank into the lunar landscape. Tumbled mountains rose around us, and wisps of dust fled from beneath us, agitated by the nearness of our rocket nozzles.

I began to believe I might live through this.

The sound of the rockets, which had been a steady, deep-chested roar, now coughed uncertainly and died away. I turned with a wild hope. Were we down? Then I stared at my feet, for, to my horror, they were leaving the deck. "Traveller!" I screamed. "I am floating once more!"

"Our fuel is gone, Ned," he said calmly. "We are falling freely toward the lunar surface. I have done my best; now we can only pray."

The lunar landscape rushed to meet us, tilting.

A thousand questions washed through my mind. How far had we been from the surface when the engines failed? And how quickly would one accrue speed, falling through the Moon's enfeebled gravity? What size of impact could the *Phaeton* withstand before she split open like an egg and tumbled us all, warm and soft and helpless, out on to the cruel lunar rocks?

There was a grind of metal on rock.

I was hurled to the deck once more. I heard a smashing of glass, a ripping of cloth and leather. The deck tilted crazily, and I slid along it for several feet, fetching up at last against a bank of instruments. Then the deck came back to a level. I pressed my face to the riveted floor, waiting for the moment when the hull burst and the air was sucked for the final time from my lungs . . .

But the noise of our impact died away; the ship settled a little further into whatever rocky cradle it had carved for itself. A great hush fell over the craft. But there was no rush of air, no more tearing of metal; I was still alive, and breathing as comfortably as I ever had.

I climbed slowly to my feet, mindful of the weak lunar gravity. Traveller stood on his couch, abandoned restraints coiled around his feet; with hands on hips and stovepipe hat fixed jauntily in place, he peered out at his new domain.

I climbed up beside him, with little effort; I saw how his

frock coat had been torn down the back, and how blood seeped steadily down his wrinkled cheek from a cut to the temple.

A city of rock lay all around us. Shadows fled from a Sun which was barely hidden behind a distant peak. The place was airless, desolate, utterly forbidding of human life—and yet conquered.

"Dear God, Traveller, you have brought us to the Moon. I could compliment your skill as a pilot, your genius as an engineer—but surely it is your sheer nerve, your audacious vision, which shines out above all."

He grunted dismissively. "Pretty speeches are for funerals, Ned. You and I are very much alive, and we have work to do." He pointed to the Sun. "Another six to eight hours, I should say, and that Sun will be hidden behind the spire, not to reappear for a full fortnight, and we shall slowly but surely freeze solid. We need water, Ned; and the sooner we get out there and bring it in the sooner Pocket can brew us a healthy pot of tea and we can set off for Mother Earth!"

Despite the feebleness of the gravity I felt as if I should fall, so weak did every one of my joints become. For once more Traveller had looked ahead in a manner which evaded me. Even if bucketfuls of precious water lay just behind those rocks over there, one of us would have to leave the craft and fetch it in. And I knew that could only be me!

[10]

AN ENGLISHMAN ON THE MOON

Traveller unfurled a rope ladder and we rejoined our companions in the Smoking Cabin. There we found an atmosphere of euphoria, aided by the deck's noticeable tilt which leant an air of enchantment to the proceedings. Traveller and his manservant settled down to opening up the access to the lower compartment of the craft. The sullen Bourne was staring out of the windows at the tumbled lunar landscape. Holden was bounding about the Cabin; with whoops of pleasure he launched himself five or six feet into the air before settling back to the deck, as gentle as a rotund autumn leaf. I could not help but smile at the crimson glow of his face. "My word, Ned, these lunar conditions are enchanting; it's exactly like being a child again," he said.

Holden was all for breaking out the brandy and celebrating our successful conquest of the Moon, but Traveller would have none of it. "There is no time for frivolities," he admonished the journalist. "This is not a picnic; we have a few hours in which to win the struggle for our very survival." He looked at me with something resembling concern—although he might have been regarding some fragile but vital component of machinery. "Ned, your comfort is of the essence now. Would you care for some tea, or even a light meal, to fortify yourself before your adventure?—and I would strongly recommend, as before, purging your system before venturing from the craft. Pocket!"

And so it was that I, surrounded by my companions and sitting in a comfortable chair, bit into sandwiches of cucumber and tomato and sipped a blend of the finest Indian teas—while all around me the desolation of the Moon, lifeless and cold, stretched to the horizon!

Though I tried, I found it impossible to purge my bowels as Traveller had recommended.

Then, all too soon, I was climbing once more into the stinking confines of Traveller's leather air suit. The hose which brought air to the suit—and which I had severed during my perilous entry into the Bridge—had been repaired by Pocket. Traveller and the others assembled items of equipment. I was given a length of rope to knot around my waist, a small electrical lantern improvised from one of the Bridge's lesser instruments, and an ice pick made from Traveller's stock of spare parts. Traveller rigged up a bag from the oilcloth which had once covered the floor. This bag, a substantial affair about four feet wide, was double-walled, and between the walls of cloth Sir Josiah inserted cushion stuffing. This satchel was intended for me to lug water ice about the lunar surface, and, said Sir Josiah, the purpose of the stuffing was to provide the precious substance with some protection from the rays of the sun.

I fixed the axe and lamp to my waist, so as to leave my mittened hands free for my climb down to the surface, and suspended the bag by two straps from my back in the manner of an outsize knapsack.

Holden began to argue that the significance of the moment—man's first steps on the surface of another world—was such that I should spend some time on some form of ceremonial.

"Out of the question," Traveller snapped. "We don't have time for such nonsense. Ned is going out to save our lives, in conditions of severe hazard; not to stand on his hands and do tricks for the King."

Holden bristled. "Sir Josiah, despite the importunate nature of our journey, we have nevertheless succeeded in landing where no explorer has arrived before. And we therefore have the duty to claim this lunar continent in the name of the Empire. I would remind you that young Ned is a representative of His Majesty's government. Perhaps the raising of the Union Flag over the dust of the Moon—"

Bourne barked short laughter. "How like you British that would be. How obscene to desecrate such a place with your ugly flag."

Holden drew himself up, thrusting his pot belly out before him. "The very objections of the Frenchie, Sir Josiah, show that such a course would be eminently suitable."

Traveller had been working at my suit seals. Now he straightened up and rested his hands on his hips, leaving me and Pocket to struggle alone. "Holden, I have never listened to such asinine balderdash. I have two objections. First, thanks to the airlessness of the lunar surface, there would be no wind to support your flag. It would hang for all eternity, limp and helpless; is this a suitable symbol of the Empire? Of course we could prop it open with some sort of crutch—a metal rod, perhaps . . ." He laughed.

"Who but the most pompous ass would consider such a course? And in any event, my second objection is rather more conclusive: it is that I do not carry flags of any description on this craft; not the Union Flag, not the tricolore, not any nation's flag. So unless you are a nimble seamstress, Mr. Holden, I suggest your ambition will remain unfulfilled."

"And," said Bourne, "the more dignity we will retain for that."

But Holden would not accept this point of view; and soon a three-cornered debate between Holden, Bourne and Traveller was raging. Meanwhile I had completed my enrobement and was standing waiting with Pocket, helmet tucked under my arm, for my adventure to begin.

After some minutes I lost patience. I raised the globe helmet in both hands and with a dramatic flourish brought it crashing down on the glass case which contained Traveller's model of the *Great Eastern.* The debate was stilled at once, and Pocket set to work with dustpan and brush to retrieve the shattered glass. With my mittened hand I reached into the ruin and extracted the model ship; it was perhaps three feet long, and I handled it with great care, endeavoring not to damage any of the detailed working. "Sir Josiah, you will forgive my impulsive and destructive act. Gentlemen, since it is I who must venture beyond these walls, it is I who should decide on the ceremonial gesture to be made.

"I will carry this model of Brunel's great ship and leave it in some appropriate place. This should take no more than a moment, and it will satisfy all our purposes. Holden, the *Eastern* is one of the Empire's greatest engineering achievements, and thus symbolizes the great civilization which has reached this pinnacle. Sir Josiah, you will surely endorse a memorial on this distant plateau to the engineer who has inspired and informed much of your work. And Bourne: I hope you will join with me in regarding this model as a symbol of the endless inventiveness and enterprise of man, which has brought us even to this astonishing land.

"And if our venture should fail," I went on, somewhat surprised at my own eloquence, "then let some future generation of mankind find this artifact and wonder at those who might have brought it here."

There was a moment's silence. Then Holden said, "Well done, Ned. You've put us in our place."

"Are we ready to proceed?"

Traveller indicated the air cupboard with a flourish. "All is prepared, Ned."

I nodded. "There is something I would like to request first, however . . ."

Once more the helmet was screwed over my head, enclosing me in a dismal miniature universe dominated by the tang of copper, the stale taste of pumped air, and the sound of my own ragged breathing. I climbed into the coffin-like air cupboard. After final handshakes from my companions—my huge mittens enclosed their tiny hands—the heavy hatch was closed down, excluding me from the cozy warmth of the Cabin. I hesitated for some moments, clutching the *Eastern* model against my leather vest; then, grabbing my courage, I grasped the wheel set in the hatchway below me and turned it with resolution.

After three or four turns the seal was broken and I heard the final sigh of atmosphere being expelled into the airless lunar environs. My joints stiffened as the suit expanded to the limits of its flexibility.

Then, at last, the hatch swung open, and I found myself staring down at a square yard of lunar soil.

This ground, some ten feet below me, looked fairly even, yet it was strewn with sharp-edged pebbles which cast long shadows in the sunlight; and the shadows were as black as ink. This cruel sharpness, and the unwavering stillness in the lack of air, spoke instantly to me of my un-Earthly situation, and I spent some minutes with the blood pounding through my ears simply inspecting that patch of soil.

At length I found the strength to proceed. I pulled a rope ladder from the air cupboard and let it unravel. Then I swung my legs down through the hatch and proceeded to climb down, pausing after a few rungs to pick up the *Great Eastern.* When my head cleared the hatchway my helmet was filled with dazzling sunlight which caused my eyes to smart; thereafter I took care to avert my eyes from the naked Sun, which lay dangerously close to the horizon.

I paused on the last rung above the ground, with my foot poised above the lunar soil. A sense of pride and occasion swept over me. That it should have been me to whom the honor had been granted of first walking on the surface of another world! I reflected on the strange chain of accidents which had led me to this point, and wondered briefly how things might have been different had it not been for that greatest accident of all, which is anti-ice. Might men have reached the Moon nevertheless? Surely a way would have been found, based upon rockets of a type not yet dreamed of; although it would have taken many more years—perhaps even until the turn of the century into the twentieth—before a successful voyager reached so far. Still, as in all things industrial and technological, Great Britain would have led the way in this parallel adventure, and so some other Briton—perhaps better prepared than I—would have stood at the foot of another ladder.

I indulged in a moment of self-pride and wished that the fair Françoise could raise her eyes from the troubled fields of France and look across space to see me in this moment of celestial glory. But this conceit did not survive a moment's reflection on the extraordinary historical significance of my situation. To set foot on another world was surely the most significant achievement in human development since the Ark—or, if Sir Charles Darwin is to be believed, since our monkey forebears desisted from hurling bananas at each other and climbed down from the trees to walk upright on the land. So, as I pressed my leather slipper into the firm, gravel-like soil, I said this prayer, unheard by any other human soul: "Lord, with this single step, like Noah I walk upon a new continent delivered to us in your grace; and I carry the hopes of all mankind with me as I take it."

I stood unsupported on the lunar soil, connected to the *Phaeton* only by a length of air hose. I could feel the keenness of jagged pebbles through my slippers; it was like walking on the breast of a young beach. I plotted each step with circumspection, for I was very fearful of rupturing the suit or the air hose.

Clutching my model ship, and with the axe and Ruhmkorff lamp bouncing against my leg, I walked down a slope into the lunar silence for some thirty feet—my hose extended only forty feet in total—and looked about me.

The landscape was a desolation of ruined and smashed rocks; these varied from pebbles to boulders far larger than the ship. The rubble extended to a horizon which, thanks to the Moon's small radius, appeared surprisingly close—a phenomenon which gave rise to the illusion that I was crossing the summit of a broad hill.

The walls of Traveller Crater were, of course, invisible to me, lying many thousands of miles away in every point of the compass.

The rubble-strewn floor was not level. It featured many hills, or hummocks; these were low, circular domes of a surprising uniformity of shape, although their size varied greatly, with the smallest scarcely taller than I was and the largest reaching perhaps fifty feet from the common level and stretching a good eighth of a mile from side to side. There must be, I speculated, some volcanic explanation for these configurations. In the invigorating lightness of the lunar gravity I imagined bounding across this landscape, leaping from summit to summit with the grace of a goat. But, of course, I was restrained by my air-carrying tether, and I was nervous in any event of the integrity of my suit.

I turned now to study the lie of the *Phaeton.* I was only some ten yards from the ship and the vessel loomed over me; overall she had survived surprisingly well, and the dull sheen of her aluminum skin glowed through a thin coating of lunar dust. The glass of the Bridge dome, though showing evidence of scorching, sparkled in the remaining sunlight and cast highlights across the shattered lunar plain. Traveller had brought us down, I saw, on the brow of one of the low hills—its summit being perhaps ten feet from the common level—and I silently applauded his skill, for we were surely safer and more stable there than in one of the narrow "valleys" which wound between the hills. But the ship was far from level, for one of its three landing legs had rested on a larger boulder and had crumpled slightly;

the leg still supported the craft, but at an angle of perhaps twenty degrees to the vertical.

As he had intended, Traveller had brought us down with the upper portions of the craft in sunlight. From the Cabin ports in the shadowed lower portion of the hull a warm gaslight shone out over the lifeless rocks; and in the windows I could make out the faces of Bourne and Holden. I longed to be readmitted to the cosiness of that interior, with its scents of Pocket's cooking and of Traveller's Turkish cigarettes; but also I experienced a surge of pride that we had brought this roomful of England to this terrible place. Even now I could see that Holden still wore his tie, neatly knotted around his wing collar!

As I stared at the ship standing proud in that hostile place I became aware that my helmet and the upper part of my air suit were becoming uncomfortably hot. I reminded myself that I had very little time to accomplish my mission before my position out on the surface became untenable. So, without further hesitation, I raised the *Great Eastern* above my head with both hands—I saw Holden applauding this gesture—and then made to place it behind a rock, sheltered from the blast of *Phaeton*'s rockets. I paused in this act, watching the ship expectantly, and was rewarded with the sight of Holden raising a camera to the port. So my final request before leaving the ship was fulfilled; by this lapse into immodesty I had ensured that my jaunt on the Moon should be recorded for all posterity.

As I held my position like an awkward statue, waiting the single second until the plate should be exposed, I felt an odd tremble from the ground below me, like a minor earthquake. But I held my pose, and the tremor passed away.

With the *Eastern* fixed in place I hurried into the

shadow of the *Phaeton,* my breath laboring, determined to get on with my mission.

I lit my Ruhmkorff coil and held it high. Pale electrical light extended far across the shattered lunar land: it could not, of course, compete with the direct light of the Sun, but it did reveal the nature of what lay hidden in the shadows of the hills and the larger boulders. I sought the reflective glint which Traveller and I had espied from space—and, perhaps five feet beyond the boundary of *Phaeton*'s hillock, I made out a stretch of soil ten feet wide which lay as flat as a millpond and returned highlights from my coil.

I moved as quickly as I could down the shallow slope of the hill, and, with my hose nearly fully extended, I crouched to reach the gleaming pool.

I was cruelly disappointed. My mitten, probing at the reflective surface, broke through it and reached crumbled soil; I raised up fragments of the surface I had shattered and held them before my face. This was no ice; rather, I held a fragment of some glass-like substance—brownish and all but opaque, but recognizably glass nevertheless. I had heard that great heat, or great pressure, can reduce ordinary sand to glass without the intervention of man, and no doubt this was the explanation of this phenomenon. Perhaps this natural pane had been formed in the very impact which had thrown up Traveller Crater itself. I was sure this substance would have formed a fascinating conundrum for the men of science—not least, I suspected, because it demonstrated the commonality of minerals on Earth and on the Moon—but it was little help to me! Had the glinting glaciers Traveller and I had discerned from orbit all been chimerae formed by this glassy debris?

In a moment of rage and disappointment I cried out and

hurled the pane of glass far from me; it traveled many hundreds of yards, its spin unhindered by any atmosphere, glinting in its treacherous fashion in the low sunlight. And the ground shook once more beneath my feet, as if in sympathy; the tremor was powerful this time, and boulders rolled across the ground, like sand grains on the skin of a drum.

I dropped to a crouch while the landscape rattled; I waited fearfully lest some boulder should roll close enough to crush me, or block my air hose . . .

And at length the trembling ceased, but it was matched almost at once by the rattling of my heart, for in the depression vacated by one large boulder I saw the unmistakable spark of frost.

I hurried to the shining patch, but as sunlight struck it the ice hissed to vapour which escaped through my fingers.

I remained elated, however, for now my path was clear. Whatever water remained on the Moon must surely lie within the deepest caves, or beneath boulders—at any event removed from the sunlight. Several large boulders lay within reach of my air hose. I hurried to one of the largest—a cube-shaped affair some four feet on a side—and spent some moments pondering how I, one man alone, should lift such a monster. I considered returning to the *Phaeton* in the hope of improvising some sort of lever; then I remembered that I was, after all, on the surface of the Moon, whose one-sixth gravity had loaned me the strength of a team of navigators. So I crouched down and slid my fingers underneath a lip of the rock. I heaved at it, expecting it to flip aside like an empty carton; but although the boulder did indeed shift, it did so slowly and ponderously—and after a great deal of plate-steaming effort from me—so that I was left in no doubt as to its substantial mass.

Thus I learned by practical demonstration the difference between weight, which is governed by the gravity of a planet, and inertia, which is not.

Imagine my disappointment, though, when the rock at last tumbled aside to reveal not even the slightest stain of frost. I stood there, lungs laboring at the thin substance provided by the hoses, and staring in disbelief at the ground.

There was nothing for it but to proceed to the next rock and try again; and when I did so, to my intense joy, I was rewarded with the sight of a thick pool of frost some five feet wide and several inches thick. Sheltering the precious stuff with my own shadow I bundled the frost into my insulated bag, using my mitten as a scoop, and came away with some pounds of lunar water.

I soon lost track of time as I worked through that changeless lunar afternoon. Boulder after boulder I tore aside, finding substantial caches of water under perhaps half of them. I filled the bag over and over, and returned several times to the *Phaeton,* soon amassing a small hill of crumbled ice in the shadow of the ship. Every few minutes the ground would tremble ominously; but I learned to ignore these small earthquakes. When the bag was more than half-full, though it did not weigh me down, its inertia, as it swung against my back, became a distracting nuisance.

Then came a massive tremor.

It was as if some giant had struck the surface of the Moon. I was thrown to the ground. I had the presence of mind to cover my faceplate with my mittens; otherwise the glass should surely have smashed. I lay there for long seconds, hardly daring to look up, expecting at any moment to be hurled into some lunar chasm or smashed beneath a fall of rock. And the Moonquake continued in an utter and eerie silence!

When only echoes still rolled massively through the rock beneath me, I climbed cautiously to my feet. My air hose, my bag of ice, were safe; but my faceplate was severely misted up—so much so that I could barely see—and my Ruhmkorff coil was smashed and useless. I abandoned it for some future explorer to puzzle over. I was uncertain of the time—not having had the presence of mind to wear a watch on the outside of my air suit!—and I stood a few feet beyond the lip of *Phaeton*'s low hill and looked about.

The landscape appeared to have changed: the look of the range of hillocks and the way their shadows lay was not as I remembered it. No doubt, I told myself, this was simply an illusion of the sunset; for even on Earth the aspect of natural features can appear to evolve as the light dies.

I hesitated for some more moments, disoriented, trying to weigh in my mind the benefits of a few more pounds of ice in my half-full satchel against the unknown dangers of this strange place—when the decision was taken out of my hands.

Another tremor erupted over the landscape. I dropped the ice axe and staggered away from *Phaeton*'s hill. After a few paces I came up against the limits of my air hose and my head was jerked back against my neck. I stood my ground, balancing with outstretched arms, and turned to face the *Phaeton*—to be greeted by a quite astonishing sight.

All around the hill cylinders of rock were rising from

the ground. There were perhaps twelve of them, equally spaced around the dome of the hill, each about a yard in diameter; they rose evenly, by several feet per second. The ground shuddered anew and I struggled to keep my feet, wondering at the power required to lift such mighty masses so rapidly. Soon the hill—and the *Phaeton*—was quite enclosed by the pillars. As the pillars grew their rate of increase slowed, until at last they settled to a height of a hundred feet. I realized that it was only by the grace of God that my air pipes had not been snagged or ruptured by the growth of this mineral flora.

The ground shook on as if in response to distant explosions, and I turned to view the rest of the landscape. Like flowers of rock, pillars sprang up around all of the hills which littered this shattered plain; some of them, I saw by tilting my fogged helmet back, towered to heights which far outshone the puny hundred feet of the *Phaeton* pillars: the largest, perhaps half a mile away, must have stretched up a full thousand feet. The pillars were as smooth as if finished by a fine craftsman, but their mineral nature was not concealed.

This sprouting growth all across the plain, conducted in an eerie silence, reminded me irresistibly of the growth of life; perhaps the pillars were analogous to the plants which dwell in desert climes and erupt into growth at the smallest drop of rain. But I wondered what sort of life it was that raised such monstrous statues, and at such speed.

At last the final pillars reached their target heights; and all across a plain newly scored by parallel shadows, the stillness was broken only by a gentle rain of dust and pebbles.

I stood my ground for a few moments, the blood pounding through my temples, wondering if it was safe to essay a return to the *Phaeton*.

Then, while I still hesitated, the next phase began.

The largest hill, some fifty feet high, was the first. Small boulders and plates of rock exploded all around the perimeter of the hill. The mound shuddered visibly and tremors raced through the rocky floor to my feet; and I had the impression of some vast animal struggling to rise from its confines of earth.

Then, with a jolt of fresh shock, I realized that this impression had been exactly right; for the whole hill was lifting bodily from the lunar soil. It rode skywards on its tube of encircling pillars. I stood there dumbfounded, scarcely able to believe the evidence of my senses. Now the "hill" lifted clear of the ground, and I saw that its dome profile was matched beneath by another, inverted dome, so that the whole formed a symmetrical stone lens; the underside of the lens, though, was scarred and fragmented. Fist-sized chunks of rock splintered from the sharp lip of the lens, which scoured at the supporting pillars.

As the lens shape rose it accelerated, reaching speeds that denied its thousands of tons mass. Soon it was soaring far above me, still sailing up its thousand-foot circle of pillars.

But this had only been the precursor: soon, all around the plain, the mounds were lifting to reveal characteristic lens shapes, and I had cause to welcome the airless nature of the Moon, for surely if there had been atmosphere to carry sound the noise of these great emergings would have smashed my eardrums at once.

Then my head was snapped backwards by a tug on my air hose and I was sent sprawling on the ground. I twisted rapidly where I lay and was greeted with the sight of the

Phaeton's hill, with the ship still on its back, riding into the sky like all its cousins.

With my ice bag bouncing against the small of my back I clawed my way to my feet, mittens scrabbling against rocks. I stood where the lip of the *Phaeton* hill had formerly been—it was now the rim of a shallow crater—and I peered up in desperation. Already the edge of the lens was some ten feet above me and accelerating, bearing the ship and all my hopes with it. Within seconds my air hose would reach its full extension. Perhaps then I would be hauled into the air, like a marionette, my legs dangling helplessly; or perhaps the hose would snap at once, spilling my precious air into the lunar emptiness . . .

I fixed my ice bag more evenly over my shoulders, bent my legs as far as my swollen suit joints would allow, and leapt from the surface of the Moon.

The lunar gravity plucked only weakly at my flight. I rose high, my hose coiling around me. As I neared the peak of my trajectory my upward speed slowed, and for an agonizing moment I thought I would just fail to grab the rim; but at last my arms and head sailed above the lip of rock and I scrabbled at it with my mittened hands, finally finding purchase in crevices in the carcass of this rocky beast.

I hung there sucking in piped air, my pack of ice thumping against my spine. As the lens accelerated into the sky the pressure on my hands and shoulders increased steadily, so that I was forced to postpone any idea of climbing safely aboard the lens; it was all I could do to hold my position.

I twisted my neck, trying to find some relief from the agony of my overextended shoulders; and as I did so I became aware of still another development. For now the rock-lens beings, having hauled themselves to the peaks of their pillar legs, were beginning to move about the plain. They scraped their way in a stately fashion across the ground toward and away from each other, in a manner reminiscent of duelling swordsmen—or of predatory insects.

This slow, silent waltz was quite as astonishing as if I had seen Windsor Castle get up and walk about.

The pillar-limbs were not articulating or tilting in any way; it appeared that, while remaining vertical, pillars were sliding one by one beneath the surface of their passenger lens; all this motion was co-ordinated in a surprisingly graceful fashion, allowing the rock-beasts to move quite freely.

All this I saw in glimpses over two or three seconds, as I soared upwards in pursuit of the *Phaeton.*

At last the pressure in my arms eased, and I realized that my lens must be approaching the top of its nest of pillars. I looked up and saw that the ends of the pillars were indeed very close—but, far beyond them, I could see the underside of another lens-beast, larger and higher than the *Phaeton*'s. It moved toward the *Phaeton* lens in a quite menacing fashion.

I had no idea what this meant, but doubted that it was a good sign; and as soon as I was able I hauled myself over the lip of the rock, dragging my hose and ice bag behind me. I had imagined that the *Phaeton* might have been shaken free, or at least, tumbled over and smashed; but, to my relief, she still clung to the hill, and even remained upright. Out of a corner of my eye I noticed that the model of the *Great Eastern* had been smashed under a fallen rock; only a few fragments of metal and glass showed where I had set her no more than hours earlier.

I hurried toward the ship. I saw how Holden and Pocket were peering from the windows in my direction—and I could see the unreserved joy with which they greeted my appearance from the dead, water-bag and all. Holden gestured at me to hurry; but I needed no urging!

Traveller had explained to me how a hatch at the lower skirt of the hull could be opened for the deposition of ice. I scrambled up a landing leg with an adroitness that surprised me, found the hatch, undogged its latches as Traveller had taught me, and was soon emptying my bag of ice into the tanks. Hastily I scooped up handfuls from my hill of collected ice and crammed them, too, into the hatch. I had to fumble at all of this with my mittened hands and the more I hurried the more I spilled ice wastefully; I was conscious the whole time that should our lens-host take it into its mind to go for a jaunt then surely I and the *Phaeton* would be hurled to an untimely death; and all the while, at the edge of my vision, I could see that other monster lens towering over the *Phaeton*'s, and drawing ever nearer.

At last it was done. I closed the hatch, hurled the empty bag far from me and dropped away from the ship's leg, waving to Holden. I scrambled up the rope ladder which led to my air cupboard, eyeing the rocket nozzles nervously; as soon as Traveller could fire his engines he would surely not hesitate to do so, whether or not I was safely aboard, and so I had seconds to make myself secure. I hauled myself through the narrow hatchway, landing in the cupboard chest first like a fish and then hauling my legs behind me; I dragged in the rope ladder and my dangling air hose and was reaching for the hatch—

—when the rockets fired.

I was thrown against the bulkhead. My body was dragged toward the still-open hatch; I scrabbled at the riveted iron with my hands and legs, and for a terrifying period I lay crucified over the open hatchway, my head dangling on a stalk of neck.

The rockets raised a cloud of dust and pebbles from the carapace of our lens-beast.

The ship lurched abruptly sideways, and I had to latch my fingers around bulkhead plates. Then the lip of the larger lens-beast, which had towered over the *Phaeton,* slid across my field of view; and I realized that Traveller had been forced to drag us across the sky to avoid this second monster.

As we lifted out of the chaos of the Moon I saw how the greater beast had moved to cover ours completely—and then, with brutal suddenness, it dropped down its tube of pillars. The pillars of the lens on which we had rested were smashed to rubble, and fragments went wheeling across the landscape; both lenses were dashed to a thousand pieces against the ground. But this was not the end of it, for the fragmented lenses seemed to dissolve in a ferment of activity—I caught glimpses of tendrils of stone weaving through the debris and knitting it, it seemed, into a new whole; and I wondered if this were some astonishing form of lunar mating. And then the rising dust obscured my view.

As we rose and the lunar landscape opened out, I realized that this extraordinary merger was just one incident among thousands, for the entire plain was covered, I saw now, with similar maneuverings, couplings, and obscene devourings!

At last I dragged myself away from the lip of the port and allowed the hatch to close, shutting out my view of the receding Moon. I lay against the thrumming metal, sucking at thin air.

[11]

A SCIENTIFIC DISCUSSION

I do not remember the stilling of the engines; I must have floated in my iron coffin for several minutes. Then willing hands drew me gently out of my box and pulled away my helmet. I came to my senses still in the suit and with the copper ring chafing at my neck, but with my head free, and with the comparatively fresh air of the Cabin sweet in my nostrils.

Holden's round face hovered before me, wearing an expression of genuine concern, and I grabbed his arm. "Holden! And have we survived? Are we free of the Moon?"

"Yes, my friend—"

"Of course we are!" Traveller barked from behind Holden. "If we aren't off the Moon what are we doing floating around the Cabin? Perhaps we have been stuffing opium into our pipes, eh? What a pity your jaunt hasn't un-addled your brains, my boy—" Sir Josiah's eyes were fixed on me, and—though he seemed to be endeavoring to conceal it—I flattered myself that there was some pleasure in his stern countenance at the evidence of my recovery.

But Holden turned to him and said, "By God, Traveller, can you not desist? For all our sakes the boy has just been through a veritable nightmare, and all you can do is—"

"Holden." I laid a restraining hand on the journalist's arm. "Do not trouble yourself; Sir Josiah means no harm. It is just his way."

Holden caught my meaning and said no more; though his face registered a reluctance to let the matter drop—and in the subsequent days I was to observe how his manner to Traveller had become noticeably frostier, a change which was evidenced in a thousand trivial exchanges.

Holden, it seemed, would have no truck with those whom he suspected of unsound views, whatever their achievements.

I was fed a clear, warming broth. Then I was allowed, for the first time in several days, a bath; and thus I became the first human to bathe in lunar water! I entertained some qualms as I entered the concealed bath, for what if the water contained some unknown agent inimical to human life?—but, now that it had been run through the *Phaeton*'s filter system, the Moon water looked, smelled and even tasted like any common-or-garden rainwater; and Traveller assured me that he had run a series of chemical tests on it before confirming its suitability for human contact and consumption.

At length I was safely lodged in my familiar seat. I was warm, bathed and dressed in my combinations and a towelling robe of Traveller's, and I held a large globe of Traveller's oldest brandy in one hand and a fine-scented cigar in the other. I began to feel rather proud of my exploits—now that they were safely in the past. Holden and Traveller sat with me, as did Bourne, who maintained his usual resentful silence. The stoical Pocket, unflappable, was working his way through several days' backlog of begrimed dishes. "So, gentlemen," I said, "in the end, quite a remarkable adventure."

Holden raised his globe and peered into the glimmering depths of the brandy within. "Quite so. And not at all as we expected. We did not find anything resembling Earthly conditions, as we had anticipated—but nor did we find the Moon to be the inert and lifeless arena favored by some theorists."

"Instead," boomed Traveller, "we found something quite unexpected—as, paradoxically, we might have expected all along. The Phoebean life forms—for such I propose we call them; after Phoebe, Moon goddess of old Greece, sister to Apollo and daughter to Leto and Zeus—the Phoebeans are quite unlike anything encountered on Earth, both in their morphology and in their astounding vigor."

I asked, "Sir Josiah, if the shattered side of the Moon were turned to Earth, would the Phoebeans' frantic activities be visible to our astronomers?"

"Surely so; if only by changes of surface hue, and the raising of dust clouds—although we should remember that, without an atmosphere, dust has no medium of suspension, and once raised will settle rapidly to the ground. But even so I think we must conclude that the Phoebeans are at present confined to Traveller Crater on the far side of the Moon.

"And," he went on, lifting his platinum nose, "this evidence of confinement supports an hypothesis I have been constructing as to the origin and nature of these lunar beasts."

He inspected the ceiling with every evidence of interest. At last the tension had grown too great to bear—even the phlegmatic Pocket, polishing his dishes, looked around expectantly; and I demanded: "And your hypothesis is, sir?"

"Let us review the facts," he said slowly, steepling his long fingers around his brandy globe. "We find these creatures at the heart of an immense crater—a crater which, we have speculated, is the result of an anti-ice explosion.

"Second. The Phoebeans muster enormous masses, and throw them about the Moon with immense vigor. From this we conclude that whatever unknown organic motors power the beasts—their equivalent of our hearts, digestive systems, muscles—must be able to call on large stores of highly concentrated energy—"

"So," Holden broke in excitedly, "are you suggesting that the Phoebeans are creatures of anti-ice, which shares the characteristic of high energy density?"

"Not at all," Traveller snapped irritably, "and I will thank you not to interrupt my series of postulates. For even a fool—" Holden winced "—could see that an anti-ice theory is rendered to nonsense by my final observation, which is that the creatures lay dormant before our arrival! If they were powered by anti-ice energy release, Mr. Holden, what in Heaven would stop them from rampaging around the Moon constantly?"

I leaned forward. "So was it our arrival that triggered such an explosion of growth, Sir Josiah?"

"Oh, good God, of course not," Traveller said sharply, with scarcely less irritation despite my heroic status. "I hardly think our blundering arrival was an event of sufficient moment to warrant the awakening of a thousand living mountains! To the Phoebeans we are rather less than a toothless flea would be to a dog. No; the eruption of the Phoebeans closely followed our arrival from a coincidence: which was that I chose to land close to the terminator."

"Ah." Holden nodded. "You mean you set us down into a lunar sunset. And, you suggest, it is only at sunset that the Phoebeans emerge from dormancy?"

"I do more than suggest," Traveller said stiffly. "I took the time to observe the surface as we departed it through my telescopes; in the day hemisphere there is no evidence of movement on the scale we observed. But the darkened side is a writhing bowl of motion, as Phoebeans swirl their complex dances around each other."

"A fascinating observation," I said drily, and wondered whether to remark on my relief that at such a time as our launch Traveller had not become so overcome with anxiety for my well-being that he had been unable to complete a few scientific observations. "But what is so special about the night, Sir Josiah?"

"In the long lunar day," Traveller said, "temperatures from the unshaded sun must reach hundreds of degrees by the Celsius measure, while during the fortnight-long night there is no air to retain the warmth of the land and heat leaks steadily into space, bringing temperatures little above the absolute zero.

"Next, I would remind you that anti-ice contains not one but two novel properties. There is the propensity of some element of it to combine explosively with ordinary matter. But there is also the phenomenon of Enhanced Conductance, as observed by Lord Maxwell and others. But this Enhanced Conductance is temperature-dependent; try to melt a block of anti-ice and the Conductance disappears, as do the magnetic walls containing the antisubstance . . . and—Boom!" He illustrated the last syllable by knocking his metal nose against the brandy globe, producing a piercing chime; we all jumped—even the uninterested Bourne. "And this, of course," Traveller went on, "is the principle on which the construction of all our anti-ice machines is based."

"I think I understand," Holden said slowly, his eyes narrowed in thought. "You are suggesting that the Phoebeans are creatures whose blood flows along veins of Enhanced Conductance. But this property is only available when the temperature is low; too high and the Conductance property fails."

"Precisely," Traveller said. "The Phoebeans must slumber through the lunar day. Then, as the first touch of night stirs their unresistive blood, they become invigorated and pursue their violent affairs. But all too soon the dawn approaches and their veins clog once more; they grow dormant in the sunshine, waiting for the night to restore their vigor a fortnight later.

"And recall that the magnetic fields associated with Enhanced Conductance circuits are quite spectacularly large—much larger than anything produced by human scientists by any other means. It is these fields, I hazard, which supply the basis for the immense strength and speed of growth of the Phoebeans which we observed."

Holden nodded. "This has the ring of truth, Sir Josiah. Just think of it, Ned! What if you spent every day unconscious, and were only able to function in the gloom of night?"

I thought that over, and replied, "Actually I have some friends who live a bit like that. Perhaps they have Phoebean ancestry."

Holden said to Traveller, "You mentioned that this

speculation tied in to the earlier observation that the Phoebeans appear confined to Traveller Crater."

"Yes. For, as you will know, the phenomenon of Enhanced Conductance has been observed only in the substance we call anti-ice. Therefore I would suggest that the life-forms we saw were brought to the Moon by the comet, or meteor, of anti-ice which we have speculated fell to the lunar surface and detonated to cause such an immense formation."

I sipped some more brandy and said, "It is an intriguing theory; but could such large and complex creatures survive such an explosion?"

"A comparatively intelligent question," Traveller said, utterly without irony. "Probably they could not. But we may speculate that the Phoebeans have emerged from some simpler animalcule, a spore perhaps, which was hardy enough to survive the impact. And we may imagine that with the vigor of their growth and activities it will surely not be many centuries before they spread around to the Earth-facing face of the Moon."

I frowned at that. "God is to be thanked that there is no possibility of these animals spreading further—to our Earth, for example." I shivered, imagining those great crystalline limbs erupting from the green hills of England.

"Perhaps," Traveller said. "But what an opportunity for scientific study such an invasion would afford us!"

"If anyone survived to carry out such a study," said Holden.

"It is to be regretted," said Traveller, "that the remaining stocks of anti-ice are so low—and mostly committed to other projects—that after our return to Earth another voyage to the Moon, by some future expedition, is most unlikely; and it may be many centuries before the theories I have expounded can be confirmed. We may never know, for instance, whether the water ice Ned collected was indigenous to the Moon, was brought there by an anti-ice comet, or has been generated since as some waste product of the activities of the Phoebeans."

Bourne grinned. "How sad for you English that you are cut off from your newest colony. You could have taught these Phoebeans how to salute your flag; or how to institute a Parliament, as you did the hapless Indians."

I laughed at this, but Holden bristled and said: "Or you Frenchies could instruct them in the techniques of revolution. They are surely mindless and destructive enough for that."

I said, "Gentlemen, please; this is hardly a moment for such squabbling." I looked at Traveller expectantly. "Sir Josiah, you mentioned our return to Earth. And so we are saved, are we not?"

Traveller smiled at me, not unkindly, and pointed to the hatch set in the ceiling. "See for yourself."

I loosened my restraint, handed Pocket the remains of my cigar for neat disposal, and left my brandy globe to hover in the air; and then, still in my towelling robe, I jumped up to the hatch and passed through into the Bridge.

The Bridge was a place of spectral beauty; the various dials and panels shone in the faint yellow glow of their Ruhmkorff lights like the candlelit faces of carol-singers; and the whole was awash in a soft blue light: this was the light of Earth, which hung directly above the glass dome of the roof.

I stared up at that lovely island of water and cloud, and at the fizzing spark of the Little Moon which soared over the oceans; and, though I knew that we had many days of travel through space still to endure, every moment that passed would bring me closer to my home, and to the world of human affairs from which I had been plucked: to the world of war—and of love.

I stared at the planet until it seemed to me that the glimmering ocean was overlaid with the soft eyes of Françoise, my beacon of hope.

[12]

THE AIR OF ENGLAND

Josiah Traveller brought the *Phaeton* back to England on 20 September 1870.

The engineer jockeyed his battered craft through the fires of air friction, the globe-circling winds of the upper atmosphere, and finally a quite devastating thunderstorm: still a mile from the ground we cowered in our seats, peering fearfully through the ports at swords of lightning which leapt from cloud to cloud; and we imagined that we had passed through Earth all the way to Hell.

And at last the *Phaeton,* having all but exhausted its precious lunar water, settled with a bump into the soft, stubble-covered soil of a Kent farm. The rockets died for the last time, and silence settled over the Smoking Cabin which had become our prison. Pocket, Holden and I stared at each other with wild anticipation. Then we heard the soft sigh of the air of England against the outer skin of the craft; and we let out yells as we realized that we were at last home.

The Frenchman, Bourne, wept softly into the palm of his hand. I noticed this and, drawn by an odd sympathy I had acquired for the fellow, might have said some words to give him comfort. But my blood was racing at the thought that I had returned to my home country; a return that had seemed inconceivable through most of our astounding flight beyond the atmosphere. And so I pushed aside my restraints, still yelling like a coot, and stood up—

—and was floored, as fast as by any brawler's haymaker, by my own astonishing weight!

My legs had crumpled like paper, and I found my face pressed uncomfortably against the deck. With arms which trembled from the strain I pushed myself upright and rested my back against the padded wall. "My word, fellows, this gravity has given us all a pack to wear."

Holden nodded. "Traveller did warn us of the debilitating consequences of a lack of weight."

"Yes; and so much for all his wretched exercise regimes. To the Moon with a set of Indian clubs! Well, I'd like to see how the great man himself is bearing up under this once-familiar strain . . ." But Holden shamed me with his reminder that Traveller was an old man who should not be encouraged to strain his heart. And so it was I who crawled like a weakened child to the large hatchway set in the wall of the Cabin.

After much effort I succeeded in turning the locking wheel, and I kicked open the heavy hatch.

A draft of cool air, the essence of a fresh English autumn afternoon, gushed into the craft. I heard Holden and Pocket sigh over the crisp oxygen, and even Bourne looked up from his introverted weeping. I lay on my back and sucked in that wonderful atmosphere, and felt the blood course through my cheeks at the nip of cold. "How stale the air was in this ship!" I said.

Holden breathed deeply, coughing. "Traveller's chemical system is a scientific marvel. But I have to agree, Ned; the piped air in this box has become steadily more foul."

Now I pushed myself upright and slithered forward until my legs were dangling over the ten-foot drop to the dark loam of Kent; I gazed out over fields, hedgerow, threads of smoke from farmhouse fires and copses.

I looked down, wondering how I might reach the ground—and found myself staring into the wide, ruddy face of a farmer. He wore a battered but respectable tweed suit, muddied wellington boots and a straw hat; and he carried a large pitchfork, held before him as if for defense. As he gazed at our unlikely craft his mouth hung open, showing poor teeth.

I surreptitiously made sure my tie was straight and waved to him. "Good afternoon, sir."

He stumbled back three paces, held up the pitchfork at me and his jaw dropped further.

I raised my hands and essayed my most diplomatic smile. "Sir, we are Englishmen; you need fear nothing, despite the extraordinary manner of our arrival." It was time to be modest. "You have no doubt heard of us. I am of the party of Sir Josiah Traveller, and this is the *Phaeton.*"

I paused, expecting instant recognition—surely we had been the subject of press speculation since our disappearance—but the worthy rustic merely scowled and uttered a syllable I interpreted as: "Who?"

I began to explain, but my words sounded fantastic even to my own ears, and the farmer merely frowned with ever greater suspicion. So at last I gave it up. "Sir, let me emphasize the pertinent fact: which is that we are four

Englishmen, and a French, in desperate need of your assistance. Despite my youth and health I cannot even support my own weight, thanks to the astounding experiences to which I have been subject. I therefore ask you, as one Christian to another, if you will forward the help we need."

The farmer's face, red as an apple, was a picture of mistrust. But at last, after muttering something about the acres of stubble we'd scorched to a crisp, he lowered his pitchfork and approached the vessel.

The farmer's name was Clay Lubbock.

It took Lubbock and two of his strongest lads to carry us from the ship. They used slings of rope to lower us from one strong set of arms to another. Then we were loaded on to a bullock cart and, swathed in sheets, hauled off across the broken ground to the farmhouse. Traveller, his voice rendered uneven by the jolting of the cart, remarked on the irony of our rapid descent through the technological strata; but his own appearance—thin, fragile and deathly pale—belied his jocular words, and none of us responded.

The rustics stared in silent fascination at Traveller's platinum nose.

In the farmhouse we were greeted by Mrs. Lubbock, a bluff, gray woman with massive, hair-coated forearms; without questions or how-do-you-do's she assessed our condition with the ready eye of a buyer of livestock and despite some protests from Traveller, soon had us wrapped up warmly before a roaring fire and was pouring thick chicken stock into us. Lubbock, meanwhile, set off to town on his fastest horse to spread the word of our return.

Traveller chafed at his confinement, protesting that he

was no invalid and that there was work to be done. He was anxious to get to a telegraph station so that the work of transporting the scarred *Phaeton* to his home in Surrey could begin. Holden calmed him. "I, too, am anxious to return to civilization," he said. "Remember I am a journalist. My paper, and others, should reward me well if I turn our jaunt into a well-turned narrative. But, Sir Josiah, I recognize my own frailty. As soon as word spreads of our return the world will surely descend on us. I have been through an ordeal without parallel in human history and am left barely capable of supporting a laden soup spoon, and would welcome the chance to recuperate for a few hours under the kind hospitality of Mrs. Lubbock. And so should you, Sir Josiah!"

Traveller did not accept the argument but had little choice but to comply; and so we were put to bed in hard pallets in small bedrooms scattered about the Lubbocks' home. Holden persuaded the farmer to station one of his lads as a guard outside the room of the wretched Bourne; I thought this was rather sour, as Bourne was hardly in a condition to shin out of the window and race off to freedom across the fields.

I lay in my pallet waiting for sleep, with my window open to admit the bright autumn air, and reflected that, despite the discomforts of this world (the hardness of the mattress under my spine, for instance, was hardly helping my new induction into Earth's gravity), the compensations—the scent of the trees growing just beyond my window, the distant rustle of a breeze through the hedgerow, the rough caress of the Lubbocks' sheets against my face—made the thought of ever leaving this Earth again seem an abomination.

In the morning I awoke to bright sunlight, feeling quite

refreshed, and was even able to take the few steps to my washbasin unaided. I found Traveller at the Lubbocks' kitchen table; he was seated in an old bath chair wrapped in his own dressing-gown, brought from the *Phaeton,* and he was enjoying a hearty meal of bacon and farmhouse eggs. Newspapers were piled up on the table and he was working his way through them as he ate; and, despite the homely warmth of the kitchen, with the morning sunlight slanting across the floor to twinkle from the polished range, Traveller's expression was as sour and thunderous as ever I had seen it. He looked up as one of Lubbock's willing lads helped me in and said, "Ned, it is no surprise that farmer Lubbock was mystified at our arrival. It was sheer vanity ever to suppose that our disappearance should have remained of interest for any length of time—not while Europe tears itself apart!"

Disturbed by these words, I began to go through the yellowing papers myself. They dated back to a few days before our departure on 8 August: apparently Lubbock stored the old journals to line his chicken coop. In general our disappearance had been overshadowed by its larger context—the sabotage of the *Prince Albert* on its launching day—and we had generally been assumed dead, lost in some chance explosion, a by-product of the assault on the ship. I was amazed to learn that it had since proven impossible to retake the *Albert* from the saboteurs, or franc-tireurs, who had stolen it; and, as best I could tell, it still wandered at large about the fields of Belgium or northern France like some escaped beast! The actions of the franc-tireurs had been linked to attacks on other British properties, at home and abroad; I wondered if the attempted sabotage of the Light Rail which Holden and I had witnessed at Dover had been committed by a Frenchman.

And, of course, there was no word of Françoise Michelet or the other trapped passengers of the ill-fated liner; and despite the pleasure of the Kent morning I felt my heart sink as I scanned those yards of barren newsprint.

Traveller remarked on my crestfallen expression, and asked what in particular distressed me. Haltingly—for Josiah Traveller was no sympathetic ear—I described Françoise: our meetings, and the immediate impression she had made on me. As I talked on I felt color steal into my cheeks; for what had seemed, in the privacy of my heart, to be an ethereal passion, became on the telling in this bright farmhouse kitchen a rather foolish infatuation.

Traveller listened to all this without comment. Then he said levelly: "The girl sounds like a franc-tireur herself, Wickers." I made to protest, shocked, but he went on, "What else, if she was so thick with that wretch Bourne?" He sniffed. "If I'm correct you should waste no more sympathy on her, Ned. She is where she chooses to be." So saying he turned to his papers again, leaving me devastated.

But, even in that first moment of shock, I perceived the plausibility of what Traveller suggested. The elements about Françoise which Holden, and even I, had noted as odd—her fascination with engineering, her angry absorption in politics—fell into place under Traveller's hypothesis as components of a far more complex character than the girl I had idealized, and whose sweet face I had projected on to the oceans of Earth.

I wanted to curse Traveller for putting such a suggestion into my head; I cursed myself for a fool even more. But still, I was not sure. And the most galling aspect of the situation was that, with Françoise lost in war-torn France, I might never learn the truth about her.

With my heart in turmoil I turned my attention to the newspapers. Reading rapidly, Traveller and I pieced together the story of the European conflict, as reported in London, since our precipitate departure.

The war with the Prussians had gone badly for the French. Reading the harrowing accounts of battles fought and lost, it was scarcely credible to me that France, with its long military tradition, its proud heritage and its model army, should have collapsed before Bismarck's aggression in quite such a craven way. French strategy seemed largely to have consisted of the twin Marshals Bazaine and MacMahon lurching about the French countryside in search of defensible positions and each other, while periodically losing skirmishes to the Prussians.

About the time of our enforced departure Napoleon III had left Paris for Châlons, while appointing Bazaine to the command of his Army of the Rhine. A few days later Bazaine, fearing encirclement by the fast-moving Prussians, had withdrawn to the west across the River Moselle. But near Metz he encountered two German corps and had finished up encircled after all; as we sat in our peaceful farmhouse reading about it, Bazaine's force was still trapped in the town of Metz, invested by no fewer than two hundred thousand Prussian troops.

So much for one half of the glorious French Army. Of the rest, MacMahon's instinct had been to stay close to Paris and so offer protection to the capital, but popular pressure, brought to bear by Parisians outraged by the violation of their precious *patrie,* had impelled him to a more aggressive course; and he had set off toward Metz in the hope of combining with Bazaine.

The Germans around Metz, commanded by the wily Moltke, had divided their forces. Bazaine was left trapped while the rest of the Prussians set off to meet the advancing MacMahon. MacMahon's forces, exhausted by their difficult march, had been encircled by the Prussians at Sedan. MacMahon himself was wounded and French command lines were paralyzed.

The Army was annihilated. The French allowed 100,000 men and no fewer than 400 guns to fall into Prussian hands.

The French Second Empire collapsed in chaos. Napoleon III himself surrendered to the Prussians, and a Government of National Defense under the Governor of Paris, General Trochu, had emerged in the capital. And meanwhile two Prussian armies had advanced on Paris itself.

Even as we had landed in our Kent field, Paris, sixty years earlier Bonaparte's capital of Europe, lay under a Prussian siege. The only hope appeared to lie with Bazaine, but he remained entrapped in Metz, and the rumors in London were that his supplies were running low. The Prussians, meanwhile, were predictably cock-a-hoop, and there was much wild speculation about plans for Kaiser William to ride in procession through the streets of conquered Paris.

I laid down the last newspaper with hands that trembled. "Dear God, Traveller. What an astonishing few weeks we have missed! Surely this humiliation of France will burn in the mind of every Frenchman for generations to come. They were already an excitable bunch—look at Bourne for an example. Surely nothing but a state of war can exist between the French and their German cousins for all time."

"Perhaps." Traveller lay back in his bath chair, his thin hands wrapped together over the robe which covered his belly, and he stared unseeing through the dusty windows of the farmhouse. With the sunlight catching the wisps of white hair which hovered about his skull, he looked as old and frail as I remembered him at that terrible moment when it seemed that even the Moon would not save our lives. "But it is not 'all time' that concerns me, Ned; it is the here and now."

"What troubles you, sir?"

With a trace of his old irritation he snapped, "Think about it, boy; you're supposed to be a diplomat. The Prussians have felled France. Surely even the wily old fox Bismarck cannot have foreseen such astonishing gains—and these in addition to his primary objective."

"Which is?"

"Is it not obvious?" He studied me wearily. "Why, the unification of Germany, of course. What better way to bully and cajole the German princelings into a political union than to set up a common foe?—and how much better if that foe is the unlovely France of Robespierre and Bonaparte. I predict that we will see a declaration of a new Germany before this year is out. But of course it will amount to little more than a greater Prussian Empire, for if those petty Bavarian princes think that Bismarck, in his pomp and triumph, will allow them much say in the running of this new entity, they will be sorely disappointed."

I nodded thoughtfully. "So the Balance of Power is shattered; that Balance which has survived since the Congress of Vienna—"

"A Balance which Britain has fought to maintain ever since." He drummed his fingers on the table top. "Let us be frank, Ned. The British government could scarcely give two hoots if Prussian guns lay Paris waste; for the French, in British minds, are bedevilled by the twin monsters of revolution and military expansionism. And these absurd franc-tireur attacks on British economic targets, like the dear old *Prince Albert,* are hardly endearing.

"But the development of a new Germany will be greeted with dread in Whitehall. For it has long been an objective of British foreign policy that there should be no dominant power in central Europe."

I frowned, and was struck by the cynicism of this view of British goals—for surely the maintenance of a peaceful settlement was to be lauded. "Tell me what you're afraid of, sir," I said directly.

His bony fingers drummed more loudly. "Ned, up to now the British have stayed out of this damn war of Bismarck's; and quite right too. But how long before British interests are so endangered by the emergence of Germany that they feel forced to intervene?"

I thought that over. "But the British Army, while the finest in the world, is not well-equipped for large engagements in central Europe. Nor has it ever been. And besides, many of our troops and officers are scattered around the world in the service of His Majesty in the colonies. Surely Mr. Gladstone would not commit us to a foreign adventure with no chance of success."

"Gladstone. Old Glad Eyes." He laughed without humor. "Gladstone, I have always felt, is a pompous oaf, and not a patch on Disraeli for wit or intelligence. Obviously Disraeli's 'flood-gate' suffrage reform of 1867 would have been a disaster for the country . . . Who knows what damage might have been done? Certainly industry would have been denied its rightful say in affairs—perhaps we would still have the nonsensical situation of London as capital! What a ludicrous thought. So perhaps it's a good thing that Dizzy retired, bruised, from politics, to concentrate on his bizarre literary adventures . . . but still, one misses the fellow's dash.

"Perhaps, though, it is a blessing that we have a Glad Eyes inflicted on us in this hour; for, as you say, he and his gang of milksop Whigs would surely be loth to commit us to an absurd adventure . . . And if the rumors are true he may be more interested in ventures to Soho than Sedan."

I guffawed at that disrespectful sally.

Traveller continued, "So perhaps Gladstone would not launch us into war in Europe. But . . . he has other options."

"Tell me what you mean, Sir Josiah."

He leaned forward now, folding his arms on the table. "Ned, you will recall your brother's experiences in the Crimea."

For a moment these dark words, uttered sepulchrally in the midst of that bright farmhouse morning, made no sense to me; and then, in a sudden, shocking moment, I understood. "Dear Lord, Traveller."

He was, of course, suggesting that anti-ice weapons might be deployed once more by the British Army; and this time, not in some distant, oddly-named peninsula of southern Russia—but in the heart of Europe herself.

I searched his face for some sign that I was mistaken in my interpretation; but all I saw in those long, somber features was a terrible fear, coupled with immense anger. He said, "Anti-ice weapons could reduce the Prussian Army in minutes. And Gladstone knows this. Bismarck has surely gambled on the unwillingness of the British to become entangled in European disputes—but the pressure on Gladstone to use this astounding advantage must be growing by the day."

I watched the fear and anger wrestle in Traveller's eyes,

and imagined this brusque but fundamentally gentle man once more forced to labor over weapons of war. On impulse I grabbed at his sleeve. "Traveler, you have brought us to the Moon and back. You have immense strength; I have every confidence that you will not allow your genius to be employed in any such fashion."

But his fear lingered; and Traveller pawed at the newspapers once more, as if seeking some glimmer of hope in their fading words.

Our idyll was not to last more than a few minutes beyond the end of that conversation. The first fist to hammer at the Lubbocks' door was that of the Mayor of the nearest town—whose name we had not even learned yet—and, as I studied this gentleman's portly, mud-spattered frame and empty smile, I realized, with a sink of the heart which startled me, that I was indeed home.

We were whisked away from our corner of Kent. We were given little time to say goodbye to each other—which is perhaps as well, for I felt a surprisingly strong bond with my fellow voyagers. I would not go so far as to say I experienced a nostalgia for those long weeks trapped in the *Phaeton,* but I did feel quite exposed without my companions close by.

Traveller soon installed himself in a pleasant inn close to the Lubbocks' field where his precious *Phaeton* lay, and threw himself into the restoration of the craft to his laboratory in Surrey. The faithful Pocket begged, and was granted, a few days' leave to visit his precious grandchildren and reassure them of his continued existence; then, as usual, he returned to work, determining and quietly serving his employer's needs.

As for Bourne, he was taken without ceremony from Kent under close arrest, and soon disappeared into the complexities of international law. The confusion of the case brought against him as a saboteur by the British, an extradition warrant issued by the Belgians, and protests lodged by the beleaguered French government—not to mention the practical difficulties of communication with that nebulous body—all conspired to threaten the hapless Bourne with a long imprisonment before even he came to trial.

Holden, as soon as he could, made for Manchester, urging us not to disclose details of our adventure to any other journalist. It was amusing to see how his ample form, reduced to the status of a sack of potatoes wheeled about in a bath chair, became filled with agitation as the size of the story he had to tell—and the subsequent fees he would command—grew ever larger in his scribbler's mind; it was as if one could see his very fingers itching.

Still, Holden's account, when it appeared in the Manchester press a few days later, did come close to doing justice to our adventure. I read through the rather lurid prose and will admit to some shivers of remembered terror as he evoked my jaunt through the vacuum and (as he overstated it) my battle with the rock monsters of Luna. The piece in the *Manchester Guardian* was handsomely illustrated by lithographs of various scenes from the account, and was topped off by a reproduction of Holden's famous photograph of myself and the ill-fated model of Brunel's ocean liner.

My only disappointment was with Holden's unsympathetic portrayal of Traveller. The journalist dwelled on Traveller's near-Anarchist sympathies in a manner which aroused adverse comment about the engineer, even at this moment of his greatest fame. I took the opportunity to read more widely on the various Anarchist thinkers—dismissing the insurrectionist crackpots such as Bakunin, and concentrating on the deeper thinkers like Proudhon, who declared that the desire for property and political power served only to encourage the violent and irrational elements in man.

Surely, I reflected, this present war in Europe was ample evidence for Proudhon's thesis, and I regretted Holden's disloyalty.

In any event, thanks to Holden's account, I became briefly famous.

I returned to the comfort of my parents' home in Sussex; my family were quite inordinately glad to see me whole and healthy. I suffered a moving reunion with my brother Hedley; his scarred face crumpled with pleasure as I described Josiah Traveller, who had become something of a fascination for Hedley since their one-sided acquaintance in the Crimea. My London friends, several of whom came to visit, urged me to make a dramatic reentrance into society, the more to capitalize on my heroic status. I looked on their faces, which seemed astonishingly young and fresh, and declined their various invitations—not from any uncharacteristic burst of modesty, for I should quite have enjoyed the admiring attention of the season's belles as I described how it hadn't been as bad as all that, really—but more from a lingering feeling of isolation. And besides, my confused feelings about Françoise were a turmoil inside me, incapable of resolution.

I went for long, solitary walks in the woods near my parents' home, exploring these odd feelings. It was almost as if, having once shaken the dust of Earth from my boots, I felt unfit to return with whole heart to human society.

And I found I missed the company of my erstwhile companions more and more.

I watched the colors of autumn spread through the trees, and wondered how such a sight would look from space.

I promised myself that I should immerse myself into the world of men as soon as my moment of fame had faded; and sure enough, fade it did—though not for reasons I would have welcomed. For as the nights of autumn drew in, so the plight of the French grew steadily more desperate.

The Prussians maintained their walls of men and guns around both Paris and Metz. In the Manchester press there were constant tales of famine stalking the streets of the French capital, and some rather more reliable accounts of how the armies of Marshal Bazaine, in Metz, were languishing in the mud, and were growing steadily more incapable even of defending themselves, let alone liberating Paris.

I perused the papers with endless, and morbid, fascination, as the leader writers discussed the choices and dangers facing Gladstone and his government. No civilized man, it was commonly agreed, would again wish to see anti-ice used as a weapon of war. But the Balance of Power was undoubtedly under its severest test, and there seemed a growing mood for some intervention before this precious and venerable guarantor of peace in Europe should be lost for ever.

Against this there were those who, remembering Bonaparte, had no desire to intercede in favor of the beleaguered French. And at the other extreme the Sons of Gascony and their like became ever more vocal in their demands that Britain should exert her evident power, not just to restore peace, but to impose order on the warring factions of Europe. The influence of these stern-minded gentlemen on the debate seemed to be growing; it was even rumored that the King himself sympathized with such views.

Reading this depressing stuff I was reminded of my conversations on the *Phaeton* with Bourne. No longer did I feel bound into such arguments, as I may have before my adventure; now I saw with a new aloofness how this national debate paralleled the internal ramblings of a deranged mind, which seeks to impose its inward fears and daemons on those around it.

At last, at the end of October, came the news that Bazaine's forces in Metz—wet, starved and demoralized—had capitulated; this time the rampant Prussians took away 1,400 guns and more than 170,000 men. Although French forces fought on in various parts of the country, it was generally agreed in Manchester that the decisive moment of the war had come; that the Prussians, victorious in the field of combat, would soon be riding through the battered streets of Paris—and that if Britain were ever to intercede in this struggle for the future of Europe, now was the moment.

The clamor of newsprint, demanding action from Gladstone, grew until it seemed a silent shout all around me, and I felt I could bear the tension no longer.

I knew of only one way to resolve these feelings; and I packed a bag, bade a hasty goodbye to my parents, and made my way by Light and steam train to the home of Josiah Traveller.

I walked the last few miles to Traveller's home. Not far from Farnham, the place was based around a small converted farmhouse, and it would not have attracted the eye—save for a brooding giant some thirty feet high which stood defiant at the rear of the house, its great aluminum shoulders covered by sewn-together tarpaulins. This was of course the *Phaeton;* and as that magical carriage loomed out of the dull landscape, I felt my heart lift.

I came around a hedgerow to Traveller's house—and there, standing before his front door, was a rather splendid brougham of rich, polished wood. I realized immediately that I was not Sir Josiah's only visitor of the day.

Pocket greeted my unheralded arrival with tremendous enthusiasm; he even begged my permission to pump my hand on his own behalf. The manservant was spry and secure now he was on firm ground, and he said, "I am sure that Sir Josiah will be delighted to see you, but at the moment he's with a visitor. In the meantime, may I offer you tea; and perhaps you would care for a glance around the premises, sir?"

He did not volunteer the identity of this "visitor" and I did not press him.

As I sipped tea I said, "I'll be honest with you, Pocket. I'm not entirely clear why I've come . . ."

He smiled with surprising wisdom, and said, "You don't need to explain, sir. In these troubled times, I'm sure I can speak for Sir Josiah in stating that this house is a home to you. Just as the *Phaeton* was."

I found myself coloring. "Do you know, Pocket, you've hit the nail exactly on the head . . . Thank you."

Scarcely trusting myself to speak further I drew on my tea.

The house itself was surprisingly small and dingy. Its main feature was a large conservatory to the south-facing rear which had been converted by Traveller into an extensive laboratory. There was also a barn used for larger-scale construction. Several acres of land surrounded the buildings. Nothing grew in these rough fields, and in several places one could see dramatic scorched scars, where rocket engine tests, launches—and even explosions—had taken place.

The conservatory was quite a grand affair, with a framework of slender, white-painted wrought iron which gave the place a sense of lightness; various tools and machines lay in that gentle light like strange plants. The laboratory was laid out something like a milling shop; a steam lathe attached to the ceiling powered various metal-turning machines by means of leather bands, and fixed to benches around the floor were small lathes, a sheet-metal stamp, presses, acetylene welding sets and vices. The fruits of these tools lay all around, some familiar from my time on the *Phaeton.* Pocket pointed out a rocket nozzle, for example, which shone in the light of the weak autumn sun, its mouth upturned like the muzzle of some unlikely flower.

"And what of *Phaeton* herself?" I asked Pocket.

"We had the very devil of a time getting the old girl home from that farmer's field in Kent. We had to take a steam crane out there to shift her, would you believe; and all the time that wretched man Lubbock protested at the ruts we were planting in his precious fields."

I laughed. "You can't blame the poor chap. After all, he didn't ask to have us drop in on him in that extraordinary fashion."

"And as for the old girl, Sir Josiah says she's fared remarkably well, considering the ordeal through which we put her: an ordeal for which she was scarcely designed, of course."

"Which of us was?" I asked with feeling.

"In the end she suffered surprisingly little damage. A collapsing support leg, a bashed nozzle, a hatful of scars and scorch marks, an overstrained airpump or two—I might say, largely thanks to your own efforts there, sir."

Now we left the conservatory and walked out into the fresh air, and so started to make our way to the front of the house once more.

"So she could fly again?" I asked.

"Could, but won't, I think, sir. Sir Josiah has refuelled her, in order to test the workings of the motors, and has spent a deal of time on fixing her up, but I think he feels she's done her bit. He has a headful of ideas for a second *Phaeton,* brighter and still more powerful than the first; I think he plans to turn the original into a sort of monument to herself."

"And so he should," I said.

Now Pocket drew to a halt and stared straight ahead. "Well," he went on more quietly, "it's only to be hoped that he's allowed to put those ideas into practice."

Puzzled by his tone, I turned to follow his gaze. Before the front door I saw the familiar figure of Traveller, his stovepipe hat screwed as incongruously and defiantly to his head as ever. He was, I saw, taking leave of his earlier visitor. The other man, now climbing into his brougham, was a wide-framed gentleman of about sixty, whose features were naggingly familiar; I studied the gray hair swept across his head, the rich white sidewhiskers, the rather lifeless eyes, the grim, downturned mouth set in a Moon of a face—

"Dear God," I whispered to Pocket. "That's Gladstone himself!"

The Prime Minister took his leave of Traveller; with a

snick of the driver's whip the brougham pulled away. Traveller walked slowly along the side of his home, absently studying the ivy which clung to the brickwork. I would have gone to him, but Pocket held my sleeve firmly, indicating no; and we waited for Sir Josiah to reach us in his own time.

At last he stood before us. He straightened his shoulders, fixed his hat more correctly at the center of his cranium, and held his hands behind his back; his platinum nose glinted in the weak November sunlight. "Well, Ned," he said, his voice as pale as the Sun. "I heard you arrive. I apologize for my—preoccupation."

I demanded without preamble: "That was the Prime Minister, wasn't it?"

"You must drop this habit of restating the obvious, Ned," he admonished; but his tone was abstracted.

"I have heard of the fall of Bazaine, at Metz."

"Yes." He looked at me carefully. "Such was in the journals. But there is also news of the *Albert.*"

Suddenly my head was filled with thoughts of Françoise; and I shouted, "What news? You must tell me."

"Ned—" He took my arms. "The *Albert* has been converted into a vehicle of war. The French saboteurs, the . . ." He groped for the phrase.

"The franc-tireurs."

"They have taken it over, installed cannon, and so have converted it into a gigantic mobile castle. And they are driving it toward Paris, where they plan to engage the besieging Prussians. Ned, it is quite insane. The *Albert* is a passenger ship, not a man-of-war. One accurate shell and it would be done for . . ."

The images conjured by his words were so fantastic that

I found it almost impossible to grasp their thread of meaning. "And the passengers? What of them?"

"There is no word."

I said, a little harshly, "And what is the import of all this? The Prime Minister of Great Britain does not call in person to deliver news, however dramatic, Sir Josiah."

"No, of course not." His eyes slid away from mine, and he adopted that strained, hunted look I had observed in the Lubbocks' farmhouse. "The news about the *Albert* was Glad Eyes' way into my sympathy. I believe he hoped to link, in my mind, the European war with my own endeavors.

"The government have reached their point of decision, you see. Metz has collapsed, yes; but Paris holds out, against all reason, even at the cost of starving its own citizens. Meanwhile the Prussians sound ever more bellicose and grandiose. There seems little prospect of a just settlement to this war; and the government rather regret that the Europeans no longer find it possible to conduct a war like good chaps, finishing according to the rules." He shook his head. "Gladstone says Europe may collapse into terminal chaos for a generation, if Britain does not intervene. He says that, but of course he believes no such thing. Britain as usual is pursuing its own aims, and Gladstone would say anything to have me cooperate. And yet—and yet, what if there is truth in what he says? What right have I to resist the tide of history?" He clapped his hand to his forehead, shoving back his hat, and shook his head.

I took his arm. "Sir Josiah, has he asked you to bring back your anti-ice weapons of the Crimean campaign?"

"No. No, Ned; they want new weapons . . . They have such ideas as you would not believe. How can human beings, men like you and me, walk around with their heads full of such thoughts? . . . And they say that if I do not cooperate, they will withdraw their investment." He laughed bitterly. "Which was precarious enough anyway. They will turf me out of my home, destroy my access to anti-ice; and a team of lesser men will be set to do their bidding in my place."

I stared into his long, tortured face, and recalled Holden's analysis of the man's poor financial acumen. Was this to be the great engineer's Achilles' heel, the flaw that would bring his work at last to ruin—just as it had destroyed, in the end, the plans of his hero Brunel?

I hoped that Traveller would have none of the government's obscene plan, but there was uncertainty in his face, and his next words discouraged me.

"Gladstone is a fool and a philanderer, no doubt; but he is also a politician, Ned; and he has planted doubts in my mind! For if I construct these devices, perhaps I can indeed make them, as he says, 'scientific' in their effectiveness. Whereas if lesser men begin to meddle with this we could face a disaster on a scale never before witnessed." His face was quite open now and full of pain. "Tell me, Ned. What am I to do? . . . I fear I must cooperate with them, for fear of the alternative—"

"In God's name, Traveller, what do they want you to build?"

He dropped his head as if in shame. "Rocket boats. Like smaller versions of the *Phaeton.* But these would not be driven by a human pilot; instead an adaptation of my navigation table, with its gyroscopic guidance system, could serve to guide the rocket to its landing point."

I was mystified. "But what would be the purpose of these manless *Phaetons*? What would emerge after they landed?" I wondered vaguely if they would carry ammunition or food in to the beleaguered Parisians, but Traveller was shaking his head.

"No, Ned; you don't see it yet. And I don't blame you, for it takes an imagination of a particular devilishness.

"The rocket boat does not land. It is allowed to crash into the earth, in the manner of artillery shells. When it does so a Dewar of anti-ice shatters; the anti-ice spills out into the heat of the earth, and a monstrous explosion ensues."

He spread his arms wide and turned about, as if drunk. "You have to admit there is a certain grandeur in the concept," he said. "From my own garden, here, I would be able to launch a shell which would reach across the Channel, all the way to Paris, and fell the pride of Prussia with one hammer blow—"

"No!"

Traveller and Pocket stared at me.

A thousand emotions coursed through my poor heart. The conflicting images of Françoise warred in me: the sweet face which had become, during our perilous voyage around the Moon, a talisman to me, a symbol of hope and the future, of all to which I would return; but underlying it, as the skull underlies the fairest visage, was the specter of the franc-tireur, a totem of all those who would unleash war and death on the fragile bowl of Earth I had watched from above the air.

How my mind reeled with these perceptions! And how far I'd come from the simple lad who had boarded the *Phaeton* barely three months earlier!

My course of action, I found, was decided.

Scarcely a second had passed since my single syllable of protest. Without thinking further I turned on my heels and ran toward the covered form of the *Phaeton.* I heard Traveller's call after me and his slow footsteps in pursuit, but the craft filled my attention.

I had to reach Paris—I had to confront Françoise, to save her if I could, to deflect the British bombs—and to do that I would travel there by the fastest means possible—at the controls of the *Phaeton*!

[13]

THE BALLOON PILOT

The Smoking Cabin had been lovingly restored. The various scuffs and rents left in the upholstered walls by our weeks of incarceration had all been invisibly repaired, and I offered up a quick, silent prayer that the craft's motive systems were in as pristine a condition.

I scrambled up a rope ladder to the Bridge. For a moment I stood there returning the gaze of the serried ranks of instrument dials, as unsure as some barbarian entering a religious shrine.

But I shook away this mood and clambered without further delay into Traveller's couch.

As the soft upholstery took my weight some hidden switch was activated, and the electric lamps within each instrument sparked to life. I fancied I heard a hissing, as pipes bore the increasing pressure of the ship's various hydraulic systems.

Like some huge animal the craft was coming alive to my touch.

I lay in that couch and surveyed the instrument constellation with dismay. But I had seen Traveller fly this craft from the Moon to the Earth, and it had looked simple enough; surely I would have no trouble with a minor jaunt across the English Channel!

With renewed determination I turned to the control levers beside the couch. The levers terminated in handles of molded rubber which were a little too large for my hands. Fixed on the handles were light levers of steel; these, I recalled, controlled the ignition and force of the *Phaeton*'s rocket motors.

As my hands closed around the handles I felt sweat pool in my palms.

I squeezed at the steel levers.

The rockets shouted their awakening. A huge shuddering beset the craft.

"Ned!"

Traveller was climbing with some difficulty through the hatch from the Smoking Cabin. He had lost his hat and his hair lay in white sheets about his forehead. He was breathing hard and sweat trickled over his platinum nose; and the glare he fixed on me was as intense as sunlight.

"Don't try to stop me, Traveller!"

"Ned." Now he stood on the deck, towering over me. With a voice whose quietness defeated the racket of the motors he said: "Get out of my couch."

"You told me what Gladstone's plans are. As a decent Englishman I cannot stand by and allow such an atrocity to proceed unchallenged. I intend to fly to France and—"

"And what?" Now he leaned over me, the sweat pooling under his deep eyes. "What then, Ned? Will you use the *Phaeton* to swat Gladstone's shells from the air? Think it through, damn it; what can you possibly achieve save your own death in the resulting holocaust?"

I stuck out my chin and said, "But at least I may be able to warn the authorities—"

"What authorities? Ned, at this moment nobody knows who the authorities are! And as for the Prussians—"

"At least the warning will be delivered. And I may rescue a few souls from the devastation which is to come, and so in turn recover a little of the lost honor of England."

His mouth worked; then some of the anger seemed to seep out of him. "Ned, you're a fool, but I suppose there are worse ways to throw away your life . . . And, of course, there is your Françoise."

I glared, as if daring him to mock me. "Mademoiselle Michelet has become a symbol to me of all those unfortunates who have become caught up in this war. If she lives still aboard the stolen land liner I pledge to rescue her—or to die in the attempt!"

"Oh, you damn idiot. I'll give you good odds that the blessed woman is precisely where she wants to be: that she'll shoot you down as you approach her, with your face split into the grin of a fool." He glared harder at me, and something of that hidden perceptiveness about folk which I'd discerned in him earlier shone through his stare. "Ah, but that doesn't matter. Does it? It's not the thought of the rescue that's exercising you so. You have to know the truth about your Françoise—"

I resented this insight into my soul. "Leave me be, Traveller! I won't be stopped."

"Ned—" Traveller reached out uncertain hands. "You cannot fly the ship. You would destroy her even before gaining the air! Why, you did not even close the hatch before trying to launch the craft."

"Traveller, don't try to stop me!—I suggest you return to your friend the Prime Minister, and, in return for the money he has promised you, proceed to build him his Angels of Death."

A frown lengthened the lines in his brow.

I felt a pang of shame, but I dismissed it. "Sir Josiah, I will grant you ten seconds to get off the craft. Then I leave for France."

With a calmness that shone through his shouted words he replied: "I disregard your ten seconds. I have no intention of leaving the ship; I cannot allow you to destroy the *Phaeton.*"

"Then we are at an impasse. Must I eject you bodily?" He sighed deeply, buried his face for a moment in his cupped hands; then lifted his head to face me. "That will not be necessary, Ned; for I see you are determined to go. And therefore I have no option but to accompany you."

"What?"

"I will fly the ship. Now, kindly vacate my couch so that we may proceed—"

I studied him with the deepest suspicion, but on his long face I could read only a new determination. "Traveller, why would you do that? Why should I not suspect you of some trickery?"

He visibly drew together some shreds of patience. "You may suspect what you like. I am not given to trickery, Ned; and I was quite sincere when I said that you will destroy this craft in seconds if you proceed unaided."

"Then assist me. Tell me how to fly the *Phaeton.*"

"Impossible." He counted the points on his long fingers. "It would take several days to impart even the basics of the flight control system design. Even," he added without irony, "to the brightest student. Second. Consider the demands of piloting a flighted craft through the atmosphere. Ned, the *Phaeton* is not inherently stable; this means that—unless you want to blast straight up in the air, like our French colleague—the pilot must be constantly responsive to the attitude of his craft; otherwise she is just as likely to flip upside down and plummet with all the force of her motors straight into the ground. This is the only flying vessel in the world, and I am the only man with experience of such arts. Third. You will recall that the *Phaeton* is a prototype. She therefore has various quirks and peculiarities which only I can anticipate and control—"

"All right!" The strain of maintaining an even pressure on the rocket levers was turning my hands into crabs of tense muscles.

Then, unexpectedly, he grinned, his hair drifting from his scalp. "You ask why I will fly the ship. I do not want you to ruin my craft, boy; that is one clear objective. Other than that—

"Well, old Glad Eyes has made it clear enough that his rocket-shells will be built with or without my participation. Now you've forced me to think about it, if anti-ice is to be used again as a weapon of war, perhaps I should witness the consequences of my own actions, rather than read some inaccurate account in the *Guardian* three days later.

"Ned, my mind is made up. Let us go seek your precious lady; let us make for Paris, the Queen of Cities!"

I searched his face again. There was no sign of guile or deception; in fact I was reminded of the impulsive enthusiasm I had reawakened in him in those last minutes of our approach to the Moon. And so, at length, I nodded.

Traveller clapped his hands together. "I have told

Pocket to shelter within the house, and so we are all prepared to leave. Now then, Ned, if you would vacate my chair—release those levers as slowly as you are able—"

And so, within a few minutes, the noise of the rockets rose to a roar; the covering tarpaulins ripped and fell away, and the *Phaeton* soared high over the Surrey countryside.

Traveller, with skill and grace, flew at a height of about half a mile above the land. He tilted the engines, explaining that by doing so the rockets could not only support the weight of the craft in the air, but also impart a significant sideways acceleration.

And so we sped southwards.

I stood with my face pressed to the windows. At such a height the land, when not obscured by clouds, takes on the appearance of a toy layout featuring beautifully detailed houses, trees and glistening rivers. It was something of a shock when we abruptly sailed over the gunmetal-gray waters of the Channel.

After perhaps an hour we reached the French coast. A harbor town lay spread out like a diagram below us, and Traveller compared the view through his periscope with the contents of a map spread over his chest. At last he nodded in satisfaction. "We have reached Le Havre. Now it is but a short hop to Paris herself!"

I imagined the simple fisherfolk below peering up and wondering at the screaming, fire-belching monster which streaked across their sky.

Our guide now was the Seine; we followed its silver course upstream through Normandy. Smoke spiraled from scattered cottages and farmhouses and, under the influence of the prevailing winds, streamed like feathers to the east. From this godlike perspective there was no sign of the war.

At one point we sailed high over Rouen—the old streets looked like a child's maze—and I recalled that it was here that we English had burned to death the Maid of Orléans. I wondered what that brave warrior would have made of our great aluminum air-boat. Would she have thought it one more vision of the Lord?

At last, at about two in the afternoon, we reached the outskirts of Paris herself.

From the air Paris is a rough oval through which the Seine cuts neatly from east to west. With the periscope we could quite clearly see the islands which lie at the heart of the city, and we studied the elegant roof of the Cathedral of Notre Dame—untouched as yet by the Prussian artillery which had been brought into close order around the city. Just to the north of the water, we could make out the Rue de Rivoli which runs parallel to the river. Tracing the road to its western extent I found the Champs Elysées, and I puzzled over fallen trees scattered over the roadway, looking like spilled matchstalks. I wondered if they had been felled by German artillery, but Traveller suggested that the grand avenue was being cut down in order to supply firewood for the city's beleaguered citizens.

Around the brown-gray carcass of the city lay the main defensive fortifications: we tracked twenty miles of walls from the Bois de Boulogne in the west to the Bois de Vincennes in the east. And, in the countryside beyond the walls, we could clearly see the encampments of the besieging Prussian armies. Officers' tents lay like scattered handkerchiefs among the woods and fields; and—when we descended a little lower—we could make out the pits in which artillery pieces had been lodged—hundreds of them, all with their sinister snouts trained on the hapless citizens of Paris. And we could even espy the flashing red, blue and silver uniforms of the Prussian soldiery themselves.

As I stared down at the wondering, upturned faces of these conquering Germans it occurred to me how simple it would be for me to drop, say, a Dewar-ful of anti-ice among them—with quite devastating effect. The Prussians could do nothing in response; we could easily rise above the range of their guns, even if they could be trained on an object floating in the air.

I shuddered, wondering if I had had a vision of some future war.

Now we were fascinated to see, rising from the brown mass of the city, the bulky, ponderous form of a hot air balloon. The Manchester newspapers had been full of the Parisians' brave attempts to communicate with the rest of France by means of such vessels, and by the even more desperate expedient of carrier pigeons; but nevertheless the actual sight was quite startling. The clumsy vessel resembled a patchwork quilt in its jumble of colors and roughly-cut panels, and it bobbed uncertainly in the brisk westerly winds which soared over the roofs of the city, but off to the east it sailed with a semblance of grace, crossing the city walls in minutes.

We scanned the horizon with Traveller's telescopes—but of the *Prince Albert* there was no sign. Traveller frowned. "Well, Ned, what next?"

I shook my head, baffled and disappointed; the scale of the martial drama laid out below me was so great that my impulsive dreams that one man could alter the course of unfolding events, even armed with such a tool as *Phaeton,* seemed foolish fantasies. "I don't know what we can do here," I said at length. "But I think I should still very much like to find Françoise."

Traveller pulled at his chin. "Then we must gather more information as to the *Albert*'s whereabouts."

"Should we land in the city itself?"

He studied the maps on his chest for a few moments. "I am reluctant to follow such a course. We would have no way of warning the citizens of our approach, or of ensuring the area was made clear—indeed, in the Parisians' present excitable state, our imminent landing might attract large crowds, who would rush into the path of our steam jets.

"No, Ned; I can't recommend a landing in the city. But I have an alternative suggestion."

"Which is?"

"Let us follow that balloon pilot. When he comes down we can land in safety and approach him."

I thought this over. I felt reluctant to waste hours in gentle pursuit of the primitive craft. But on the other hand the balloon's pilot would surely have a wider understanding of the situation than the average Parisian, for otherwise he would not have been assisted to escape. A few moments quizzing this intrepid fellow might replace hours of scouring the Parisian mobs.

"Very well," I said to Traveller. "Let us pursue this brave pilot, and hope that he can assist us."

To the east of Paris lies the Champagne region of France; and it was here, some twenty miles from the city walls, that the westerly winds deposited our balloon pilot. Amid neat little vineyards his deflated vessel lay like a colorful pool, quite unmistakable from the air.

Traveller landed the *Phaeton* a quarter of a mile to the north. Before the rocket nozzles had cooled we unraveled rope ladders and scrambled to the ground. It was now late afternoon and we stood for a few seconds, blinking up at a cloudy sky. The *Phaeton,* having arrived in its usual spectacular style, sat at the center of a disc of charred and fallen vines; never again would these plants bear fruit! And just beyond the burned region a young man in a simple smock stood staring; even from here I could see how his mouth hung open.

Traveller strode confidently toward this rustic and pressed money into his hands. The engineer told the fellow, in broken French, that he was to take this offering to his employer as recompense for the destruction of a portion of his vines. Bemused, the poor chap unfolded the money and stared at it, as if he had never seen an English five-pound note before. But we left no time for further explanations; with the curtest of farewells to our reluctant host we strode off through acres of hedgerow and vine.

Five minutes later we came upon the balloon. The craft, deflated now, was constructed of crudely-sewn oddments of cloth—I spotted tablecloths, bedsheets, curtains, and even a soft, white fabric which reminded me of the gentler items of ladies' apparel. The sac was breached by panels attached to lengths of twine; these panels were clearly intended to be ripped open in order to deflate the sac; but around these neat rectangles the balloon wall had torn, and so the craft must have descended with more velocity than the pilot intended. I remarked to Traveller, "Good Lord, Sir Josiah, this whole affair is nothing more than an improvisation."

Traveller said, "One would need more courage to take to the air in such a vessel than to travel to the Moon in the

Phaeton. The inhabitants of Paris must be truly desperate to—"

"Actually," came a voice, in French, from behind billows of cloth, "this Parisian is only desperate to get on with his business without the accompaniment of arrogant English remarks, and—ow!"

Traveller and I exchanged startled glances; and we hurried around the fallen balloon.

The craft's basket was nothing more than a large wicker laundry box, fixed to the sac by lengths of leather. The basket lay on its side, and scrolls and bundles had spilled over the soft soil; and in the midst of all this debris sat a young man. He was about my height and age, with dark, Gallic good looks. He was dressed in the plain, dour clothes of the city worker; so that he could have been, for example, a bank clerk. But his gray jacket was torn and muddied. His left leg was stretched out before him, and he was pushing at the ground, trying to rise to his feet; but every time he put an ounce of weight on that left leg he winced in pain.

Traveller bent to examine the damaged leg. I said, in English, "You must rest there. Your leg has clearly been hurt, and—"

In French he replied, "My name is Charles Nandron. I am a deputy in the Government of National Defense. Sir, you are on the soil of France, no doubt uninvited; you will have the courtesy to address me in the tongue of my country, or not at all—ow!" Traveller's probing fingers had reached his ankle. Nandron threw back his head and clenched his teeth.

Using my fluent French I introduced myself and Traveller. "We came here in the *Phaeton,* which is an anti-ice—"

"I have no interest in English gadgets," sniffed the deputy. "I have risked my life in order to communicate with our provincial government in Tours—"

In his snapping English, Traveller said, "If you don't sit still and show some interest in this leg, young man, you won't be communicating with anybody except a few grape-growers for a long while." He turned to me and said, "I'm no doctor, but I don't think there's a break—just laid-open skin and a nasty sprain. In the *Phaeton* I have some linament and poultices; if you keep our haughty young gentleman from crawling away I will fetch the medication."

I nodded briefly. As Traveller stalked off Nandron's arrogant eyes flickered curiously at Sir Josiah's platinum nose; but he soon returned to his inspection of the sky.

I said in French, "The accounts in Manchester of the state of Paris are fragmentary, based largely on the news brought out by intrepid escapers like yourself—leavened with a healthy dose of speculation."

He nodded, closing his eyes. "Paris is in grave peril. The Prussians clearly intend to starve her into submission."

"You receive news of the war in there?"

"We know that Bismarck holds all of France to the north and east of Orléans, save Paris alone. Just as in 1815, France will stand or fall as Paris stands or falls; but this time we will repel the invaders . . ."

"Yes. And is there an army inside the walls of the city?"

"An army of citizens, sir. The National Guard has been doubled to over three hundred thousand men; every able-bodied man in the city, practically, has risen to save his country. Even we politicians are expected to serve in the breach!"

I studied his proud face, plastered now with the perspiration of pain, and reflected that if the history of the hydra-like Parisian mob was any guide, these hapless politicians probably had little choice but to man the barricades with the rest. But I forbore to comment on this, asking instead: "And what is the situation in the city?"

He shook his head. "You know that food cannot be brought into the city; the prevailing winds make it impossible to fly in even a few pounds by balloon. But there is much food remaining; our difficulty as a government has been one of distribution, both by region and through society." He laughed with a mild cynicism. "It surprises no one that the poor suffer most. Shopkeepers too are seeing their businesses ruined. But the best restaurants maintain full menus." He fixed me with a glare and tried to sit up straighter. "Perhaps you and your dilettante companion would care to call on one such during your visit. I apologize in the name of all Parisians for the lack of such items as fresh vegetables and seafood; but the menus have been made more exotic than ever with the addition of such items as kangaroo, elephant and cat—"

I laid a calming hand on his shoulder. "Sir, we are not your enemies. We are risking our own lives in this theater of war; we are searching for someone."

With a stab of curiosity he demanded, "Who?"

"Have you heard of the *Prince Albert?*" I explained the circumstances of the craft's stealing by franc-tireurs, and the accounts of its moving south toward Paris.

But Nandron shook his head. "I know nothing of such a vessel," he said dismissively. "And in any event our franc-tireurs are now much more profitably employed on the disruption of the Prussians' long supply lines back to Berlin . . ."

Disappointed by this fresh failure, I nevertheless spent the remaining minutes waiting for Traveller's return drawing further details from this haughty young Parisian of the condition of his city. He told me, for example, how even now the program to rebuild the thirty-year-old defensive walls was beset by wrangling and delays as rival groups of engineers argued over the selection of the most elegant and appealing design. I could not help but recall my brother's accounts of the simple but efficient earthwork fortifications thrown up by the Russians around Sebastopol.

In the calm, fading light of that rustic French afternoon I found it difficult to accept as truth the harrowing details of Nandron's tales.

Paris's best hope of salvation seemed to lie with the Minister of the Interior, Gambetta, who some weeks earlier had ballooned out of Paris. This Gambetta had, it seemed, raised a new army from the very earth of France itself, and had already struck at the Prussians with some success, at Coulmiers, close to Orléans. Now Gambetta was making for Orléans where he intended to make a fresh stand against the invaders. But vast Prussian forces, formerly kept busy by the siege at Metz, were moving to meet him; and it appeared that Orléans might become as decisive a battlefield as Sedan.

Traveller returned and efficiently applied a poultice to Nandron's leg. As Sir Josiah worked Nandron went on, "It is said that General Trochu"—the head of the provisional government—"has no fears for the future of France; for he believes that Sainte Geneviève, who delivered the country from barbarians in the fifth century, will return to do so again." He laughed with some bitterness.

I asked, "You do not share his beliefs?"

"I would rather have truck with the rumors flying around the bars of the city which state that Bonaparte himself has returned from the dead—or perhaps did not ever die at all, in his place of British exile—and is returning in a great chariot to join Gambetta's armies at Orléans and drive out the Prussians."

I nodded. "Old Boney himself, eh? What a charming idea . . ."

But Traveller waved me silent. "This 'great chariot,' " he snapped in his broken French. "Do these street tales bear any details?"

"Of course not. They are the gossip of the ignorant and ill-informed—"

I looked at Traveller with a new surmise. "You think this chariot could be the *Albert?*"

Traveller shrugged. "Why not? Imagine the great anti-ice vessel driving through the fields of France, piloted by these intrepid franc-tireurs. Might not news of such a development reach the desperate city of Paris in a garbled form, becoming mixed up with this nonsense about the Corsican?"

"Then we must make for Orléans!" I said.

But Nandron snapped, "Your analysis is wrong. No self-respecting son of France would have any truck with the gaudy machines of the British. For it is the opinion of the Government of National Defense that the technological invasion of France by Britain is every bit as odious as that of the Prussian barbarians—"

"If a little harder to define, eh?" Traveller said cheerfully. "Well, my boy, you may despise the very name of Britain; but unless you accept British help now it is going to take you rather a long time to reach Tours on that foot, despite my miraculous healing powers."

The Frenchman said frostily, "Thank you; but I would prefer to make my own way."

Traveller slapped his forehead in frustration. "Is there no limit to the stupidity of young men?"

In heavily accented English, Nandron said, "You must understand that you are not welcome here. We do not want you. We must throw off the hand of the Prussians with the blood of Frenchmen!"

I scratched my cheek. "I wish you'd tell that to Gladstone."

He looked puzzled. "What?"

"Never mind." I straightened up. "Well, Sir Josiah; that seems to be that."

"To Orléans?"

"Indeed!"

We bade Nandron a goodbye which was not returned, and set off once more across the neat vineyards; my last view of the stubborn deputy showed him struggling on one sound leg to gather together the papers and other materials he had transported with such difficulty from besieged Paris.

[14]

THE FRANC-TIREUR

"We have not an hour to lose," I insisted to Traveller. "Even now the *Prince Albert* may be closing with the Prussian forces; and we can be sure that when battle is joined the situation of those innocents on the cruiser will become even more perilous."

Traveller rubbed at his chin. "Yes. And your foolhardy plans to extract Françoise will scarcely be aided by Prussian and French shells lacing the air. We must aim to rendezvous with the liner before it joins with the Prussians. And there is another cause for urgency which may not occur to you."

"Which is?"

He clenched one bony fist. "The anti-ice weaponry."

I said, "Surely the preparation of the devices you have described will take some time—especially since you have removed yourself and your expertise so precipitately from England."

He shook his great head. "I fear not. Various rocket

craft—prototypes for the engines of the *Phaeton*—lie completed in my laboratory. It would not take long for Gladstone's men to adapt them. And Ned, you must not exaggerate my personal importance: the principles of my anti-ice engines would have been comprehensible to Newton; a few minutes' examination should more than suffice for any competent modern engineer. Even my more original contributions, like the gyroscopic guidance system, are hardly opaque."

His remarks were troubling. "My God. Then we must take off at once!"

"No." Traveller indicated the failing light—it was already five of an autumn afternoon. "It would hardly be practical to land the *Phaeton* in the middle of a battlefield in the pitch dark. And besides," he added, "this has been a long day for both of us; it is barely a few hours since I greeted Old Glad Eyes in my study."

I argued against this delay with all the force I could muster; but Traveller was unmoveable. And so it was that we prepared to spend another night within *Phaeton*'s aluminum walls. I scraped together a meal from the replenished stocks of pressed meat; Traveller poured globes of his fine old brandy; and we sat by the light of the mantles in the Smoking Cabin, just as when we were between worlds.

The centerpiece of the Cabin, the elaborate model of the *Great Eastern,* had been replaced by a replica, as far as I could see an exact match in every detail. Traveller's little piano remained folded in its place, a sad reminder of happier moments.

For a while we reminisced on our voyage into space, but our minds were too full of the morrow. At length I proposed, "It is not, of course, merely the availability of your experimental rockets which will determine the schedule of this war. For the government will surely use the diplomatic channels available. The knowledge of British determination to use anti-ice will focus the minds of these continentals wonderfully."

He laughed. "So, merely on Old Glad Eyes' admonishment, they will lay down their arms like good chaps? No, Ned; we must face the facts. Bismarck knew all about our possession of anti-ice before he provoked this awful war, and must therefore have discounted Britain's will to use it. Only the detonation of an anti-ice shell in the midst of his battle lines will convince him otherwise. And as for the French—Ned, these fellows are fighting for their lives, their honor, and their precious *patrie.* They are scarcely likely to respond to the abstract possibility of a British super-weapon. Again, only the deployment of such a device is likely to change their minds. So diplomacy is meaningless; there is no argument for delay. And this, I am sure, is the calculation which Gladstone and his Cabinet have made."

His words were somber; I pulled a deep draft of brandy. "Then you feel all the arguments are for the use of anti-ice."

His eyes roamed around the flickering mantles. "I can see no alternative."

I leaned forward. "Sir Josiah, perhaps you should have stayed in England and argued against this course of action. Perhaps your force of argument might have made some difference."

He looked at me, a flicker of amusement in his cold eyes. "Thank you for that well-thought-out and rounded piece of advice: from the man who gave me no choice but to accompany him away from the scene! But in any event, my presence would have made little difference. Gladstone did not come to my home to debate the issue, but to force me to comply with his decision."

So the evening passed.

As darkness closed in we settled down once more into our narrow bunks. I lay still all night, but, my head whirling with the possibilities of the morrow, failed to sleep a wink.

We both rose as the first graying of dawn reached the windows. The Little Moon was high in the clear sky, a beacon of brilliant white illuminating the awakening landscape.

With few words we washed and dressed ourselves, ate a hasty breakfast, and—not an hour after dawn—took the *Phaeton* once more into the skies of occupied France.

The old city of Orléans is situated some fifty miles south of Paris, on the banks of the Loire. Four centuries ago it was relieved from an English siege by Joan, called the Maid of Orléans; now it was in the front line of another war, with France in still more desperate peril.

Traveller insisted that the water tanks needed filling, and—to my intense irritation—put down the *Phaeton* on the river bank. Grousing loudly, I helped him wrestle lengths of hose to the reedy water's edge and stood by impatiently while the craft's pumps sucked up the liquid the motors required.

We reached Orléans a little before seven-thirty. Despite Gambetta's recent victory at nearby Coulmiers, Orléans herself was still occupied. And, as we hovered perhaps a quarter of a mile above the rooftops and spires of the city and inspected the upturned faces of the citizens through our telescopes, everywhere we saw Prussian troops and officers. One soldier—a cuirassier, splendid in his white metal breastplate and dazzling cockade—raised his rifle to us and let off a shot. I saw the flash of the muzzle and heard, a few moments later, the distant report of the explosion; but the bullet fell harmlessly to earth.

There was no sign of the *Prince Albert.* I suggested landing to seek fresh news, but Traveller pointed out Prussians emerging from billets all over the city into the early morning light; a column was forming up in marching order on the northern outskirts of the town. "I think discretion is the wisest course," he said. "A blundering descent by the *Phaeton* would scarcely put at ease these battle-ready Germans."

"Then what should we do?"

The engineer, lying in his control couch, snapped a fresh eyepiece to his periscope. "I would say the Prussian column is making ready to march to the west—perhaps toward Coulmiers, there to engage the French once more. Our best chance of encountering the *Albert* surely lies in that direction."

"And if we fail again?"

"Then we will indeed need to put down and hope to acquire more information without getting our heads blown off. But let us meet that difficulty when we come to it. To Coulmiers!"

From Orléans, Traveller traced the shining path of the Loire to the west, then veered off north, crossing a broad plain crudely delimited by hedgerow. But as we neared the town of Coulmiers itself I noticed on the approaching horizon a great carpet which lay across these dull French fields, a blue-gray sheet of dust and motion and the glint of metal. Soon I could discern that this sea of activity was making its way slowly but purposefully to the east, back toward Orléans!

So we came upon the French Army of the Loire, Gambetta's new *levée en masse.*

We swooped like some bird of prey over the advancing army. Close to, this great ragged force was less impressive. Artillery pieces labored like horse-drawn rafts of gunmetal in a river of soldiery; but the infantrymen's dark blue greatcoats, their red caps, their battered white haversacks and bivouac tents, all showed the signs of many nights' hard usage in the fields. And their faces, young and old, seemed full of fatigue and fear.

Once again potshots were fired at us, to no effect; but when an artillery piece was halted and its muzzle raised toward us Traveller rapidly increased our altitude.

As the soldiers merged once more into a monstrous sea of humanity my sense of the scale of this force returned; it seemed to stretch from horizon to horizon, a tide set on sweeping away the cockaded Prussians like so many Canutes.

"Dear God, Traveller, this is surely an army to end all armies. There must be half a million men here. They will crush those Prussians once more by sheer weight of numbers."

"Perhaps. This Gambetta chap has obviously done well to raise such a force. Although some of those artillery pieces look a little elderly; and did you notice the wide variety of rifle makes? One wonders about the availability of ammunition to these brave fellows, too."

I had observed none of this. I said, "Then you are less optimistic about their chances of success against the Prussians today?"

He pushed away his periscope and rubbed at his eyes.

"I have seen enough of war to know more than I would wish to know about its science. Numerical superiority, while a significant factor, is far outweighed by training and expertise. Look at the poor Frenchies' formation, Ned! As they march they are already deployed into their battle units. Clearly they are incapable of short-order maneuvers; and so their commanders must draw them together like so many sheep and herd them off into battle.

"Meanwhile the Prussians are marching comfortably and competently to meet them . . .

"Ned, I fear we are about to witness a day of blood and horror; and if it is decisive it can only be in favor of the Prussians—"

But I was scarcely listening; for on the eastern horizon I had made out something new. It was like a fortress whose walls loomed over the flashing bayonets of the French soldiery; but this was a fortress which rolled with the infantry across the plain . . .

Unable to contain my excitement I turned to Traveller and grabbed his shoulder. "Sir Josiah, look ahead. Will those Prussians not turn and flee before—that?"

It was the *Prince Albert.* We had found it at last!

The land liner was an ingot of iron adrift in this ocean of greatcoated humanity. Behind the vessel we could make out tracks of churned earth stretching in a perfect straight line to the horizon. Traveller was pleased by this, seeing it as proof that his anti-ice propulsive system had performed as desired.

There were clearly plenty still left aboard the *Albert* who understood its provenance, and its link with the extraordinary aerial boat which hovered above; for we were greeted with cheers from the Promenade Deck and from soldiers who walked close to its muddy tracks. I waved back, hoping I could be seen through the *Phaeton*'s dome. It was, I reflected, a pleasant change from potshots.

But Traveller's expression was grim; he inspected through his periscope the damage his craft had suffered.

Five of the six funnels still stood, though their proud red paintwork was scarred and mud-spattered; where the sixth had stood there was only a black and gaping wound which led, like the mouth of a corpse, into the dark stomach of the ship. Peering into this wound, and recalling the details of the ghastly August day of the craft's launch, the blood surged to my head with an almost audible rush.

The rest of the damage seemed more superficial. The glass-covered companionways which had once adorned the flanks of the craft had been hacked away to be replaced by rope ladders—for speed of retraction in case of attack, I supposed. A thousand irregularly-placed slits had been knocked through the hull. Through these slits I could see—not the elegance of salons or the delicate wrought-iron work which had characterized the ship's sparse elegance—but the ugly snouts of small artillery pieces.

The land liner had indeed been transformed into a machine of war.

Traveller's anger was deep and bitter. "Ned, if the Prussians only realized how fragile the *Albert* truly is, they surely would not have allowed it to penetrate so deep into France unchallenged."

"But you can see it's an icon, a rallying-point for these Frenchie infantry."

"It's a symbol, but can be no more. Ned, it's more likely to lead these poor lads to their early deaths than victory."

I frowned and turned to the east-facing window. "Then we'd better land without further delay, Sir Josiah, for—look!"

On the horizon, under the gleaming Little Moon, was a line of glinting silver, of dark blue tunics, of the looming mouths of artillery pieces, of the nervous movements of horses: it was the Prussian Army out of Orléans, drawn into battle order.

War was perhaps half an hour away.

Albert's ornamental pond had been boarded over, and its garden reduced to a pool of mud punctuated by the snapped stumps of trees. The whole upper deck swarmed with artillery pieces and soldiery; these assorted troops ranged from the magnificence of Hussar officers, in their sleek black lambswool busbies, to citizens—both men and women—in the ragged remains of fine clothes. On seeing these last my heart gave a leap; if such noble folk had stayed with the ship since its ill-fated launch, perhaps there was indeed a chance of finding Françoise still alive.

Traveller held the *Phaeton* steady for some moments, until his intention evidently became apparent; and one of the Hussar officers began to clear a landing area.

The *Phaeton* set down as gentle as an eggshell. Without waiting for the nozzles to cool I undogged the hatches, lowered a rope ladder and scrambled to the deck.

I was dazzled by the strengthening sunlight. (By now it was past eight-thirty.) As the noise of the engines echoed away the inhabitants of the Promenade Deck, soldiers and citizens alike, began to approach us. Every one bore a rifle—even, I was shocked to see, a woman! This extraordinary person wore the remnants of a silk gown reminiscent of that worn by Françoise on the launch day; but the gown was bloodied and torn, revealing expanses of undergarments that, in less grisly circumstances, might have seemed indiscreet. Her face obscured by shadow and dirt, she held a chassepot before her, the muzzle pointed in my direction, with as much evidence of competence and command as any of her male companions.

From this suspicious crowd emerged the officer who had earlier cleared the deck. He was a tall man of about thirty who bore well the brown tunic and white sash of his regiment, and his fierce brown eyes and pencil moustache, all framed by a brass chinstrap, spoke of strength, intelligence and competence. But his eyes were deeply shadowed, and his face was covered with the stubble of several nights. He introduced himself as a Captain of the Second Hussars, and inquired as to our business; but before I could reply a sound like a suppressed cough came from the eastern horizon.

The Hussar dropped to his face, as if felled; Traveller and I followed his lead more slowly. Traveller whispered, "Prussian artillery."

"What? Are we close enough?"

"Undoubtedly. Let them find their range and—"

A whistling shriek tore the air, somewhere to my left; a shell fell to earth some distance from the sea of French troops and exploded harmlessly, evoking a ragged cheer from the *Albert*'s passengers.

But they were less keen to applaud when a second shell plowed into the ground perhaps a quarter-mile behind us, scattering troops like skittles. The deck shook beneath me, and before my horrified eyes a great gout of rust-colored soil spewed into the air. The mingling of earth and human flesh was such that it was as if the Earth herself had been wounded.

"Traveller, is this war?"

"I'm afraid so, lad."

The Hussar officer turned to us and said, in rapid French, "Gentlemen, you can see how we are fixed; if you do not wish your fancy toy blown to pieces I suggest you fly to some quieter spot."

I grabbed his arm. "Wait! We are seeking a passenger on this ship; she was trapped here when—"

But the Captain shook away my hand with angry impatience and hurried to his troops.

I turned to Traveller. "I must find her."

"Ned, we have but minutes. One good shot by those Prussians—"

I grabbed his shoulders desperately. "We've come so far. Will you wait for me?"

He pushed me away. "Don't waste time, boy."

I wandered as if in a nightmare over the Deck. Within, I could not accept any image of Françoise save that of trapped passenger, of victim. And so I searched for her in places where she might be cowering, or might be locked away. I peered down stairwells which led into the interior of the ship; but where once champagne and glittering conversation had filled the air, now I was reminded of nothing so much as the interior of one of Lord Nelson's battleships. Artillery pieces protruded like the muzzles of dogs through pushed-out hull panels, and everywhere there was the stink of cordite, the fumes of formaldehyde, the heaped bandages of an improvised field hospital. I found the Grand Saloon—or what was left of it; where the funnel had once passed through the room concealed by decoration there was only an obscene, gaping chimney, and the interior of the Saloon was uniformly blackened and destroyed. But men and women moved purposefully about, tending weaponry. The elegantly painted panels, battered and charred, looked down with exquisite incongruity over scenes their painters had surely never anticipated.

But there was no sign of Françoise. My tension and anxiety wound to snapping point.

I climbed back to the Promenade Deck. All around me there was shouting. Peering beyond the rim of the Deck to the field below I could see that the ragged French formations were already exchanging rifle shots with their Prussian opponents. Shells continued to whistle over us, splashing into the bloodied ground throughout the body of Frenchmen. The *Albert*'s guns had also begun to speak now; and with every shell they blasted away, the whole fragile edifice of the liner bucked and shuddered.

Then I heard, like the note of an oboe amid the din of a great orchestra, the voice of Traveller, calling my name. I looked back toward the *Phaeton.* When the engineer saw he had my eye he pointed skywards.

Squinting against the climbing sunlight I made out a line of white, like a very thin cloud, sketched across the heavens and arcing past the Little Moon. The line was growing, as if being writ by the hand of God . . . and it was passing over our battleground in the direction of Orléans. This apparition made no noise, and went unnoticed by the eager and terrified troops on the ground.

The meaning was clear. It was an anti-ice rocket. My heart sank, not only out of personal fear, but out of shame to be British at that hour.

I shook my head and returned the focus of my attention to the growing chaos around me, wondering how I could complete my search in the few moments the anti-ice shell had left me.

I espied the woman "soldier" I had noticed earlier. This

ferocious damsel had now lodged herself at the rail at the bow of the ship and had raised her rifle to her shoulder, aiming at the Prussians. I resolved to speak to her. Surely the few remaining women on board the craft, no matter what their attitudes to this conflict, would help and support each other in this arena; and so perhaps this modern Joan would be able to direct me to Françoise, whose rescue had become my only fixed point in all this turmoil!

I made my way forward. It was slow going. Excitable Frenchmen rushed from side to side of the craft, the scent of Prussian blood in their nostrils, more than once bowling me over. Prussian shells continued to burst in the air all around, and every few seconds I was forced to duck, or flatten myself to the plates of the Deck.

But at last I reached the warrior lady; by now she was squeezing off shots with clinical efficiency, and when I laid a hand on her shoulder she turned to me and snapped, in rapid Marseilles-accented French: "Damn you! What do you want? . . ." Then her voice tailed away and her eyes narrowed—sky-blue eyes which were still, behind their mask of dirt, quite lovely.

I stepped back, oblivious to the falling shells. "Françoise? Is it you?"

"Obviously! And who the Hell—Ah, I remember. Vicars. Ned Vicars." Her face seemed to recede from me, as if my eyes had been transmuted to telescopes; my face felt numb, and the crash of battle seemed far away.

So it was true. As Holden had suspected, as Traveller's quick insight had discerned, as I in my foolish naïvety had refused to accept.

She shook her head, wonder briefly breaking through her tension and anger. "Ned Vicars. I thought you were dead in the explosion."

"I was aboard the *Phaeton*, and she was not destroyed. Frédéric Bourne stole her. We flew off—Françoise, we flew to the Moon!"

She looked at me as if I were mad. "What did you say? . . . But what of Frédéric?"

"He survived; and is safely locked away. But you—" I laid my hands on her shoulders, and felt only knots of muscles. "Françoise, what has happened to you?"

She punched away my arms and clutched her rifle against the oily remains of her dress. "Nothing has happened to me."

"But your manner . . . this gun—"

She laughed. "What is so strange about a gun in the hands of a woman? I am French, and my country is in mortal peril! Of course I will use a gun."

"But . . ." The stink of dust and cordite, the shriek of the shells, the shuddering of the Deck—all of it rattled loudly in my head. "I thought you might have been killed when the funnel exploded; or, if you survived, perhaps you had become a prisoner."

She leaned closer to me and peered into my eyes; her face, which once had seemed so beautiful to me, was a mask of contempt. She said, "Once I thought you and your like . . . sweet. Harmless, at worst. Now you seem criminally stupid. Ned, listen to me. I was not injured in that funnel explosion because—*after I set the funnel stopcock,* during our tour with that dour engineer—I made sure I was in a far, far corner of the ship."

I knew, now, why I had determined to come to this terrible place. I had come to confront the truth at last: and here it was, in all its bare horror. I could scarcely speak.

An approaching shell shrieked, more loudly than ever;

over its noise I shouted, "Françoise . . . come back with me."

Now she opened her mouth and laughed out loud; I saw how spittle looped across her perfect teeth. "Ned, you Englishmen will never understand war. Go home." She turned away from me—

—then the Deck lurched beneath me, and I was thrown to my back; a great shout filled my ears.

The *Albert* was hit. The land liner ground to a halt. Traveller had been right: one accurate shell had been enough to stop the ship. Four funnels still pumped out steam, but from the fifth there came only ominous black smoke; and from somewhere in the depths of the craft there was a low, agonized grinding, as if the ship's metal limbs still strove to propel it over the earth.

The Promenade Deck was bent into great metal waves. Plates had been torn apart from each other, their rivets snapped.

Soldiers and guns had been scattered like toys. But all around me there was already purposeful movement, as men climbed over their companions to seize their fallen weapons.

Of Françoise there was no sign. She may have recovered before me—or she might even now be lying sprawled and broken among her countrymen, a new Maid of Orléans.

There was nothing I could do for her now—it seemed there never had been—and I must concentrate on saving myself. At the far end of the deck the *Phaeton* still stood, a little crazily; as I ran toward her the land liner was racked by a second explosion, and I was thrown again to the bloodied deck. It seemed the *Prince Albert* would tear itself to pieces without further aid from the Prussians.

Steam belched from the *Phaeton*'s nozzles. I scrambled up the rope ladder, dragged it in after me, and slammed home the hatch; then, with what was left of my strength, I hauled myself into the Bridge.

Traveller lay in his couch, his face a grotesque mask; for his platinum nose had been smashed away, and the gaping socket was a pit of dark, still-trickling blood. From above this hole his cold eyes flickered over me once—and then he wrenched at his control levers, and the *Phaeton* shot without ceremony into the air.

But even as we rose the Bridge was flooded with light. I clung to the deck while the vessel bucked in the roiling air like a frightened horse!

The *Albert*'s Dewars had failed. The anti-ice energy they contained was released in a flood, and the fragile frame of the liner burst like a paper bag. A gust of heat like a wind from hell rushed up and caught the *Phaeton,* hurling her upwards like an autumn leaf over a bonfire. For long seconds Traveller fought with his controls, and I could only wait, thinking that we should surely flip over and fall crashing at last into the earth.

. . . But slowly, as one emerges from a storm, the boiling of the air subsided. The *Phaeton*'s bucking settled to a gentle roll, at last becoming still.

I stood cautiously; every inch of my body felt as if it had been systematically pummeled, but I remained intact and unbroken, and once more I offered grateful prayers to God for my deliverance.

Traveller turned his terrible mask of a face to me. "Are you all right?"

"Yes. I . . . Françoise is a franc-tireur."

"Ned, she is certainly dead now. But she chose her own path . . . As must I," he added darkly.

I looked out of the glass dome. The French and Prussian infantries had joined now. Below us was a bowl of dust, splashed blood, and a thousand small explosions: it was a field of battle from which we were mercifully so aloof that the cries of the wounded and the stink of blood were lost.

Traveller pointed, off to his left. "Look. Can you see? The trail of Gladstone's shell from London."

I looked up into the sky. By squinting hard I could make out the strange line of vapour which stretched across the sky, a little more ragged now. Was it only minutes since I had stood on the deck of the *Albert,* studying that trail?

"Traveller, where is it going?"

"Well, it's surely intended for the battlefield. What better way to demonstrate His Majesty's displeasure than to flatten the pride of Prussia and France with one blow? . . . But Gladstone's bunglers have made a mess of it. They've overshot. I knew I should have stayed home to get it right for them. I knew . . ."

His voice was steady and rational, but it had a strange undercurrent; and I sensed that his control was about to snap. "Traveller, perhaps the shell's inaccuracy is a blessing. If it falls harmlessly into an uninhabited area—"

"Ned, the shell will be tipped by a Dewar containing several pounds of anti-ice. It is unlikely to be 'harmless' . . . and in any event, I have observed it long enough to be sure of where it will fall."

"Where?"

"It will be any second now, Ned; you should shield your eyes."

"Where, damn you?"

". . . Orléans."

First there came a flowering of light, quite beautiful, which fled along the ground in all directions from the center of the old city. When that had faded, and we were able to open our dazzled and streaming eyes, we saw how a great wind was scouring after the light across the plain; trees snapped like matchstalks and buildings exploded to rubble.

Within seconds of the impact a great bubble of cloud formed over the city center. The cloud lifted to the sky, a monstrous thunderhead growing out of the ground; it blackened as it rose, and was lit from below by a hellish red glow—undoubtedly the burning of Orléans—and from above by the flickering of lightning between plumes of cloud.

It was all quite soundless.

I became aware that the clashing armies below had grown still, that their guns no longer spoke; I imagined hundreds of thousands of men straightening, facing their erstwhile opponents, and turning to this monstrous new apparition.

Traveller said: "What have I done? It makes Sebastopol look like a candle."

I sought words. "You could not have stopped this—"

He turned to me, a bizarre smile superimposed on his travesty of a face. "Ned, I have dedicated my life since the Crimea to the peaceful exploitation of anti-ice. For if I could get the damn stuff used up on peaceable, if spectacular, purposes, then men would never again use it on each other. Well, at least the stuff will be exhausted now by these follies of Gladstone's . . . But I have failed. And more: by developing ever more ingenious technologies for the exploitation of the ice, I have brought this day upon the Earth.

"Ned, I would like to show you another invention." His face still disfigured by that ghastly smile he began to open his restraints.

". . . What?"

"A conception of Leonardo's—one of the few Latins with any sense of the practical. I think you'll find it amusing . . ."

And those were the last words he spoke to me before his fist came crashing into my temple.

Cold air slapped me awake. I opened my eyes, my head throbbing.

The Little Moon filled my eyes.

I was sitting in the hatchway near the base of the Smoking Cabin. My legs dangled out of the open hatchway; the battle-strewn ground was many hundreds of feet below. A strange khaki pack, like a soldier's knapsack, was fixed to my chest.

Startled to full wakefulness I made to grab at the lip of the hatchway. A hand rested on my shoulder; I turned and stared at long fingers dully, as if they comprised some odd spider.

It was Traveller, of course. He said, shouting over the rushing air, "It is nearly done, Ned. The supply of Antarctic anti-ice is all but exhausted. Now I must finish it." He laughed, his voice distorted by the hole in his face.

His tone was terrifying. "Traveller, let us land in safety and—"

"No, Ned. Once, our young French saboteur told us that to waste a few ounces of anti-ice was worth the life of a patriot. Well, I've come to believe he was right. I mean to destroy the *Phaeton,* and in this act of atonement to hasten the removal of the anti-ice curse from Earth."

I searched for words. "Traveller, I understand. But—"

But there was time for no more; for I was administered a kick to the small of my back, which propelled me feet first from the vessel and into mid-air!

As the chill air whistled past my ears I screamed, convinced I was to die at last. I wondered at the depths of despair which had compelled Traveller to commit such an act—but then, after a fall of fifty feet, there was a sharp tug to my chest. Cables fixed to my pack had tautened, and now I dangled, slowly descending. I looked up—uncomfortably, for the straps of the pack had bunched under my armpits. The cables were fixed to a construct of canvas and cable, an inverted cone which was catching the air as I fell and so slowing my fall to a safe rate.

Squirming in my straps I looked down, beyond my dangling feet. The anti-ice thunderhead, still growing, climbed high over the corpse of Orléans. The armies of France and Prussia lay spread out beneath me, but there was little sign of movement; and I found it inconceivable that men should resume killing each other after such an event. Perhaps, I reflected in the silence and calm of my mid-air suspension, now that the world's anti-ice was virtually exhausted, this ghastly—accident—would serve as a warning for generations to come of the perils and horror of war.

Perhaps Traveller had at last achieved his goal of a warless world—but at a cost he would find difficult to accept.

From somewhere above my canopy there came a roar, a flash of steam and fire. I twisted my head back once more—there was the Little Moon staring down, bemused, at this tortured Earth—and there went the fabulous *Phaeton,* rising for the last time on her plumes of steam.

The ship continued to climb, unwavering. Soon only a vapor trail, reminiscent of Gladstone's shell, marked out her path; and it became obvious that Traveller had no intention of returning again to the world of men. At last the trail thinned to the near-invisible as Traveller reached the edge of the atmosphere . . . but it was a trail that pointed like an arrow at the heart of the Little Moon.

Now his intention was clear; he meant to drive the craft into the bulk of the satellite itself.

Some minutes passed. Traveller's trail dispersed slowly, and I swung impotently but comfortably beneath Leonardo's canopy; I kept my eyes fixed on the Little Moon, hoping to be able to detect the moment of the *Phaeton*'s impact with it—

The world was flooded with light, from horizon to horizon; it was as if the sky itself had caught fire.

The Little Moon seemed to have exploded.

Barely able to see, I fell heavily to the ground among a group of wondering French infantrymen.

[Epilogue]

A LETTER TO A SON

November 4, 1910
Sylvan, Sussex

My Dear Edward,
I trust this parcel finds you as it leaves me: that is, in good health and spirits.

No doubt you will be surprised, on opening this latest package from home, to find the customary missive from your dear mother replaced by these few pages of scrawl from myself. And I hope you will forgive me if I omit the usual bulletin of news of home; of these matters I will only say that we all remain hale and hearty, and miss you tremendously.

My intention in writing to you is to try in my own inadequate way to make up for the deficiencies in understanding which should exist between us as father and son. I accept full blame for this; and you may have realized that our last lengthy conversation before your posting to Berlin—you remember: that affair of pipes, whiskey and carpet slippers before a dying fire, late one Saturday evening—was an earlier attempt to break through this barrier between us. I failed, of course. And yet, in the purity of your anger that evening, how my heart was rent to see in you so much of myself, the self of thirty or forty years ago!

Let me simply say this. I am your father. I do not regard myself as a coward, or less than a patriot. You need have no shame on that score, I assure you. But my views on the coming conflict with Prussia are clearly not ideas you feel able to share.

I have no desire to impose my philosophy on you; you are an Officer in the finest army in the world, and I am very proud of you. But I want you to understand me. When war comes—as I believe is inevitable—then, praying God preserve you, it will assuredly change you, for better or worse; and I want to try, one last time, to explain myself—my life, since those fateful days of 1870—to the young man I have raised.

You have read my own manuscript account of the adventures which befell me forty years ago—as well as the more polished rendering by Sir George Holden. George, before his untimely death from an illiberal intake of port and other substances, managed to parlay his experiences into a lucrative and rewarding career. He made his fortune, of course, with his scientific romance *The New Carthage,* whose premise was the discovery of anti-ice by the inhabitants of that ancient city, and their subsequent and spectacular revenge on their enemies, the Romans. The critics thought it "a smooth read but hardly plausible" . . . which was exactly the judgment of Josiah Traveller when he threw Holden the idea all those years ago aboard the *Phaeton*!

I begrudge George none of his windfall earnings—good luck to the fellow—but such self-publicity was not for me.

After my return to England in the aftermath of the use of that first Gladstone Shell, I resigned my post in London and returned home to Sussex. I studied, took my articles and have since worked quietly—and as far as possible anonymously—as a solicitor of no more than modest achievements in the local area.

But I have watched the unraveling of global events following that cataclysmic autumn; and it has seemed to me sometimes that human affairs have unfolded like a shabby flower about the single, dazzling point of light that was the Gladstone Shell.

I will not dwell on what I saw of the devastation of Orléans. I pray God you are spared such sights, Edward. But perhaps your career will take you to that ghastly site where the *Prince Albert* still rests, immobile since receiving its little gift from the Prussian artillery, a rusting monument to another war.

The Shelling marked the end of the European war, of course; if a new fear of British intervention were not sufficient, I believe the will to fight of those men who had been gathered on the plains of the Loire was expunged by their salvage work amid the stink of Orléans. I remember watching the Prussian columns form up, filthy, slow and solemn, to make for home; and I knew then that here was one generation for whom war was done.

Edward, it shocks me now to see references to the Shelling of Orléans as if it were some great triumph for Britain. It was an accident—the Shell was not even aimed at the city—and the fact that the intervention achieved so many of Gladstone's ends is due only to the sheer horror and scale of the carnage that was wrought.

A formal settlement between France and Prussia was reached, under British chairmanship, at the Congress of Tours during the spring of 1871. After such a costly reverse Bismarck's ambitions to unify Germany were perforce abandoned, and that wily old gentleman struggled to maintain his own position of influence and power. (But survive he did, of course.) Thus today Germany remains a cozy mish-mash run by princelings and dukes, with the eagle of Prussia pent up in one corner; and this is surely preferable, in British eyes, to the great middle-European German Power which might otherwise have emerged.

Meanwhile in France the new provisional government, under Gambetta, welcomed British assistance in quelling the continuing rebellious unrest in Paris; and Gambetta even engaged the advice of eminent English parliamentarians in drawing up a constitution for a new Third Empire. And so it is that a Parliament—indistinguishable in every key particular from the Mother of Parliaments in Manchester—now meets daily in Paris herself, and for four decades the British-style constitutional settlement which underlies all this has filtered down into every nook of French society.

Yes, we have a Europe settled as the most fair and scrupulous—British—statesman of 1860 might have requested it; and to back it all up we have garrisons scattered through such traditional danger spots as Belgium, Alsace and Lorraine, Denmark—and even on the outskirts of Berlin herself. We may not have built the Norman fortresses dreamed of by the Sons of Gascony, but nevertheless we can say we have achieved a British Europe.

And if all this political and military dominance were not sufficient, there is the continuing wonder of anti-ice technology. The Light Rail network spreads ever deeper into the Continent, and air-boats for both passengers and freight, large enough to swallow the dear old *Phaeton,* skim daily above the clouds, bringing Manchester and Moscow no more than a few hours apart. Trans-atmospheric broughams flit between Earth and Moon, and every year the Royal Geographical Society regales us with accounts of the exploits of its newest explorers, in Traveller Crater and among the Phoebean rock animals.

And, of course, in silos hidden under Kentish fields, the Gladstone Shells await, one for every European city.

It is strange to recall now that Josiah Traveller believed—at the very end of his life—that, with the exhaustion of the known supply of anti-ice at the South Pole, the exploitation of that substance would, for good or ill, come to an end. . . . How ironic it is that in his last, desperate act he should have shown humankind how to reach out greedy hands to more anti-ice—more than he himself could have imagined—a supply so large that it could be considered practically inexhaustible!

Who would have imagined that the Little Moon should be composed almost entirely of anti-ice? It was clear immediately to observing astronomers that an explosion of the magnitude generated by the *Phaeton*'s final impact could only be the result of an anti-ice detonation. The scientists now understand that the Little Moon is a fragment of that comet which destroyed itself in scouring out Traveller Crater on the Moon—a fragment which fell into orbit around Earth—perhaps after several bruising, but slowing, scrapings along the roof of Earth's air. All this happened in the eighteenth century, the savants say; and so at the same time as the Australian aboriginals were watching another fragment of the comet streak across their skies to Antarctica, the Little Moon settled into the skies of Earth.

So an immense supply of anti-ice energy circles the Earth, kept from melting and exploding by its own rapid rotation and its frequent sojourns into Earth's shadow.

Once Traveller had inadvertently shown the way, the remaining Earthbound stocks of ice were used to build new *Phaetons,* just able to reach the Little Moon and return with precious Dewars full of frozen power. And now every European can watch the tiny sparks which are British orbital boats endlessly climbing to the Little Moon and falling back into the pool of air, further consolidating our power.

How poor Traveller would have hated to see this outcome! I often wonder if, in those final moments as that awful light burned through the aluminum walls of the *Phaeton,* he understood the implications of what he had done. I pray that he did not; that his great, inventive brain was stilled long before the final destruction of his ship, the thwarting of his purpose . . .

But I digress.

Edward, I return to the subject of our debate that Saturday evening. Is the world a better place for this Pax Britannica which we have imposed with our anti-ice and our industry and administration?

My answer must be, sadly: no. Not even, in the end, for us British ourselves.

I know your fascination with politics is sketchy at best, Edward, but even you must have followed the recent ghastly developments at home, such as the strikes against Balfour's new food taxes—taxes which seem specifically designed to hammer the disenfranchised poor—and the brutal suppression of those strikes by Churchill's troops.

Not for centuries has England seethed with revolt in

this manner. How have we British, with our talent for accommodation and compromise, come to this pass? For, historically, the British way has been to give a little to avert bloodier discontent. For instance, perhaps further reform of Parliament—like Disraeli's failed reform of the 1860s—would, however partial, have served as a sop, to relieve this new pressure for change. A compromise now might be for Balfour to take in some ideas from this Welsh chap David Lloyd George, who advocates tax reforms aimed at the super-rich and the landowners. Yes, Edward; I mean Lloyd George the rabble-rouser and recent convict! Are you shocked? Well, perhaps if such men were invited to contribute to the government we should find a happier solution.

But in Britain today we have no room for accommodation, however slight. Edward, this is the malevolent influence of anti-ice and the new technologies, which have given such power to the industrialists—at the expense of other unrepresented sections of our society. We have changed for the worse, and now—as a Frenchman of my acquaintance once predicted—we are in danger of being torn apart by our own contradictions.

I do not expect you to agree with any of this: merely to respect my views for what they are.

The picture is scarcely happier abroad.

Let us take France. Edward, I know the French. Do you suppose they have accepted the imposition of a British parliament? I will tell you it sticks in their throats, much as their dry French bread sticks in mine. I have no case to make here about the merits or imperfections of the British system. My point is only that *it is not French;* should we not therefore have allowed our Gallic cousins to continue their groping toward a constitutional settlement which might address the issues of their own national character and past? But we did not; and so the French dream on, of the glorious days of their Revolution, and of their precious Bonaparte.

As for Prussia, there is that wily old fox Prince Otto von Schönhausen Bismarck, still ruling the Berlin roost at the age of ninety-five. The new Emperor, the second William, is putty in Bismarck's liver-spotted hands.

For a long time it was argued that Bismarck had become a friend, if a reluctant one, of the British—for consider the trade and cultural exchanges which have proceeded in the intervening decades between our two nations.

But surely recent events—principally Bismarck's disgraceful intervention in the question of the Austrian succession, so reminiscent of the intervention in Spanish royal affairs by which he provoked his earlier war with France—have proved the lie of this.

Bismarck has played out the intervening decades like the opportunist and devious politician he is; and by a series of ruses, feints and stratagems has maintained his own position in Prussia, and Prussia's position in Europe.

Bismarck is no friend of Britain. Britain stopped him achieving his life's goal: the unification of Germany. It is as if Bismarck refuses to die until this goal is achieved—or at least until Manchester is rendered impotent to intervene.

Now he is ready to strike. And we await the new Ems telegram which will provoke the armed conflict with Britain. What role will France adopt? If the Prussian goal is the scrubbing of British influence from the plains of Europe, then the best we can hope for is that the Frenchies stay neutral. Let us not forget the ghosts of Orléans . . . And it does not help that the present French foreign minister is one Frédéric Bourne.

But surely, you insist, even now Bismarck is only testing our nerve. Surely he will never risk calling down a rain of anti-ice fire on his own countrymen.

But he will, I say. For, Edward, I believe that Bismarck now has anti-ice weapons of his own with which to reply; the security of our stock of anti-ice, however thorough, cannot have remained inviolate for all these decades. The Prussian weapons will be every bit as powerful as Britain's—or more so, given the application of Prussian military ingenuity.

What, then, will be the outcome?

A new Balance of Power might emerge, I suppose: a face-down between two states, Britain and Prussia, each bristling with anti-ice weaponry, each deterred from further warfare by the devastating capability of the other . . . Will this Balance guarantee peace? Perhaps. But these past decades of British hegemony will not be easily forgiven in the halls of Europe. Recall the address to the Commonwealth of His Majesty at the dawn of the new century, in which he described the future. A thousand years of British power . . . the shadow of the Union Flag stretching across the centuries—such ranting has only added to the stockpile of disaster which awaits ourselves or our descendants.

Edward, I fear war is now inevitable. The embittered old men of Berlin and Paris will scarce blink an eye at the destruction of their own populace, if it means the erasure of Britain from the European map; and so, deceived by our own vain and arrogant complacency, we face a darker war than man has yet seen.

I pray that you now understand my fear and dread; and

I pray, of course, that we all survive the coming days of darkness, and are reunited at last in the sunlight of a better and more just world.

I Remain, With Love,
Your Devoted Father
NED VICARS